SCREAMSCAPES

TALES OF TERROR

Evans Light

SCREAMSCAPES: Tales of Terror
Copyright © 2013 by Evans Light
All rights reserved.

THIRD EDITION

February 2015

ISBN: 1484056388
ISBN-13: 978-1484056387

Primary editing provided by Andrea Harding,
Express Editing Solutions.
Primary editing for *Arboreatum* provided by Catherine Depasquale.

SCREAMSCAPES

TALES OF TERROR

Evans Light

EDITED BY ANDREA HARDING AND CATHERINE DEPASQUALE
WITH ADAM LIGHT AND DOUGLAS PRYER

DEDICATION

To my wife, who makes me get it done,
and my kids, who make me want to.
To Adam Light for always telling me it's perfect,
and to Doug Pryer for always telling me it's not.
This book wouldn't exist without
your generous help and encouragement.
Thanks to my Dad and family for their love.

In memory of Ray Bradbury.
A tip of the hat to Joe R. Lansdale and Joe Hill.

CONTENTS

CRAWLSPACE

"THOMAS! Are you even listening to me?"

The sharp tone of his wife's voice burst the haze of his reverie like a bowling ball through a minefield.

Tom let out a long sigh, loud enough for Kelly to hear. The sound of it escaped his lips in a leisurely way, perfectly matching the pace of the steam as it floated up and out of his shower stall and into the cold farmhouse bathroom that lay beyond. He wished he and his hot water could be together forever and that she would just give up and go away.

"Tom? *Tom!*" she continued, irritation prickling along the edges of her voice.

He grunted and turned off the shower, watching sadly as the warm water swirled down the drain away from him, leaving him alone and naked, cold and wet. He missed the warmth of its embrace already.

"God damn it, Tom!"

He stepped from the shower, grabbing a towel from the rack to wipe the steam from the vanity mirror above the sink. As the moisture cleared, he caught sight of his wife's stern reflection glaring at him from over his shoulder. It had been weeks - maybe months - since there had been genuine eye contact between them, he realized. The icy look he now saw in her eyes unsettled him.

"Well?" she said. "Is it going to be finished before I get back or not?"

Tom closed his eyes and took a deep breath. If she didn't leave to visit her mother soon, he might like to finish *her* instead, he thought.

"Yes Kelly. It will be done before you get back," he said calmly, though his teeth were clenched. "You have my word." His words echoed in the quiet tension of the tiled room, making a sound that reminded him of marbles spilling onto a glass table.

"Good." Kelly said coldly.

"So when are you leaving?" he asked in a lighter tone that he hoped would relieve the tension and hurry the process along.

She wasn't so easily deterred.

"I'm serious, Tom. If I come home to find you passed out in bed in the middle of the afternoon again with nothing done," her voice trailed off, the threat implied rather than spoken, as she glanced down at his naked body. The harshness of her expression let up for a second, replaced by a look of surprise.

Tom, seeing this, quickly covered himself with the towel and turned to face her.

"Look, I don't want the floor to rot out from under our feet any more than you do. I already have all the materials - I swear I'll spread all the lime under the house before you get back."

Still seeing doubt on her face, he reinforced his statement. "If I don't meet my deadline, I'll move in under the house until it's done. We've thrown so much money into this pit it would be stupid not to keep it up properly now."

She relaxed visibly, but her eyes remained cool, calculating.

Tom tried to smile at her but failed.

"What?" he shrugged nonchalantly. "What more do you want me to say? Are you leaving today or not?" He feigned exasperation, hoping she would turn and leave in a huff.

She stood her ground, evaluating him.

Did she know? He wondered. *How could she?*

"I don't want you to say anything," Kelly said, after a long pause that spoke volumes of disappointment without a single word. "The only reason I'm still here is because I thought you might like to say goodbye to your daughter before we leave. You do remember that you *have* a daughter, don't you? Six years old, four feet high, blond hair, first grade - sound familiar? *She'd* like to say goodbye to you - although for the life of me, I have no idea why."

Tom turned his face away, embarrassed for her to see the flush of shame he knew was spreading across his face. She was right - about that one thing, anyway. In his eagerness to have his wife out of the house, he *had* forgotten about Emily. He pictured her sitting in the other room, a sad look on her face, waiting patiently to tell her worthless daddy good-bye.

Guilt slapped Tom like a hot rag across the back of his neck. It was an emotion he was not used to feeling.

"Give me one minute. I'll be right there," he muttered, grabbing his jeans from a hook on the wall by the bathtub and tugging them on.

***

TEN MINUTES LATER, the luggage had been loaded into the minivan and his daughter Emily had been kissed good-bye.

Tom was turning away from his still-angry wife to head back towards the house when Kelly grabbed his hand, stopping him.

She surprised him by putting her arms around him, holding him close to her for a moment.

Then she kissed him.

As she pressed her lips against his, he realized that it was the first time they had kissed in a very long time, maybe since he had lost his job. Had six months passed already? It was only a brief kiss, but still, it surprised him.

Time really does fly, he thought, *whether you're having fun or not.*

Kelly climbed into the minivan and drove away without saying a word. Tom shivered in the bitter cold of the Pennsylvania morning air and waved goodbye until the red tail lights disappeared into the distance.

The warmth of his wife's lips still tingled on his own. He wondered what surprised him the most about that kiss: that it had happened in the first place, or that it had made him realize that he had no love left for her at all. Ten years of marriage, and love had left the building. Unlike his wife's absence, however, he was pretty sure his feelings weren't temporary.

It mattered little either way, Tom figured, and he brushed the thought of the unexpected kiss aside.

***

CUP OF JOE IN HAND, Tom strolled out onto the porch into the frosty morning, ready to hurry up and get the day's work behind him.

The brisk sting of winter in his lungs felt almost as satisfying as seeing his wife's rear-end disappear from view for an entire week, he thought as he took in a lustful breath of the cold morning air.

He sipped from his coffee, smiling as steam drifted from his lips. The first rays of the morning sun were streaming through a shroud of trees - an omen of better things to come, he hoped.

Finally life was good, he thought - even if he did have to spend the entire day crawling around on his belly in the muck underneath the house, spreading lime. It was a small price to pay for the week of freedom that lay before him; freedom from accusing looks and random nagging, freedom to allow joy to flood back into his life. Life was good and would get a whole lot better when Miranda showed up.

Just one more day and she would be in his arms again, the two of them alone in the house together. Tom's heart quickened at the thought. He figured he'd gladly spread lime in crawlspaces for the rest of his life if Miranda were waiting for him at the end of the day.

Darkest before the dawn, Tom thought to himself and smiled.

Miranda was more than the dawn to him. She was as hot as the sun itself, the light of his miserable life. She made him feel totally and completely alive, born again. With her, he had a second chance at happiness, a fresh opportunity to do everything right.

His reflection on the front window drew his attention. Tom sat his coffee down to check himself out, running his fingers through his dark, still thick hair.

"Not bad," he said out loud, "you've still got it, Tommy-boy." He shot a smile at himself, zipped up his wool-lined work jacket and shoved a pair of utility gloves into his pocket.

As he surveyed the frost-covered yard, he still felt satisfied with his decision to purchase this old farmhouse in the country. True, it was a journey to get anywhere; the nearest person that could reasonably be called a neighbor was the better part of a mile away.

Regardless, it felt good to know this land belonged to him - especially since his career had gone down the shitter. Even if he would never be able to fix the place up the way he had once dreamed, he was sure he could find a way to live without riding stables and a swimming pool.

Tom thought of his recent downfall less frequently now than he used to. But every now and then, his thoughts would drift back to the event, like an accident replayed in slow motion, over and over again, his mind trying to figure out what he could have done differently.

His career in the finance industry had been a lot like the final Space Shuttle Challenger mission: a straight-up trajectory that was all smiles and hope and promise, right up until the point where everything exploded into a million pieces. His wife

6

was the survivor left behind, barely able to comprehend what had happened, still trying so hard to pretend everything was normal.

What was that old joke? *I'll feed the kids, you feed the fishes?*

His career was sleeping with the fishes, anyway. This thought amused him, and he chuckled aloud.

His new job had been a high-profile, high-paying position, one he had assumed he wouldn't have a shot at for at least another fifteen years; but fortune had smiled upon him and handed him his dream job on a silver platter when he least expected it. They had told him this was the gravy train to ride into retirement with style; the fantastic salary, stocks and bonuses were a certainty for at least the next decade, no sweat.

It had seemed too good to be true, but he still took the bait, hook, line and sinker, and for a while life was grand. He and Kelly and Emily were happy together, maybe the happiest they had ever been as a family. The fat checks started rolling in as promised. His wife had been able to quit her job to raise their daughter full-time, and the future, as they say, was wide open. If only it had lasted a little longer.

Tom snapped out of his daydream, back to the reality of the present, to the dozens of bags of lime that waited patiently for him at the end of the driveway. Not that long ago, there wouldn't have been a pile of cash big enough to convince him to climb inside a filthy crawlspace, even for a brief visit.

He realized now that his dream was long gone. Now he was simply one of a million other unemployed, middle-aged men, struggling to keep up with a deteriorating house that he could no longer afford. He had been forced to exchange his fine tailored suits and unending possibilities for manual labor that he would rather not touch with a twenty-nine foot pole.

As he squinted against the bright winter sun, delaying the inevitable labor as long as possible, his mind continued to wander back to that fateful day a few months after he had taken the promotion - the day when his phone had chirped with the tinny voice of a stranger telling him that his big shot job had come to a sudden and untimely demise.

Financial mismanagement had been revealed by an internal audit, he was told. It had all occurred under his area of responsibility, and the board of directors had decided to let him go.

In that instant it had dawned on him for the first time that he wasn't the golden child; he was the fall guy.

He would not be prosecuted, he had been informed - but he wouldn't be receiving severance, no golden parachute or retirement package - only game over, the end.

Those had been the worst of times, the bad days, the big depression. Kelly had begged to get her job back, and did – but at only half the former pay. During that dark period, Tom only got out of bed for the briefest moments, just long enough to get his daughter off to school and help Kelly out of the door to work; then he would retreat back into the safe womb of his bedcovers, lured by the promise of dreamless sleep. There he would lie, motionless in the darkness, for hours upon hours, day after day.

He had gained weight, avoided his wife and daughter, and generally behaved as though his life was over.

His inconsolable sulking ultimately led to two serious incidents.

Twice his daughter had gotten off the school bus to find the front door to the house locked, and twice was stranded on the porch, frightened and alone, for several hours. Kelly had arrived home from work on both occasions to find her young daughter outside, panicked and in tears. She had been distressed and enraged, as both times Tom was fast asleep inside the house - fat, unshaven, unshowered – and deaf to the cries of his little girl banging on the front door, pleading for him to let her in.

That was what had led to Kelly giving him a final ultimatum: either he could get his life together, or he could get out.

She had suggested that perhaps he should go back to school and learn a new profession. It would be good for him, she had argued; it would open his eyes to new opportunities, get his mind off the past and help him focus on the future – or some such blather. He had thought that even she, herself, hadn't believed what she was telling him.

She had lectured him for what seemed like hours, rivaling a brainwash session in a gulag. Eventually, her relentless barrage of rhetoric had broken his will and Tom had agreed to go back to school, to community college in a nearby town.

After his high-flying business experience, it felt like the ultimate humiliation. He was only in his early forties, but the disintegration of his career had dealt such a blow to his ego and self-image that he felt like a man twice his age. He had showed up to his first college class feeling like an elderly man being forced from his room at a retirement home to attend an arts-and-crafts social.

He had hated the classes at first, had only agreed to go because it had required less effort than packing his stuff and moving out of the house.

It was the lowest point in his entire life, he was sure. He had been about ready to pull the plug once and for all on his cryogenically frozen dreams, but then one day he had met the most amazing creature.

"Miranda." she had stated simply. She had offered him her hand and flashed a smile, confident and beautiful. Her coal-black hair was trimmed neatly at the shoulders, framing blue eyes that shimmered with intensity.

The instant her hand touched his, it set his cold, sorrowful heart on fire.

It had been his first day in a new art class, an elective he had chosen to take, and the instructor had given them an assignment to complete together.

"We're going to be perfect partners for this project," she had said, "you work on *it*, and I'll work on *you*. I want to find the artist in you for everyone to admire."

Tom remembered that he had stared blankly at her for a moment, speechless, stunned by the power of her passion, her sheer presence – her eyes.

He was amazed to have found himself interested in something, or more accurately – *someone* - for the first time in longer than he could remember, and a whispered "okay," had been the best response he could muster.

She had hugged him, probably out of pity for his devastated sense of self-esteem. But that one simple hug had left him a changed man. The moment he felt her arms around him and took in her scent in one deep breath, he knew he was in love, had a reason to live again.

Not too long after that, they had made love for the first time in the back of her Chevy Malibu, parked behind the campus canteen. He remembered calling Kelly afterwards that day to tell her she didn't have to pick him up from school - he already had a ride.

Kelly had never asked him about his new friend at school, but seemed pleased to find his attitude on the mend. He had started speaking up more frequently at dinner than was usual, and helping around the house more, too.

But mostly, he eagerly anticipated going to class each morning.

He and Miranda had made love every chance they could since then, sometimes in her car, sometimes in an empty classroom, or a private study room at the college library. Whenever they had a moment alone they were all over each other - inseparable, insatiable.

Tom finished off his coffee in a final gulp, set the cup down on the porch rail and began collecting the things he would need for the task that lay ahead.

He would tell Kelly about Miranda; he would. He knew it was the right thing to do, and he would do it. Not yet, but soon; it would be better for him to reveal the truth about Miranda himself, rather than allow Kelly to find out accidentally. He would need to stay in control of the situation, if he were to have any chance of keeping things from getting ugly.

He grabbed his thick woolen hat from the rocking chair and zipped his coat up to his chin. He slipped his cell phone and keys into his coat pocket and tucked a small mag-light into his jeans.

He locked the front door, descended the stairs and headed for the corner of the house. His boots crunched on the frozen ground as he approached the thousand pounds of powdered lime, stacked in fifty-pound bags, that waited for him there along with several large rolls of plastic sheeting.

Tom was no handyman, nor had he ever been. Hanging up a picture was the closest Kelly had ever gotten him to engaging in actual physical labor, and then only after incessant nagging.

But paying someone to do the job for him was no longer an option, and the moisture under his house had to be controlled soon, or else he would have a much more expensive problem on his hands - one he wouldn't be able to afford, either.

He started to work, heaving the sacks of lime onto his shoulder, one at a time, and then dropping them off in a heap next to the small hole that led underneath the house.

The crawlspace entrance was little more than a gash in the stone foundation of the old house. The rusty door that kept the crawlspace sealed from the outside world swung open inwardly - a somewhat awkward arrangement - and was propped open with an old crowbar, wedged into the mud under the house.

He squatted beside the crawlspace entrance to catch his breath, the moisture of his lungs huffing little white puffs into the frigid air. He shielded his eyes from the bright sunlight as he tried to see what awaited him underneath the house.

Darker than the devil's asshole under there, he thought. The doorway gaped open before him – its maw black, cold and soulless. It reminded Tom of a cold-blooded carnivore, a dead-eyed crocodile, motionless on a river bank, waiting to clamp onto the flesh of an unsuspecting victim and drag its startled prey deep into the inky black below. He remembered reading somewhere that they would sometimes hold the unfortunate catch underneath the water until it lost hope, stopped struggling, and finally surrendered to the unyielding darkness of the croc's bowels.

The thought made Tom cold, and he shivered. He had never experienced claustrophobia, but he thought he might soon understand that irrational fear.

"Fuck," he said. "This sucks!"

Got to get it done, he reminded himself. Even though he had insisted to Kelly this would be an all-week project, he felt sure he could knock it out in a single day, easy. Miranda would be here in the morning; there was no way he was going to waste precious time that could be spent with her back under the house tomorrow.

After a solid hour of work, Tom dropped the final bag of lime on top of the others. The exertion of carrying a thousand pounds of lime had made his clothes too warm, and he unzipped his coat to let it air out.

He realized he was no longer afraid to break a sweat, to get his hands dirty; Miranda had seen to that. He had started doing push-ups and sit-ups each morning, and the effort was paying off. He had lost twenty pounds during the two months that had passed since he met her.

He recalled the look of surprise that had flashed briefly in his wife's eyes earlier that morning, when she had seen him naked in the bathroom. Even though she had tried to hide it, he knew his newly-fit physique had surprised her.

He wiped the sweat from under the edge of his hat as he knelt and peered into the dark muddy hole he was about to crawl into. His coat had to go, he decided. He didn't want to be a sweaty mess before he even got started under the house.

He slipped off his outer layer and draped it neatly over a stack of bagged lime. Hot trails of steam rose from it into the frigid winter air like phantom snakes.

He took a deep breath for courage, pulled the flashlight from his pocket and slipped on his work gloves. He got down on his knees and stuck his head into the hole to have a look around.

A foul stench greeted him as he waited for his eyes to adjust to the darkness. The smell was a dank mixture of several equally unpleasant scents – mold, rust, rotting wood, stale dust and an earthy shit smell that he figured was a fairly accurate recreation of what it must be like to stick your head up a cow's ass and inhale deeply.

He could hardly see a few feet ahead of him in the limited area the sunlight was able to penetrate. He could see that the crawlspace floor was still very muddy from the faint sheen of reflection on its surface, but it was nowhere near the lake it had been a couple of weeks ago.

Leaving the crawlspace door open had helped dry things out a bit, but Tom was disappointed to see that he was still going to have to contend with a fair amount of moisture.

He flipped the flashlight on and panned the beam of light back and forth across the tight crawlspace. It shone on only the first few rows of rough-hewn crossbeams that supported the floor of the house, barely a foot or two above the muck.

He leaned further into the hole to try and find the permanent light fixture that would illuminate the space while he worked. Tom loved his mag-light; the flashlight's beam chased the darkness from its path nicely, and in a few seconds he spotted the lonely and ancient light bulb, nailed to a beam in the dead center of the crawlspace. A thin pull string dangled from it.

Tom sighed. Why couldn't the light have a power switch next to the door? How much more would that have cost? Whatever the amount, he was confident it would have been money well spent.

He pulled himself back out of the crawlspace and sat for a moment, plotting his plan of attack. The door was small, barely wide enough for a man of average size to fit through. He thought for a moment how fortunate it was that he had slimmed down recently. On the other hand, perhaps it was unlucky; if he were still overweight he wouldn't have been able to do the job even if he wanted to.

He grabbed a roll of plastic sheeting and slid it through the narrow opening, careful to keep the end of the roll out of the soft mud.

Once the first roll of plastic was tucked safely underneath the house, Tom turned to soak up a few last rays of sunlight before he crawled into the waiting gloom. Fragile beams of the midmorning sun shot here and there through the sparse foliage of several enormous elms, making the trees look like giant glowing sea urchins hovering in the air.

A deep breath of the fresh winter air brought him a rush of pleasure with its mingled scents of pine, snow, and fallen leaves. Miranda had brought him back from the edge of extinction, had made him once again able to appreciate the little things, the simple wonders that life could bring.

The thought of her renewed his vigor, and he turned to face the crawlspace; it still lay in wait for him, mouth agape.

Without further hesitation, he dropped to his knees, took a deep breath and squirmed through the narrow opening.

The aging farmhouse sat atop a much tighter space than Tom had realized. The darkness, combined with an oppressive odor, created its own unique brand of claustrophobia. If the temperature hadn't been like a meat locker, he wasn't sure he could have handled it.

He now realized exactly why the plumbers he had hired previously had insisted on raising their rates halfway through the job. He had always held the grudging thought that it was because the Lexus in his driveway had made him an easy mark for blue-collared types. He knew better now, though, as he stared into the horrid space underneath his house. He had no doubt that those plumbers had earned every penny, regardless of how much they had charged him.

There was little room to maneuver between the cold, muddy ground below and the rough wooden beams above. He rolled onto his side and turned on the flashlight, panning the light back and forth to scope out the area in which he would be working.

The ground underneath the house was fairly level, from end to end and side to side. No spot he could see offered more comfort than any other – it was all one big soggy, subterranean field of mud, punctuated with supports at regular intervals.

The beams above him were so low that he had no hope of achieving an upright sitting position anywhere beneath the house. He realized, to his dismay, that he would be spending the entire day in a slightly elevated low-crawl, at best. He could move across the ground without completely dragging his body through the mud, but not by much.

He attempted to raise himself onto his hands and knees, and hit his head on a crossbeam in the process; not hard, but painful enough to get the job off to a bad start and fully illustrate the physical limitations the task would impose.

Knees and elbows were going to be the best he could manage to keep himself off the ground. It was such a tight fit he couldn't even lift his head up enough to look ahead. To look in any particular direction, he had to turn his entire upper body, head cocked to the side. Contorting himself into awkward positions all day was going to be a serious pain in the neck, he thought - pun intended.

The small flashlight didn't help much. Tom hoped an increase in the amount of light would make his cramped situation more bearable, so he turned his attention to finding the bulb.

He located it quickly. The glass bulb reflected the beam of his flashlight like a buoy bobbing in the middle of the ocean during a starless night.

Tom grabbed a roll of plastic and positioned it in front of him. He ran his fingers around the roll, found the loose edge of the sheeting and clamped it to the ground with his palm, rolling the plastic out ahead of him with his other hand. A dry pathway unfurled before him, as he crawled towards the dormant light bulb. The low crawl towards his target was slow going, and required more effort than he had imagined.

He was halfway to his destination in the center of the house when his back snagged hard on something. He was hooked, stuck on a low crossbeam, unable to move in any direction. Panic pushed the air from his lungs and he couldn't breathe.

He was held immobile between the house and the earth, his body wedged like a hatchet in a piece of dried kindling. Every attempt he made to free himself only served to ensnare him further. He visualized in fast forward what would happen next – his futile struggle, reaching the point of exhaustion while his strength and hope faded.

Fear sent his imagination into overdrive. In his mind's eye, Tom pictured rats creeping from their dens in the darkness beneath his house, one at first, timidly – then others, emboldened by his helplessness. He imagined the vermin gathering by the dozens around his face, curious darting black eyes observing him calmly, before they charged him and devoured the skin from his face.

Tom closed his eyes and became still, his body locked in a half-crawling, half-lying position on his knees and elbows.

There are no rats, he reassured himself. An exterminator had thoroughly inspected the property before he purchased it, and it had been given a clean bill of health, as far as pests were concerned. He tried to remind himself of this fact, although in his current state it brought him little comfort.

After a few minutes, the paralyzing panic that had gripped him passed. His breath began to come more easily, and soon he was once again drawing in the sour air freely.

"Fuck." Tom muttered, once he realized that the absence of pain meant that it was only his shirt that was stuck, not his actual body.

He unbuttoned his shirt and wriggled out of it, left arm first, then the other.

Once out of it, he was free. He was now naked from the waist up, and the cold air bit at his exposed flesh as viciously as the pack of rats he had imagined seconds before.

Tom saw that his shirt had snagged on a rusty nail sticking out from a crossbeam. He realized how lucky it was that the nail had only hooked his shirt, and not dug deep into the meat of his back. He pushed the offending nail out of the way with his thumb and made a mental note to keep a closer look out for hazards.

He squirmed his way back into his shirt and got down to business, rolling his way towards the light bulb like a man possessed, as though at any moment the ground beneath him might give way and swallow him whole if he dared linger too long in any one spot.

Then, there it was: the light bulb, only inches in front of his face. He turned his body awkwardly to the left, head to the side to look back towards from where he had come.

The crawlspace entrance looked a lot smaller from here, and it seemed further away than he knew it really was. It occurred to him that his feelings about that opening had completely changed, now that it had become an exit, now that he was on the inside.

When he had looked at the entrance from the outside, it had been foreboding, threatening in its dark gloom; but from his new vantage point, deep in the belly of the beast, that same opening had assumed a different meaning entirely. It now shone with radiant light, beckoning him to hurry to it, to thrust himself into the glorious sunlit wonders that lay beyond.

It's all a matter of perspective, Tom thought, and smiled.

His fingers found the light's drawstring; as he grasped the small ball-bearing-like beads, he suddenly realized he should have brought a spare bulb along, in case this one was burned out.

He rolled onto his back underneath the bulb, the clearance so low that he could barely roll over. He gave the chain a gentle tug, and the light popped on with a scratchy but reassuring "click".

Thank God.

For the better part of two minutes Tom lay flat on his back underneath the increasingly warm bulb, eyes closed against its hot brilliance. The exertion required to get the plastic rolled out even this far had been a lot more than he had anticipated.

Eyes closed, he imagined himself back in his comfy bed, with his goose down comforter pulled up to his neck, warm sunshine streaming through the window onto his face and the soft warmth of Miranda snuggled up beside him.

Tomorrow can't get here soon enough, he thought.

He took a deep breath. Rest time was over. He had to get this done as fast as possible. He rolled back onto his belly, again squeezing his body as he turned in the tight space.

The shining brightness of the light bulb brought a new warmth and semblance of comfort to this terrible place. This job might not be so bad after all, Tom thought – especially if he didn't have to crawl around with a flashlight the entire time.

The sole downside to the improved lighting was that it revealed that the crawlspace was even more filthy and disgusting than the flashlight's narrow beam had cared to show.

Decades of abandoned cobwebs drooped overhead, weighted with hundreds of long-hollowed shells, insect corpses that waited for his unwitting face to brush them free from where they dangled, in eternal slumber, as he crawled by. Tom wondered how many of these cobwebs were already stuck to the back of his head and shivered at the thought.

Further away, towards the far end of the house opposite the crawlspace door, the ground had a glossy green sheen, probably moss – even though he couldn't imagine how it could grow here, deprived of even the slightest sliver of sunlight. Maybe leaving the crawlspace door open for the last week had been enough to allow it to take hold?

Tom scrunched his nose in displeasure and realization hit him – how much he had lost with his job, how much he missed his freshly pressed suit and his fine office, where the air was always a pleasant mix of coffee and corporate sanitation. This is what he had been reduced to: crawling around in the dark, alone.

He rotated around to face the crawlspace exit again, trying his best to stay atop the narrow plastic path he had laid. Every wayward knee or elbow that slid off the plastic meant another part of him that was wet, muddy, and most importantly - freezing cold. The temperature had dropped since he started and he had let the sweat on his body cool too much.

Tom fought the urge to shiver as he struggled to catch a glimpse of sunlight coming through the open crawlspace door, the same portal that had glowed with such transcendence a few minutes before. The brilliant incandescent glare of the light bulb behind his head cast sharp shadows that stretched out along the ground in front of him.

He looked intently from right to left, but could see nothing beyond the bright ring of light in which he was immersed.

A sudden urge to stand, to stretch, to breathe fresh air possessed him, and Tom scooted along the plastic path toward the crawlspace exit as fast as he could.

The light bulb revealed the limitations of its reach, as Tom quickly found himself submerged again in an inky darkness as he approached the periphery of the house. *Where the hell was the opening?* It should have been in full view by now.

He fumbled in his pocket for the flashlight he had stowed only a few minutes earlier, thinking he would not need it any longer.

He propped himself up on both elbows and clicked the light on, illuminating the area in front of him.

He was startled to see the inside of the crawlspace door a couple of feet in front of his face, concentric circles of light reflecting off its rusty steel surface. Happy to be so close to the exit, Tom let out a sigh of relief.

Then it hit him. The door was closed.

He had difficulty processing it. His mind began to spit out possible explanations, like coins from a slot machine. He sorted through the numerous options and settled on the most likely explanation as to why the crawlspace door he knew beyond a shadow of a doubt had been firmly propped open with a crowbar was closed: the wind must've blown it shut.

He crawled forward and gently pulled at it with one hand, hoping it would swing open, but it didn't budge.

He pulled again, harder, but still the door refused to give.

Maybe someone had passed by and seen the door ajar and decided to close it? He had been in this house almost a year and had yet to see a single neighbor set foot on his property, but he supposed it was possible.

"Hey!" Tom yelled. "Anybody there?"

He waited. Silence.

"Hello?" he called again, more urgent this time, louder. "There's someone working under the house. Please open the door!"

Again he listened, half expecting to hear snickers of laughter; maybe teenage boys had cut through the yard, seen the door open with his materials beside it and thought this would be one hell of a prank.

He held his breath and listened for any sound from the world on the other side of the door.

Nothing.

"Fuck this," he said and twisted himself around, ignoring the plastic sheeting he had so carefully spread on the ground beneath him. It wound around his knees as he turned, rolling onto his back. He stuck his knee into a sludgy puddle; cold water seeped into his jeans and up his bare back chilling him to the bone. He placed the soles of his boots solidly against the steel door; the heavy rubber tread gripped the rusty surface nicely.

He took a deep breath and kicked with all his might. The shock of the impact traveled like electricity up his legs and into the base of his spine, but the door didn't budge in the slightest.

"Fuck! Fuck, fuck, FUCK!" Tom screamed, grasping at his legs but unable to bend his body enough to reach them.

"God damn it, open the motherfucking door!" He screamed so hard it felt as though his throat was turning inside out.

"Open the door! Open the door! Open the motherfucking door!" his voice started out strong and demanding, but the sound of desperation in his voice was growing more prominent.

He planted his feet against the door and kicked two, three, four times more, with the strength of his entire being, but to no effect.

He lay still, panting. His backside was soaked, his jacket slathered in mud, the freezing cold held at bay only slightly by the heat of his exertion.

After a few moments, Tom worked his way around to face the door again, and cupped a single naked ear against the door's frozen metal, listening intently.

The silence beyond the door was complete. In a hoarse whisper, he began to plead earnestly to anyone who might be within earshot on the other side of the door.

"Look, this isn't funny anymore." His voice was barely more than a whimper. "Please open the door. I promise I won't be mad. I promise there won't be any trouble."

He grew still and listened again.

No reply. Not a sound.

He glanced up at the floor of the house above. It felt as though the weight of the entire structure was pressing down on him, crushing him into the mud. He had to summon every ounce of self-control he possessed to keep from descending into a full-blown freak-out.

He listened for sounds coming from above – hoping to hear someone walking around inside. He listened for thirty seconds, perhaps forty, but his ears detected no movement, nothing but the sound of his own labored breathing, his adrenalized heart pulsing in his chest. He realized then that there would be no muffled footfalls from above unless the person who had trapped him here had broken into the house and was robbing him blind. If that were the case, he doubted they would be keen on letting him out when they were finished.

It would be at least a week before his wife would return; what if he really were trapped under here? Would he still be alive by then?

Would she even bother to call to check on him while she was gone, he wondered. It was unlikely. And if she did, would she be concerned if he didn't answer the phone? He guessed not. If anything, she would probably think he was back to moping in bed and wouldn't bother trying to call again.

Thinking about his wife calling to check on him reminded him of his own cell phone – it was in his pocket right now. Getting reception at the farmhouse was a fifty-fifty chance at best, and that was being charitable; but trying to make a call from under the house was definitely worth a shot, Tom thought.

If he could get through to Miranda, even for a

second, she could come and set him free. She would come running to help him. Then, afterwards, they could have a good laugh in a hot bath about his misadventure.

Tom eagerly slipped his hand into his pants pocket to retrieve his cell phone; not finding it, he remembered putting it in his coat pocket – and his coat was outside.

His momentary hope deflated faster than a balloon in a pin factory, but all was not lost. Miranda would be here tomorrow. No matter what happened, the very thought of her, his new love, always filled him with hope. He was sure he would find a way to get out before then, but if worst came to worst, at least she would be here soon.

He decided not to let it come to that; he would find his own way out of this predicament.

Tom took stock of his equipment: A small flashlight, a box cutter, four rolls of plastic sheeting, and the wet muddy clothes on his back. The box cutter might be useful, he thought, and perhaps he could use the plastic sheeting to keep warm.

He rolled onto his knees next to the crawlspace door; the space was so tight that he couldn't lift his head without hitting the floor above.

He pulled his filthy gloves from his fingers and inspected the door frame of the entrance. The doorway was about two feet high by three feet wide, constructed from solid steel tubing welded at the corners. Whoever had built the door had wanted to make sure it would never need to be replaced.

He ran his fingers around the edges of the steel frame. The door fit so snugly that he was unable to slip even a fingertip into the hairline crack that remained between it and the jamb.

The steel door extended over the jamb on the side opposite the hinges, and he realized kicking it open would be impossible. He would have to pry it open.

He tried his best to move the door back and forth, pushing lightly and releasing. But the door had zero give, not even the slightest hint of a jiggle.

His flashlight was starting to give out. He turned his attention to the crawlspace door, hoping to unscrew the two big hinges with the blade of the box cutter. But the screws had been welded into place; escape was going to be trickier than he had hoped.

No, he decided, he would have to find something he could use to pry it open. Maybe a forgotten tool, a loose pipe – he might have to pull out his own plumbing to climb out through the floor, he thought. Whether or not he would have to do something that drastic before the day passed - before Miranda got here and could help him out - he wasn't sure.

He remembered that the door had been propped open with a crowbar; perhaps it had fallen over in the soft mud and was lying somewhere nearby?

Tom shone the flashlight around, illuminating the ground near the crawlspace door.

To his left, he could clearly see a hole in the mud, now half-filled with water, the spot where the crowbar had been. He maneuvered his head to the left and the right, careful to avoid striking it on the low-hanging beams only inches above, feeling for the crowbar in the sludge, but it wasn't there. Whoever had closed the door must have taken it out.

Tom turned around and rested, with his back pressed against the sealed exit, his neck bent sharply forward due to the low clearance. He wished desperately that he could sit up straight, for even one minute.

He panned the weak light around the crawlspace again, intently looking for anything useful. The maglight was only bright enough to see a small radius of the ground around him. The naked incandescent bulb still burned steadily in the center, but he wasn't ready to try to crawl back to the far side of the house to look around just yet.

He leaned his head back against the steel door and sighed deeply. His breath emerged into the cold air as a phantom of steam, illuminated in the flashlight's dim beam.

He set the flashlight on the ground beside him to put his gloves back on. A reflection in the light's beam caught his attention, something small and white on the ground a few feet away from where he hunched.

He dropped his gloves, picked up the flashlight and scooted himself through the mud to see what it was. It seemed odd that anything he might find in the muck under the house could look so shiny and new.

It was a small piece of glossy paper, sturdy cardstock with handwriting on it. Tom peeled it gently from the mud. The ink was smudged, but the neat manuscript lettering was still very legible.

"Enjoy your fresh young meat," it read.

What the fuck? Tom wondered.

He flipped the paper over to find the other side completely smeared with mud.

He wiped it clean with his thumb, positioning the flashlight to get a better look.

It was a photograph.

The face of a beautiful young woman beamed a smile at him through the grime, her eyes sparkling and full of joy.

His curiosity turned into shock as he realized who she was; the realization felt as though someone had kicked him in the stomach.

It was a photo of Miranda - the only one he had of her. He kept it hidden deep inside his wallet, and would pull it out whenever he was alone and feeling sad. Seeing her face, even in a photograph, always made him feel so much better.

But right now, here, her photo had the opposite effect. Seeing her face smiling at him through the smeared filth felt like an icicle plunged deep into his heart.

He flipped the photo back over to take a second look at the writing. Everything was coming together now – the handwriting was unmistakable, he was surprised he hadn't recognized it instantly.

It was Kelly's.

He began to shiver uncontrollably, hugging himself for warmth, but to no avail.

Kelly had found out. That was what had happened. She had found out about his affair with Miranda and now she was punishing him. He almost felt relieved at the thought.

He had been planning to tell her, he knew it was the right thing to do, but the right moment had not yet presented itself. That was the only way he could explain his procrastination.

So much for that now; things had never felt as out of order as they did at that precise moment.

A new realization struck him - he now had hope of getting out of the crawlspace today. He imagined how events had played out: Kelly had found the picture and decided to get revenge on him, to shake him up. She had dropped their daughter at her nanny's house this morning instead of going to visit her family, and had then come back here to confront him. If that was what had happened, that would mean she was *here*. No wonder she had been so adamant about him promising to finish this job. She must have been planning to lock him under here as punishment for his indiscretion all along.

He took some comfort in the understanding that no matter how angry she might be, at least it meant he was not alone. The thought of being trapped in this crawlspace - even for one day – scared him more than almost anything else he could imagine. A pissed-off, cheated-on wife was a frightening thought – but Kelly was no killer. She would relent, she would let him out. She would probably be crying in his arms looking to him for comfort by the evening's end.

She was probably standing outside of the door right now, he thought, trying to decide what to do next. God, he hoped that was true. He realized he hadn't looked forward to seeing his wife's face so badly in a long time.

He slid the photo back into his pocket.

"Kelly?" he called in a gentle voice through the steel door.

"Baby? Are you there? Talk to me."

He heard nothing but icy silence, but in his mind he saw her standing there, fists clenched, mulling over her next move.

"Kelly, I know you're there and I know you're very upset with me…" He paused for dramatic effect. "…and I know I deserve it."

He smiled to himself. This was a game he knew, a game he would win. That bitch wouldn't know what hit her, after he manipulated her into letting him out of here.

Shit, I might lock her ass under here and be done with it, he thought to himself. *I like the sound of that.*

He pressed his ear against the stinging coldness of the door and listened with all his might for her reply, for a muffled sob, for the sound of the padlock being lifted out of the collar, anything.

Silence.

She was being exceptionally stubborn, he thought. It wasn't like her for more than thirty seconds to go by without some sort of bitching spewing from her mouth.

"Sweetheart?" he tried again, using the most humble voice he could manage. "I never meant to hurt you. I love you. I am so, so sorry. Let me out so we can talk about it, okay - about where we go from here."

There was still no response, only maddening silence. Minutes ticked by. Without his watch or his cell phone, he had no way of knowing how much time had passed.

OK, think, Tom, think. How long can she keep me under here before she gives in? When did she find the picture – this morning? Last week? What else could she know about it, other than the fact that he had a picture of someone she didn't know in his wallet?

He didn't know how long Kelly might have had the picture. He hadn't looked at it recently himself. It had only been two days since he had last seen Miranda in person, so it was possible that Kelly had taken it several days ago, if not more.

She would cool down, Tom knew. She couldn't leave him under the house forever; she wouldn't kill him, it wouldn't be worth it. He had not been the best father lately -that was true. But Kelly would not take her daughter's daddy away.

It wasn't like she had had much use for him since he had been laid off anyway, he figured. They hadn't had anything resembling a true conversation for months. Now that she knew about the other woman, she would probably be glad to see him leave, to be able to get on with her life.

Regardless of how she had found out or how she felt about things, here he was: trapped under his own house, freezing cold, soaking wet, and powerless to do anything about it.

Fuck that, he thought, *and fuck her. I'm getting out of here, and she can go fuck herself. There's got to be a way out. I'm not going to lay here and freeze my ass off while she sits upstairs fingering herself while I suffer.*

Tom scanned the crawlspace in earnest for any other way to escape. He knew there was only one door, but he scanned the perimeter of the foundation.

The usual small vents usually built into the foundation walls were missing, since the house had been built long before building codes had required them. He wouldn't have been able to fit through a little vent anyway, he knew. It would have been nice to be able to see sunlight, though - for his sanity's sake if nothing else.

Previous owners had upgraded the house's heating and cooling to a central system decades ago, but the air ducts ran inside the attic, not the crawlspace. Unfortunate, because that eliminated the possibility of pulling an air duct loose from the floor and breaking his way up into the house through the hole.

Too bad, he thought. He could've knocked loose one of the air ducts to blow warm air down here while he plotted his escape.

His flashlight was losing its brilliance and cut weakly through the darkness. He thumped the head of the flashlight against his palm, and it brightened back up. Near the front corner of the house, he could make out what looked like a neat stack of objects, but details were lost in the gloom. Cinderblocks, he guessed. Maybe an abandoned tool might be nearby?

He crawled forward to inspect, full of renewed hope. His elbows and knees made a wet sucking sound as he pulled them from the mud.

After sloshing his way through twenty feet or so of mud and muck, he was surprised to find himself looking at several very new-looking, shrink-wrapped packages of bottled drinking water.

He wasn't sure what to make of this discovery. Did the plumbers leave this when they were working down here a few months ago? If they were that forgetful, perhaps they had left some tools behind too - a wrench, hopefully a crowbar?

No, a crowbar was too unlikely, a fantasy - but a wrench? That was possible. Didn't all plumbers carry giant monkey wrenches around with them? If he could get his hands on one of those, maybe he could bust his way through the foundation and create a hole big enough to escape through.

He surveyed the immediate vicinity around the bottled water for stray tools. Then he saw something, something odd-looking in the corner. He shoved the cases of bottled water excitedly out of his way and crawled towards it as fast as he could manage. It looked like a duffel bag – what if it was full of tools?

Something thin and shiny stuck out from one end of the sack. It reflected the beam of the flashlight back towards him from the sea of near-total darkness; some sort of tool, perhaps? Maybe a screwdriver?

He covered the ground that lay between him and the object in a few seconds, and grabbed for it as soon as it was within his grasp.

It felt different in his hand than his mind had expected it to, and he knew instantly that it wasn't something the plumbers had left behind. He trained the flashlight on it.

It was the pointed stiletto heel of a woman's shoe; black and dressy, with a tasteful silk bow on top, a sharp four-inch heel underneath.

The heaviness of the shoe startled him as he lifted it. It took several seconds for his mind to process the fact that the shoe was heavy because someone was wearing it.

"Fuck!" Tom shouted. He recoiled reflexively, dropping the shoe along with the foot it contained, and again struck his head against a sharp corner of an overhead beam. A streak of pain burned through him, creating a lightning-like flash in his eyes.

Temporary blindness and harsh pain halted his retreat. Every instinct in his entire being commanded him to flee, to get out, to get away from this situation, but there was nowhere he could go.

Tom cradled his throbbing head in his hands; his panicked eyes darted here and there in the dim light, like the beady eyes of the rats he had envisioned not long since, desperately searching for an escape route and finding none, stuck to die in this sinking ship of a crawlspace.

He looked back at the human being that lay like a

crumpled sack in the corner, only a few feet away.

I'm not alone after all, he thought, but the idea brought him no comfort.

"Hello?" he called optimistically to where the person lay silent and motionless in the corner, shrouded in shadows. His voice was not much more than a crackling whisper, so hollow and soft it sounded like an answering machine recording from long ago.

"Are you OK?" he asked, but as soon as the words left his lips he realized that an answer would probably frighten him more than anything else ever could.

He took a deep breath and cautiously crept to where the person lay. The flashlight's ever-weakening beam caressed a distinctively female shape; it traversed along a feminine, slender calf with porcelain skin, over a muddy knee on its journey towards a bright blue dress hiked up over a shapely thigh. The person was lying motionless, in what would have undoubtedly been a very sexy pose, under almost any other circumstances.

The woman was on her side, facing away from him towards the stone foundation, her bottom leg sticking straight out, the other leg pulled up slightly; ankle resting daintily on calf.

He placed his hand on her shoulder and pulled her gently towards him. Her head flopped back and her empty gaze met his.

"No, no, no, no!" Tom whimpered in a low sobbing tone as he recognized who it was.

It was Miranda. The new light of his life – *no, fuck that* – the only light his life had ever known. The light had been extinguished.

He had been anticipating her arrival all morning, all week – in a manner of speaking, his entire life. Now, he realized she had been here all along.

He didn't want to believe it – the body couldn't be Miranda, it couldn't; but deep inside he knew the awful truth, no matter how much his mind tried to persuade him that *it wasn't, it couldn't be, how could it be?* - Tom knew with horrible certainty that it *was* her.

As he stared through tears into her lifeless eyes, he realized she didn't quite look like his Miranda anymore. The sparkle in her eye that made her different from every other woman he had ever met was gone, replaced by a glassy coldness that was nothing like her, the *real* her - not this wax-museum quality replica of her laying in the mud underneath his house.

As he began to weep - something he hadn't done since he was a small boy, the flashlight shook violently in his hand.

Maybe she was still alive, and he could save her; he hoped it wasn't too late. He slid his arm under her head and pulled her close into his chest, cradling her like a child.

"Miranda," he pleaded. "Talk to me. Say something. Come back, baby, come back – I love you so much."

His warm tears rolled down her cold cheek as he laid his sobbing face against hers. He pressed his fingertips against her slender neck, checking for a pulse. Her skin felt like fossilized wood: cold, smooth and rigid.

Her eyes were wide open, bulging half out of their sockets, mapped with dark red bloodshot veins, her eyelids dried and curled back much farther than they should have been. She stared past him, at some point off in the distance, over his right shoulder.

Her mouth was frozen in a snarl, teeth slightly bared. It reminded him of a dog growling a warning: "Stay away, or else."

He wanted so badly to close her staring eyes, to bring together those soft lips that had kissed him with such tenderness only a couple of days before. He wanted to give her back the dignity that had been stolen from her in death. She had been murdered and discarded like garbage, a total calamity in which he had played an unwitting role.

She was wearing a blue dress, a gift from him. It had perfectly matched her stunning periwinkle eyes, those eyes that had sparkled with delight when he had surprised her with it.

She loved it, she had said, and had wanted to try it on immediately. He had said no, to wait. He had asked her to wear it when she came to see him at the farmhouse this week. He couldn't wait to see how beautiful she would look wearing it while lying across his bed.

Well, here she was, and he was finally seeing how beautiful she looked in the dress. Except she wasn't reclining gracefully on his bed, she was laying in the mud underneath his house, about six feet below where his bed would be. The blue of the dress now more closely matched the color of her pallid skin than her eyes. Those eyes that once contained a bottomless sea of blue were now wide and black in the center, pupils dilated like big black pennies.

This is not real, he thought, but it was. The cold heaviness of her body in his arms was proof enough of that.

An odd thought occurred to him, the thought that at any moment she might spring back to life, full of hatred for bringing her to this tragic end. He pictured her setting upon his flesh, intent to devour him with canine fangs gleaming, glistening in the dim glow of the solitary light bulb here in the squalid mud beneath his house.

He resisted an urge to drop her into the mud; instead he laid his hand upon her clammy leg, stroking the smoothness of her right calf, so cleanly shaven and porcelain white, as if to say *"I'm sorry. Oh, my dear sweet Miranda, I am so sorry."*

But she didn't jump to life with eyes blazing and teeth bared to devour his flesh and his forever damned soul as he had feared. Instead, she did what the dead do: nothing. She ignored his touch as though *he* was the phantom, and something much more important than him occupied her entire attention, somewhere over his right shoulder.

The texture of her skin reminded him of silly putty he had played with as a child. For a moment, he had the perverse idea of pushing a color Sunday comic up against her skin to see if a reverse image would remain imprinted on her leg.

He pictured a comic strip with Charlie Brown sitting in front of Lucy's psychiatric advice stand, *5 cents, please*; except instead of Charlie Brown sitting on the stool it was him and instead of Lucy seated at the stand it was Miranda, dead and stiff and staring off into the distance with those glassy, bloodshot eyes.

His sorrow at finding Miranda lying dead in the mud under his house had come to him fast and hit him hard, a sucker punch to the heart. But now he felt another emotion pushing his sorrow away: a sense of anger stronger than any he had ever known before flushed his cold body with a raging heat that boiled in his marrow.

Kelly would pay, he decided.

Kelly had done this. Kelly had killed his true soul mate. His fucking bitch of a wife had stolen the last single joy he had left on this whole entire planet.

Why hadn't she killed *him*, instead? Why did she have to murder a perfectly innocent young woman, so full of life and beauty? What had she ever done to hurt anyone?

Tom pictured his wife standing outside the crawl space door again, arms still crossed in her typical disapproving manner; but this time he imagined seeing her eyes full of delight as she listened to the cries of his sorrowful discovery seep through the door.

He wanted to kill her, to drag her worthless life straight out of her body and give it to Miranda. Life for the worthy, for the beautiful – not the worthless cunt his wife had become.

He would kill her himself, he decided.

Tom let Miranda's lifeless corpse fall back into the mud; her head landed with a dull plop, free arm dangling over the backside of her body.

Tom stabbed his dying flashlight into the darkness ahead of him as he crawled furiously back towards the closed crawlspace door. He splashed through the mud and threw himself towards the sealed exit of what had become in his mind a cursed crypt.

The only remaining vestige of thought in his mind was of revenge: immediate, unyielding and unmerciful retribution.

The rusted steel door stood resolute before him. As he faced it, he became possessed with the conviction that no mere obstacle of brick, mortar or steel could prevent him from inflicting carnage on the person responsible for the horrendous death of his beloved.

Tom squatted on all fours, every muscle of his body tensed like a lion, set to pounce on its prey. He lunged at the door as though it were his mortal enemy, letting out a feral growl as he slammed his shoulder into it with every ounce of his rage-fueled strength.

"You killed her, you bitch!" he snarled through rusted metal with inhuman ferocity. "You killed her. There's nowhere you can hide, I'm coming for you."

He hurled himself against the door again and again, bruising muscle, tearing tendons, ignorant of the absolute futility of his efforts.

Despite the fury within his soul, his body was human and could only withstand so much abuse. Tom launched himself forward one last time before allowing his body to drop into the mud, but he was far from finished.

He clenched his muddy hands into fists and began pummeling on the door in a sick, steadfast rhythm, like a drummer settling in for a solo at a rock concert. Tom already knew how this performance was going to end: with that fucking cunt's head ripped clean from her body, that's how.

Unceasing curses billowed from his mouth like an incantation from the depths of hell, a stream of pure hatred manifested in auditory form.

His effort was wasted; the door absorbed his

abuse with stubborn indifference. His fists were not so unaffected; the rough, rusty surface efficiently shredded his skin, creating a foamy mush of blood and flesh above his wrists.

"I'll kill you, I'll kill you," he screamed, his threats in time with the pounding of his fists. His voice faded to a rasp, his breathing labored.

He twisted himself around in the small space and lay flat on his back in the mud, planting the soles of his feet solidly against the crawlspace door. He resumed stomping on the steel again, with the full strength of both legs at once, not missing a single beat of the rhythm he had established with his now battered and bleeding fists.

"How dare you lay a finger on her? She never did anything to you! You killed her for making me happy? You had no right!" he screamed at the wife he imagined must be standing just outside. His voice began to change, to falter, to tire out. What had started as a lion's roar had been reduced to a pathetic whimper.

WHAM-WHAM-WHAM slammed his feet against the steel.

"I'LL – KILL – YOU!" His threat had become a mantra.

Yet the door stood firm, unyielding. Some tiny part of Tom's brain knew that the door would never kick open, that it only opened inwardly – but the rest of his mind didn't care.

Time stopped for Tom. He continued pounding for what might have been hours, but what was more likely only a few minutes longer. His voice grew softer and softer as his exhausted body continued its increasingly hopeless flailing in the cold, wet mud, the gasping spasms of a fish in a drying puddle, taking its final breaths.

"I'll... kill... you." His last statement of malevolent intent amounted to little more than a thought in his head and a small wisp of steam above his lips.

Tom's feet dropped to the ground beside the doorway. He lay there, as spent as three-inch ash on an abandoned cigarette.

Then silence set in, a quiet so dark and deep and real that his heavy labored breathing seemed to belong to it, not him.

Tom lay motionless as his body slowly sank into the cold mud. He wasn't sure how much time had passed since he had come to be here, but it was long enough for him to be certain that he was, in fact, completely and utterly alone. He knew there was no one in the house, no one outside of the house, no one for miles.

He felt the reality of his solitude with so much certainty it was as though a sixth sense had emerged. His wife had never been there listening, smirking as he had imagined. The silence that greeted him from outside the door and from the house above him was complete. It contained not a hint of a presence other than his own, and even that felt as though it was in danger of slipping away.

The flashlight, tossed aside during his rage, lay in the mud somewhere off to his right. Its filament was a dying ember, a soft red halo of light in Tom's peripheral vision.

Then, as quickly as he noticed it, the glow extinguished.

Silence had arrived first; now its companion,

darkness, announced itself. Tom barely had time to register these sensations as actual thoughts before the next unwelcome guest arrived, like the third horseman of the apocalypse: the cold.

A bitter chill gripped Tom's body with a sudden rushing ferocity. The hot heat of rage that had burned in his veins only minutes before was replaced with a torrent of frigid water, ripping through every capillary in his body like tiny jagged shards of ice.

Tom tried to roll over onto his front, but found he was unable to move. He lay terrified, half-paralyzed, teeth clenched as his entire body convulsed; shivering as the excruciating pain of the cold drew him into its arctic embrace.

The unholy trinity of cold, darkness and silence now owned his soul. With enormous effort, Tom dragged himself onto his stomach; his shredded hands dripped blood that clotted in sticky spiral ribbons on his forearms. He wanted to crawl from his muddy puddle back onto the dry plastic sheeting, but the exertion of his rage had completely depleted his energy.

He looked towards the light bulb in the center of the crawlspace that still burned like a distant sun in the darkness; it seemed as though it was a million miles away. He wanted to go there, to be close to its warmth and light, but he felt like a planet at the farthest end of the solar system, spiraling out of control, about to be flung into the nether regions of the uncharted void of the universe, never to return.

***

TIME PASSED. Tom didn't know how much. He'd been

EVANS LIGHT

trapped in the crawlspace for days, weeks – maybe
even months; he didn't know or care anymore. Tom
no longer had a sense of time, of day or night.

Everything was night now. Everything was cold.

He had kicked at floorboards, pulled at pipes,
pried at foundation stones, but to no avail.

He had survived as best he could. He had moved
the water bottles nearer to the light bulb in the center
of the crawlspace, had pulled the plastic sheeting
there as well. He had created a makeshift shelter
around the light, to capture its warmth in a bubble of
plastic.

He had tried to dry his sopping clothes, but there
was never enough heat to make a difference. They sat
in a soggy pile, unworn, forgotten. He had ventured
from his shelter from time to time to revisit his useless
attempts to escape, to sit nude and freezing by the
crawlspace door and call for help until the cold drove
him back to the warmth of his shelter by the light
bulb.

That had been back in the good old days here in
the crawlspace, back when he had still had light and
warmth, before he had accidentally broken the
solitary incandescent bulb.

Since the light bulb had gone, there had been
nothing but dark and cold and silence.

Tom lay on his back in the dark, nude and
wrapped up in plastic in the spot under the house
where the dirt was the driest. The clearance there was
only fifteen inches, but Tom didn't mind. He'd rather
lie flat on his back pinned under the beams in dry dirt
than to be in the cold mud with more room.

Things were better that way, he would probably
have told you; but Tom didn't talk anymore. He'd

44

been quiet for a very long time.

Tom's plastic cocoon was surrounded by a strange variety of objects, tossed about him in no particular order, stuff he had pried from underneath the house a long time ago, back when he still believed escape from the crawlspace was possible.

One of the objects was a three-foot length of pipe he had managed to detach from the plumbing, flooding half of the crawlspace in the process. In a pile of stuff next to his feet was quite a bit of insulated wire of various lengths; he'd once had an idea for how to use it, but had since forgotten and the project had been abandoned.

Further off to his right side were a dozen or so water bottles filled with stale urine, neatly lined up along the edge of the crawlspace wall. A few more bottles, slightly fresher, were carelessly littered here and there around him.

In the corner of the crawlspace, near the place where Miranda's undisturbed corpse once lay, was a small, smooth circular indentation in the dirt. It was the remnant of a puddle of tears, long since dried. There was another indentation in the dirt near Tom's waist - a puddle of urine, still quite full and wet.

Situated about thirty feet from where Tom reclined motionless in the dull, dreary and otherwise unremarkable crawlspace was a large and rather comprehensive collection of human bones.

Tom had discovered that dark, cold and silence weren't the unholy trinity; they were the first three horsemen of his own personal apocalypse. He had realized this when the fourth and most fearsome horseman arrived: hunger.

Tom had fought valiantly to resist this strongest

temptation of the flesh, but had lost the fight in the end.

The larger bones in the collection had been picked mostly clean of flesh, and were still attached to the festering, open carcass of a nude young woman, sprawled out in the mud up against the crawlspace wall.

The cold had provided plenty of refrigeration for Miranda's tender young flesh. Tom had gnawed her thighs, calves, and biceps down to the bone; only her face and the furry parts between her legs remained entirely unmolested.

"Enjoy your fresh young meat," Kelly had written on the back of Miranda's photo, and Tom had done precisely that. He had been devastated to find her body here at first, but eventually discovered that Miranda was a companion with truly exquisite taste.

**

TIME AND LIGHT are almost always connected in one fashion or another and so it was with Tom. Time for him had evaporated in the darkness and left him alone with eternity.

Then, one day, light returned to the crawlspace. With it, time returned as well.

The light arrived with no sound or fanfare.

Tom was lying in his usual spot, from which he moved only on the most infrequent occasion to feed or to drink, or occasionally to void elsewhere, although more often than not he would let go wherever he lay. His eyes were open, unseeing in the darkness, when the crawlspace door pushed open.

Light streamed through the opening, and the

early morning sun peeked into the darkest corners of the crawlspace.

Tom did not react at all at first, his sense of sight so wasted in the darkness that his eyes were unable at first to interpret the forgotten sensation.

After a few moments, Tom licked his dry, cracked lips and blinked. His scarred hands, fingertips blackened and dead from the frost, clenched into fists as he turned his head towards the open crawlspace door.

The warmth of the sunlight caressed his face like some long-forgotten but cherished childhood dream. His body, as if by instinct, began to slowly move towards the light.

The radiance beckoned him, and he dragged himself through the mire hand over hand, clawing at the earth beneath.

With great effort, he squirmed his way through the crawlspace door, slowly emerging into the sunlight. Anyone who might have seen his expulsion from the small dark hole could be forgiven for thinking they were witnessing a house giving birth to a human.

He lay panting on the ground, covered in afterbirth of dried blood, mud, and other bodily fluids, his nude body still mostly wrapped in the womb of plastic sheeting he had created during his long gestation underneath the house.

He made his way to his feet, wobbly and uncertain at first like a newborn foal; his eyes blinked rapidly in the bright sunshine, as he tried to comprehend the new world around him.

A look of awareness, of remembering, rose slowly in his eyes. He surveyed the house for a moment, the

EVANS LIGHT

crawlspace door, the yard around him and the world that lay beyond.

He made his way toward the front of the house on shaky legs, dragging his feet along in a clunky shuffle, finally arriving at the steps that led up to the main entrance.

He ascended the stairs one at a time with great care and deliberation, stopping to rest briefly on each one. After what seemed like an eternity, he reached the top. The front door to his house stood open. It beckoned him and he entered.

The aroma of freshly-prepared food floated into his senses like angels on clouds. He saw his wife watching him from the kitchen down the hall. How long had it been since he had last seen her? She looked younger than he remembered. Her demeanor was relaxed, refreshed, like she'd never felt better in her entire life. Her eyes sparkled.

Tom stood motionless in the front doorway, naked and covered in his own filth, lost in the sight of her. She smiled and unfolded her arms, bidding him forward.

"Come here," she said softly in the most silken voice he had ever heard.

He stumbled to her.

She wrapped her arms around him and pulled his ravaged body close to hers with a gentle embrace, rocking him gently like a mother with her child.

She smelled of lavender and vanilla.

"I love you, Tom," she whispered, and kissed him lightly on his filthy cheek.

He rested his head on her breast, closed his eyes, and began to cry.

***

CRAWLSPACE *is one of my earlier stories, and ended up being longer than originally envisioned. I'm rather fond of the final section, the somewhat poetic outro on which it culminates.*

Reactions to this story have been interesting to follow, and seem to vary depending on gender. There are two sides to every story, the axiom goes, and CRAWLSPACE is no exception. Regardless of whether you choose to place your loyalties and sympathy with the main character, or if you feel that he is getting his just desserts, the ending should still satisfy most.

As a side note, the original draft ended in a much more brutal and conclusive manner, but I think the ending as it is now puts the reader in a much greater state of psychological discomfort, and leaves the "where do they go from here" open to the imagination.

WHATEVER
POSSESSED YOU?

READING WEIRD TALES and horror novels were his guilty pleasure. He felt certain he could write them, too - as brilliantly as the best of them.

Gerard Faust had long harbored the notion of quitting his job at the university, of saying *fuck it all* and finally doing what he really wanted to do: write horror for a living.

Common sense had kept him from ever giving it a try, at least until recently. He was a Professor of *Literature*, for Christ's sakes. Why would he dare sully his reputation - maybe even risk his tenure - by writing bloody pulp? Even the best, most literate horror was despised and ridiculed by academia until long after the poor author was dead. Gerard was sure his own death, by starvation most likely, would be swift in coming if he tried to make a living by writing what he loved.

It *was* tempting though. He had his entire first

novel completely formed in his thoughts, written in his mind. The book would be amazing, he was certain. All he had left to do was actually *write* it, to take some time off from teaching and get it done.

"You know the difference between a pizza and a horror writer?" Sonia, his wife, used to tease, whenever he'd bring up the subject.

"A pizza can actually feed a family of four?" he'd mutter. Gerard knew the answer well enough and had taken its meaning to heart, so his wish to become a full-time writer had remained simply that – *an idle wish*, a daydream.

But sometimes wishes do come true, he secretly believed.

He had gone out for dinner with a long-lost college friend who had made something of a name for himself in the publishing industry. Casual conversation, along with a couple bottles of wine, got Gerard talking about his long-dormant book idea. His friend loved it.

To his utter surprise, a few days later Gerard found himself signing an honest-to-goodness publishing contract, complete with a hefty advance payment and a brutal six month deadline.

It seemed too good to be true, and he was afraid that maybe it was.

The challenge of turning his idea into a finished novel proved much trickier than he had anticipated. The words in his head had skillfully eluded his efforts to capture them on the page for weeks at a time. A feeling of helplessness and impending doom grew inside him as the final deadline approached; the sands of time seemed to fall faster with each passing day.

Some days, the words poured from his fingertips and the stack of pages on his desk would begin to grow. A faint glimmer of hope sparkled somewhere on the distant horizon, he felt confident.

But the feeling didn't last long. A profound case of writer's block once again settled over his mind like a dense fog. He knew he had to get the words flowing, and fast - his deadline was only two weeks away, and his unpaid sabbatical from teaching would end shortly thereafter. The advance for the book, half-spent already, would have to be repaid in full if he couldn't deliver.

The thought made him shudder.

After wasting the afternoon staring at a blank screen, the inactivity of his fingers relentlessly mocked by a blinking cursor, he decided to abandon his desk and go get some fresh air. A change of scenery might help clear his mind, at least he hoped, so he hopped in the car and headed for the one place where he could almost always find fresh inspiration.

A small bell chimed overhead as Gerard pushed open the vintage stained-glass front door and stepped inside the used bookstore. He inhaled deeply, savoring the aroma of ancient inks and yellowed paper, as a connoisseur of fine wine might appreciate the bloom of a vintage year. A sense of calm washed over him.

He made his way through the racks of books towards the register at the back counter, the worn planks of the floor knocking loudly underfoot as he walked. The store was mostly empty, only a single other individual browsed through the dusty titles quietly as Gerard made his way to the back of the shop.

The register was untended. Gerard sidled up to the counter and rang the bell, glancing through the small window in the office for a sign of the clerk. The rare editions that he had come to look through were sitting in a stack behind the counter, just out of reach. He wished the shopkeeper would hurry.

He rang the bell again, impatient.

"Mr. Faust?" A soft voice came from over his shoulder.

Startled, he spun about to find a young man wearing a hoodie standing behind him. He was dirty and unkempt, and seemed extremely nervous.

"Yes?" Gerard asked, trying to recall if he knew him from somewhere. "Can I help you?"

"I hope so," the man said, slipping his hand inside his coat as he fumbled about for something concealed within.

Gerard wondered if he was about to be mugged. He knew he was being irrational, but his pulse still quickened as he pictured the floor of the bookstore covered in his own blood and guts.

The man located whatever it was he was looking for and withdrew his hand. He wasn't holding a weapon, to his relief. Instead, the man tightly clutched a folded square of paper between his grimy finger and thumb.

"The clerk here said you were a writer, said that you drop by sometimes, said you might be able to help me," the man said. "I need a professional opinion on something real bad."

He offered the folded paper, his hand trembling.

Gerard took it. The stock of the paper was heavy and the grain coarse on his fingertips. Two words were written on the outside in exquisite calligraphy:

Maazo Maazo.

"Read it," the man said, insistent.

Now curious, he unfolded the brittle parchment-like paper. It appeared ancient, and he was careful not to rip it along the seams.

In the center of the paper was a single stanza, handwritten with accomplished penmanship. It appeared to be a poem, perhaps, or the verse of a song. Gerard read the first few words to himself and realized it was in a foreign language. It looked a little like Portuguese, but he wasn't sure.

He looked up, puzzled.

"I don't know this language, sorry," he said, and tried to hand the paper back, but the man refused to take it.

"It's not a foreign language," the man said, a hint of derision in his voice. "It's a new art form, one the world has never seen before. That's why I need your opinion."

"How can I give you an opinion on something I don't understand?" Gerard said.

The man took a deep breath, clearly growing irritated. Gerard wondered if something was wrong with the man. He seemed *off*, somehow.

"You have to read it *out loud*," the man said, making clear he was stating the obvious.

"Words and music are inseparable," he said, "no dividing line exists between one and the other. Music permeates every word ever uttered."

His suspicions about the man's mental state now seemed justified, and he looked for a way to make a graceful and rapid exit, as the man continued rambling.

"For this to work - for you to hear the actual song

embedded in the words," he said, "you have to speak them with your mouth. You can't just think them in your head. Your vocal cords are the instrument on which the music of those words will be played. It's the physical act of saying them that releases the music they contain. Try it, you'll be amazed – I promise."

"Okay, I'll read it, *once* - but then I have *got* to go," Gerard said, laughing weakly. "My wife is going to have the cops out looking for me if I'm even one minute late for dinner tonight,", he said, hoping it sounded remotely plausible - especially if this nut job had any more weird ideas in store for him.

Gerard spoke the strange words aloud, sounding them out phonetically as he read.

"Mah-zoe Mah-zoe toso nimi so, tumay noso oolaya ma-yi, Noso olaya anona ya na-mi..."

He paused. The man's expression had changed from irritation to pure anticipation. His eyes were eager, pupils dilated.

"Go on, go on," he urged, "the good part's coming."

Gerard continued.

"Tumay noso oolaya ma-yi, Mah-zoe Mah-zoe toso nimi so," he finished.

"Yes! Yes!" the man growled, and his voice became surly and strange as he spoke.

He grabbed Gerard by the face before he could react, pulling him forward until their noses touched, snatching the paper away, crumpling it in his fist. The fragile parchment disintegrated almost instantly, its remnants drifting like brown snowflakes to the floor.

The man's pupils began to flash open and shut, like a camera aperture, snapping photos one after the other, and his breath blew hard against Gerard's lips.

It was hot, too hot, almost scalding, like steam blowing from a kettle. Gerard tried to pull away, but the man's hand was like a vice clamped over his jaw.

Gerard felt steamy breath entering his mouth, crawling over his tongue like it was alive, sliding down the back of his throat. Then he felt it somewhere deep inside him, moving.

The man's pupils stopped flashing. He released Gerard, stumbling backwards, as though he had been punched in the stomach by an invisible fist.

Gerard's heart pounded, making a hot angry noise as it beat louder than ever before. The pulsing throb of the muscle in his chest sounded like muffled words being spoken inside him, words that repeated over and over.

Maazo Maazo, Maazo Maazo, it said.

"I'm sorry," the man mumbled, his voice little more than a whisper as he gasped for breath. "I had no choice. He made me do it."

Gerard could barely hear the man over the sound of his own pulse thumping in his ears.

"What did you do?" Gerard asked, frantic. "Who are you?"

"*Free*," the man said simply, then turned and ran from the store. The little bell rang overhead as the door slammed behind him. Within seconds, he had disappeared into the descending gloom of the rainy evening.

***

THE OWNER OF THE STORE finally poked his head out of the back office after hearing the scuffle, but wasn't able to identify the deranged man, telling Gerard that he had only spoken to the man once before, a few days ago.

Gerard drove straight home, wheels splashing through puddles on tree lined streets. He was shaken but otherwise unharmed, and eager to get back to the safety and comfort of his family and home. He knew it would be a while before he would have the courage to visit the bookstore again.

As he drove, his throbbing heart eased back into its regular rhythm, the words *"Maazo Maazo"* still reverberating loudly inside him. It was like having a second heartbeat – not in his chest, but in his mind. The hum of it in his head was both energizing and comforting. It felt as though something had been missing from his life until today, and now he was whole.

"Maazo Maazo," he said out loud, and as he spoke the words, a powerful feeling of energy surged through him. A new sense of determination to finish his book, to complete what he had started, took root in his gut. That feeling continued to blossom as he turned the car into his driveway.

Maazo Maazo, Maazo Maazo, the rhythm whispered.

He would finish his book, and it was going to change the world.

***

GERARD TURNED THE KEY to his front door and stepped into the foyer.

He was greeted only by darkness and silence, which was unusual. He wasn't terribly late getting home, not late enough to make Sonia get angry and take off, anyway.

Besides, he had a good excuse - no, a *great* excuse.

"Sonia?" he called into the darkness.

He was relieved when she answered.

"I'm in the living room, could you please help me with something?" she called in a happy, sing-song voice.

Gerard fumbled along the wall, looking for a light switch.

"Did a breaker trip in the garage again?" he asked as his fingers located a switch beside the living room door. He didn't expect it to work, but flipped it into the "ON" position anyway.

He was startled when the lights came on like they were supposed to, and then again when he found the living room full of balloons and smiling people.

"Surprise!" everyone shouted. The room was draped with decorations; a big banner over the fireplace read, *"Lordy, Lordy, Gerard is Forty!"*

A few minutes later, Gerard was seated at the head of the dining room table, and refrains of "Happy Birthday" filled the air.

Maazo Maazo. Maazo Maazo.

The refrain was still pounding in his head like a mantra, and it was making him feel as though he would burst if he didn't start working on his book soon, or even better – *right now.*

His fingers started tapping on the tabletop, impatient to begin typing. Gerard clutched his hands together in an effort to make them be still, but his fingers continued to struggle, as if they had a mind of their own and were eager to get to work.

Sonia handed him the first slice of cake, but he only took two bites before he excused himself and darted off to his study.

***

HE SETTLED into the soft leather chair at his desk and realized it had never felt so good before. He looked at the hopeless stack of papers piled on his desk - that was his draft, the one that needed to be completed in two weeks. Finishing his book had seemed almost impossible until tonight; he had been sure he would miss his deadline, and hadn't been confident he would be able to make the project coherent enough to publish, much less sell enough copies for him to quit his day job.

But those doubts had gone, replaced by a vigor and determination he had never felt before. He pulled his keyboard towards him, caressing its keys with his fingers as he waited for the computer to boot up.

Beside the monitor was a functional dipping pen and matching ink well, a thoughtful gift Sonia had given him when they were dating. He remembered that she had wrapped it in glossy red paper dotted with little white hearts. It had been a permanent fixture on his writing desk ever since.

Gerard picked up the pen, its metal surface cool and smooth against his skin. On its silver stem, the pen was engraved with elegant lettering: *"To the best man who ever wrote his way into the story of my life; make sure it has a happy ending! Love, Sonia"*.

Once the computer was ready, Gerard slipped the pen back into the ink well and began to type. The noise of the party in the other room seemed to drift from somewhere now far away.

Gerard began typing with a slow and steady pace

at first, but the tempo of his fingers on the keyboard grew faster and faster as he went - a locomotive picking up steam and headed down the straightaway, a full load of coal in its boiler and the devil on its heels.

***

SONIA AND THE KIDS found Gerard still working hard at his desk the next morning, dozens of printed pages strewn across his desk. It looked as though he had written his way through the entire night.

After much pleading, she convinced him to take a break from writing and join her in the kitchen for breakfast.

"I'm so sorry," he said as he poured a coffee. "I shouldn't have acted like that."

Sonia smiled.

"It's okay," she reassured him. "I told everyone you were under a lot of pressure to meet your deadline, and they seemed to understand. I probably shouldn't have sprung a party on you like that - I just thought you could use a night off. You've been working yourself to death with that book."

Gerard remembered the previous evening, and an excited expression lit up on his face.

"Something happened yesterday at the bookstore, before the party," he said.

She shot him a quizzical look.

He searched for the right words as he settled into the seat beside her, but came up empty.

"I don't know, something...I feel...clear, different." He blew the steam from the top of his coffee and took a sip before continuing.

"I read something at the bookstore that inspired me, I think it was a song – it changed me somehow, I don't know exactly. Now that I'm trying to explain it to you, it sounds, well, pretty stupid."

Gerard shook his head and covered his face with his hands.

She laughed, relieved, and hugged him. When he raised his eyes to meet hers, she was surprised by the dark look of resolution she saw there.

"I will finish my book," he said, "and it will change the world."

***

GERARD WROTE like a man on a mission from God from that day forward, determined to see his project through to the end, to keep his eye on the prize. The energy that had entered him in the book store, reading strange words out loud on a rainy afternoon, hadn't subsided.

Neither had the words *Maazo Maazo*. They reverberated inside his skull continuously, a rhythm to his work, his walk - everything he did was to the soundtrack of *Maazo Maazo, Maazo Maazo*. He put the new vitality it gave him to good use. He would finally vanquish the novel he had been carrying inside him all these years.

He would finish it, once and for all.

Gerard found himself drawn to the keyboard at his writing desk like a moth to flame, typing for hours at a time. Sonia was happy to see him finally buckling down and making his book a reality - at least at first.

As the deadline drew ever nearer, writing became something more than his dream job: it transformed into an outright obsession. Whenever his fingers touched the keyboard he would fall into a trance, as if intoxicated. He waved away dinners offered by his wife. His children's pleas for attention were ignored.

He wrote like a man possessed. Sonia began to worry.

Gerard worried, too. The charge he got from the words *"Maazo Maazo"* echoing inside his head was no longer comforting. The repetition was relentless; the pace of the incessant mantra grew faster, more urgent, with each passing day the tone became more sinister. He feared the manic pressure of it might at any moment cause his head to explode in a spray of gray and red.

He had to make it stop.

As the days rolled by he realized that he didn't even know what his fingers were typing anymore. He no longer cared whether he finished his book or not; all that mattered to him now was to make those infernal words *stop*.

The only relief he could find was to write. Whenever his fingers touched the keyboard, the sound in his head would die away, leaving him with the sweet silence in his mind he so desperately craved; but it lasted only for as long as his fingers could type.

Everyone that knew Gerard thought he was a man extremely determined to finish writing a book. They were wrong.

He was writing to save his life.

Sonia had never seen her husband so passionate about anything before, but she suspected he might be losing touch with reality. She dealt with his obsessive typing as best she could, but the late night typing marathons and his deteriorating personal hygiene were beginning to take their toll, on both of them – and their relationship. She wasn't sure how much more she could take.

***

TWO DAYS before his deadline, Gerard sat down at his desk in the study and quickly fell into the sweet embrace of silence that only came when his fingers danced across the letters. He woke up several hours later, surprised to find himself in bed, with no recollection of how he had come to be there.

He pushed his pillow aside and squinted at the alarm clock through the darkness; it was very early morning.

His head and fingers throbbed with pain – it must have been a long evening at his desk again, he figured. The blackouts were happening more frequently, with him stumbling to bed later and later each night, exhausted and mumbling incoherent nonsense. The endless hours of typing were taking a toll. He had to find a way to make it stop.

He slid out of bed and tiptoed to the bathroom, being careful not to wake Sonia. Her irritation with him and his erratic writing and sleep habits had been growing. The last thing he needed right now was to wake her up; then he'd have to deal with a fight on top of a splitting headache.

Gerard pushed the bathroom door shut behind him and flipped on the light. The sudden incandescent glare stung his eyes and caused his head to throb even more. He reached for the cabinet above the sink to get some Motrin, but stopped when he caught a glimpse of himself in the mirror.

The sorry person reflected there startled him. He had never been so thin before; his sallow complexion belonged to someone in the final throes of a terminal illness. No wonder his wife was fed up with him. He had let himself go.

"What's wrong with me?" he asked himself out loud.

The moment the words crossed his lips, his hands gripped the counter, and his body stiffened in a spasm. He watched in the mirror, helpless, as his mouth began to move by itself. The thought occurred to him that he was having a seizure.

His mouth spoke.

"You want to know what's wrong with *me*?" it asked, his voice sarcastic and strange. "There's nothing wrong with *me*! There's something wrong with *YOU*!" His own face grimaced at him in the mirror.

"Look me in the eye when I'm talking to you!" he commanded himself. "Look me dead in the eye and I'll show you exactly what's wrong with you."

Unable to do anything else, Gerard looked himself in the eye, his manic reflection staring back at him.

The pupil of his right eye began to dilate. As he watched, the black circle in the center expanded slowly until no white remained. Something wriggled like a maggot inside the clear viscous fluid of his eye.

The sight of it panicked him. He tried to jerk back, to look away, but his hands and body held him fast.

"Stop trying to get away. Look at me!" his voice commanded again, the tone severe.

The thing inside his eyeball pressed itself against

the interior of the transparent lens; it bulged from the pressure. He could see every detail of its shape. It reminded him of puckered petals on a still-closed morning glory blossom.

The petals unfurled, revealing a small twitching eye. It stared back at him - an eye inside his eye, centered where only the darkness of his pupil should have been.

"Shit!" he yelled, and discovered that he had regained control over his body. He backed away from the mirror, knocking over Sonia's White Diamonds perfume in the process. The glass bottle made a racket as it clattered against the hard tile floor.

"Shit, shit, shit!" he stammered, breathless. His heart was pounding in his ears.

"What are you doing in there?" Sonia yelled from the other side of the bathroom door. She sounded pissed.

"I'm about sick of this crap," she said bitterly. "Some of us have to go to work in the morning."

Gerard thought it best to say nothing. He leaned over the sink to examine his eyes in the mirror again, dreading what he might find. But they looked fine; bloodshot, but otherwise normal.

Then his lips began to whisper.

"So now you know what's wrong with you," they said, in a hiss at first, but then shouted: *"SO DON'T FUCK WITH ME!"*

The lamp clicked on in the bedroom. The squeak of mattress springs confirmed to Gerard that he was in trouble.

"What did you just say to me?" Sonia screamed as she flung open the bathroom door. "I refuse to live like this! Go sleep on the couch," she yelled, her index finger trembling with rage as she pointed towards the bedroom door.

Gerard flicked off the bathroom light switch and padded past his glaring wife to the sofa downstairs. He was sure he wouldn't be able to sleep again that night.

Within minutes he was snoring.

***

HE AWOKE the next morning delighted to find that his headache was gone. He wasn't sure if what he had seen in the bathroom the night before had been real or a wicked dream. He examined his eyes carefully in the hallway mirror. Everything looked normal.

Gerard desperately needed someone to talk to, someone to help him figure out what was going on. He hoped Sonia would understand if he opened up to her. He knew he'd have to approach the subject carefully, or else she might think he was losing his mind.

After packing the kids out the door to school, he took a deep breath and told her everything that had been going on.

The conversation went downhill fast.

"What do you mean you can't remember what you write?" Sonia asked, visibly irritated. She trembled as she sipped her coffee.

"Sonia, I don't know. I can remember sitting down to type, but I can't remember *what* I wrote. I don't even know how I got to bed last night, and it's been like this for a while. Honestly, I don't know how much longer I can go on like this."

Sonia's face flushed with anger. She slammed her

mug down on the granite counter.

"You don't know how much longer *you* can go on like this?" she snarled at him. "You can't remember when *you* went to bed last night?"

Gerard realized this conversation had been a big mistake, especially this morning. He should have waited.

She was getting revved up. "That's so funny," she sneered, "because *I* remember the exact moment you came to bed last night. I remember very well, because I tried to go back to sleep for several hours. I remember seeing '4:44 AM', and thinking how strange it was to see those numbers on the alarm clock."

She glared at him, daring him to speak.

"You don't have *anything* to say?" she asked sarcastically. "That's odd, because you sure had a lot to say last night, didn't you? What was it you said when I asked you to please let me get some sleep? Was it 'I'm sorry'? No, no – that's not it. What *did* you say? Oh wait, I remember – *'DON'T FUCK WITH ME'*. Yes, that's what you said, didn't you? You are such an inconsiderate *asshle.*"

She turned away from him and began tossing dirty breakfast dishes into the dishwasher.

Gerard attempted a recovery.

"I'm so sorry," he said, "you're right – I am an asshole, a *major* asshole. But I'm also a very, very sorry asshole."

Sonia didn't bother to look at him as she wiped the table.

Gerard grabbed a broom and began sweeping the floor. He was going to need to change his strategy or else this argument was going to become the opening salvo of their relationship's World War III.

"I have to finish this *one* book. I *have* to finish it," he pleaded with her, "I'm going to go crazy if I don't get it done. In fact, I think I'm starting to go a little crazy already."

He smiled and stuck out his bottom lip like a sad puppy, hoping she would find it hard to stay mad at someone so cute.

She finally relented.

"Okay, okay," she said. "At least you got it done before your deadline. Now maybe you can take a little break from writing for a while."

"My deadline is tomorrow," Gerard said. "I promise I'll do my best to have it completed by then."

Sonia stopped what she was doing and gave him a funny look.

"What are you talking about?" she said. "You already finished it - I mailed the manuscript off yesterday, overnight mail. I have the tracking number around here somewhere."

She dug through her purse.

"What manuscript? Gerard asked, confused. "I haven't finished writing it yet! What did you mail? *To who?*"

Sonia's irritation returned with a vengeance.

"Are you just screwing with me now? I'll tell you *what manuscript* - the three hundred and fifty-two pages you left by my side of the bed yesterday with a handwritten note asking me to overnight it to your agent in New York - Jerry something-or-other."

She turned her frustration back to the search in her pocketbook. Seconds later she withdrew her hand, clutching a shipping receipt.

"I didn't give you anything to mail," Gerard

stated flatly.

Sonia glared at him, squeezing the shipping receipt into a ball inside her clenched fist.

"You know what? I'm done," she said. "You can take your stupid book and you can stick it straight up you-know-where. I'm finished."

She threw the receipt at him. It hit him square in his forehead and rolled under the table.

He stared at her, blinking and confused.

"I'm taking a shower and going to work," she said, trying to calm herself down. "I've let you waste enough of my time, *my life*, already. We can figure out what we're going to do about living arrangements later."

Gerard felt the pounding in his head growing louder, faster.

Maazo Maazo, Maazo Maazo, it thumped, each word stabbing like a knife deep into his brain.

The room began to sway around him, and Gerard saw the edges of his vision turn black, like he was being sucked into a dark tunnel. He held onto the kitchen counter to keep himself from falling.

Then his voice started talking, but he wasn't trying to say anything.

"Sonia, baby," he heard himself say, but his voice was different, like it was coming from somewhere else, somewhere far away.

Darkness swallowed him. He was passing out.

***

HE STARTLED back into consciousness, clawing at the kitchen counter to keep from falling. He was surprised to find himself clutching linen sheets and a comforter instead of a smooth granite counter top.

He wasn't in the kitchen anymore, he realized; he was lying in his bed, nude, the sheets cool against his skin. A shower hummed in the master bathroom.

How did I get here? he wondered.

"Are you going take the whole day off, or only the morning?" His wife's voice echoed cheerfully from the stall in the adjacent room.

He jolted up in the bed and looked at the clock on the nightstand. It was almost noon. The shower stopped.

"You want to go grab some lunch with me?" she sang in a delighted tone as she danced into the bedroom, hair wrapped in a towel.

She shook her glistening naked hips.

"What?" he asked, confused.

"Oh, did I bang my poor baby's brains out? Is that why you look so silly?" she baby-talked, and kissed him hungrily on the mouth.

He struggled to get away, but she jumped on the bed, straddling him.

"What time is it?" he asked.

She bounced up and down on his crotch, eager and playful.

"It's almost noon. C'mon, take the rest of the day off. I'll let you have your way with me for three more hours," she begged, sounding hopeful.

"No, I need to get ready for work myself. Shouldn't I save some strength for later?" he asked, trying his best to go along.

"You'd better, lover boy!" she squealed and rolled off him. She started getting dressed for work.

He touched his head, checking for sore spots.

"Sonia, did I hit my head when I passed out in the

kitchen?" he asked.

"What are you talking about, silly? You didn't pass out in the kitchen! Practically raped me in the kitchen, yes – and in the hallway and on the bed - but I wouldn't exactly call that passing out."

"So I didn't fall down?"

She laughed at him, and slipped on her shoes.

"Only once, when you were trying to screw me *and* carry me down the hallway at the same time, remember? You might have to keep working on that move. Why do you ask? Did you hurt yourself?"

"No, I thought...never mind."

"Well, don't you think about it - keep on lovin' me like that and we'll never fight again, I promise. I'm just jealous of your keyboard. If only you fingered me half as much as you do that thing," she laughed, only half joking.

"It's okay," Gerard mumbled. He still had no idea what was going on.

Sonia grabbed her briefcase from beside the dresser and headed for the door. She stopped and looked back at him, a wistful expression on her face.

"You know I love you, right? I'm really sorry about this morning – and I do hope you have good luck with your book. I didn't read your finished manuscript, but it did look very nice, very professional. I bet you it sells a ton."

"Thanks. Fingers crossed," Gerard said. He felt more confused at that moment than he had in his entire life.

As soon as Sonia's car left the driveway, he threw on some clothes and went into the kitchen to find the shipping receipt Sonia had thrown at him earlier. He fished it out from under the table, and headed for his study.

A thick ream of printed paper was stacked neatly in the center of his desk. He was sure he hadn't printed anything so large in the last few weeks. Curious, he picked it up.

A cover sheet read in large, bold lettering:

Serenity's Termination
A Novel by Gerard Faust

It was the title of his novel, the one he had thought he would never complete. The heft of it in his hands quickened his pulse. He flipped to the last page. Three hundred, fifty-two pages - like Sonia had said.

His book was real.

He had no recollection of finishing it, though; no memory of printing it, no idea how his book could have been completed.

Had he been working on his book the whole time, managed to actually finish it while banging away in a daze? He opened it to a random page and began to read.

The writing was a lovely flowing prose; its literary sophistication and tonal resonance surprised him. He had no idea he was capable of such elegance.

The beauty of the writing stood in stark contrast with the depravity of the content, however. Sordid, revolting images bloomed to life inside Gerard's head as he read. Deeds so vile, he was filled with shame.

Gerard flipped through it, reading snippets here and there. It was foreign to him; the things he read barely resembled the book he had intended to write under the same title. Entire passages of the book had been written in an unknown language. Notes from the author encouraged the reader to repeat those passages aloud, in order "to fully appreciate the alliterative and musical properties they contained".

Those tonal passages were followed by English-language descriptions of unspeakable brutalities, acts so profane and malicious Gerard was repulsed by even the possibility they had been written by his own hands.

One such section told the story of a man bound by wire to a luxurious, velvet-covered chair facing a golden vanity, complete with desk and mirror.

Beside him sat another man, dressed in white and holding a gleaming scalpel.

The man in white began to slice the skin from the bound man's face with the razor-sharp scalpel, piece by piece - not saying a word, his face expressionless.

As the story told, the man bound by wire to the velvet chair was powerless to do anything other than watch his misfortune unfold in the vanity mirror before him. As each new sliver was cut from his face, it was placed beside the others neatly arranged on the vanity's tabletop.

Slice after slice, his face was removed. After the last piece was cut away, the bound man saw that his former face had been transformed into a grotesque mask that stared at him from now-empty sockets, a bloody jigsaw puzzle of human flesh.

The short tale ended by telling that, once finished with the task of cutting, the man in white plunged his scalpel into the bound man's heart, and then began to feast upon the delicacy he had so carefully prepared.

Gerard tossed the stack of pages away as though diseased. It slid across the smooth surface of the desk, knocking over the ink well Sonia had given him. The shipping receipt slipped off the desk, catching his eye as it fluttered to the floor.

His heart sank when he finally realized what the receipt meant. Had he left a note asking his wife to mail this profanity posing as his finished draft to his agent? Was he insane?

Panic surged inside him. He had to get that manuscript back; he had to destroy it. Were the stories in it even legal? What if the publishers had called the police? Was it possible he might, even now, be mere minutes away from being arrested and dragged from his home for mailing such obscenities?

Gerard sat down at his computer to compose an e-mail letting his agent know that someone was playing a prank on him, that what he was receiving was some elaborate joke that wasn't funny.

He opened up a new e-mail and began typing *Jerry Rogers*, the name of his agent, into the address field but his fingers typed something different: *Maazo Maazo*.

He tapped the delete key several times and tried again. Still, the words *Maazo Maazo* appeared every time he typed.

"Maazo Maazo," he muttered out loud. He felt a spark of energy as he said the words, and then his hands no longer belonged to him. They typed, dancing across the keyboard

Words scrolled across the screen: *Maazo Maazo. Maazo Maazo was me. Maazo Maazo is now we. Stop resisting and listen up. This is your one chance to make it, to get published, to be a big-shot writer. Do you want that opportunity? Then you had better take it now or else they're going to say you are crazy and lock us both away.*

The writing stopped.

His hand grabbed the mouse and opened up a word processor program. His fingers resumed typing.

Are you reading me Gerard? The words taunted him.

I'm going crazy, he thought.

Say something Gerard. Say YES if you read me, his fingers typed.

"Yes," Gerard whispered.

Good, the writing on the computer screen resumed, Gerard's fingers dancing along the keyboard.

I want to be a writer, too. If you are successful, I am successful. I am trapped inside you. You don't want me here forever. I don't want that either. Your wife might be the only person that wants me inside her forever, judging from how many times she came when I fucked her with your sorry body this morning, – but that's not important. Are you still with me, Gerard?

"Who are you?" Gerard asked.

Maazo Maazo, of course; you invited me in by name - don't you remember? How good you felt when I first came into your body that day. I bet you felt almost as good as your wife did when I came inside her body this morning – but I shouldn't brag. We can't all be good lovers - or good writers, for that matter. But at least I can make you look good, and you can enjoy my success, too – if you listen up.

"What do you want?"

The same as you: to be a famous writer. I want to be the world's MOST famous, most widely-read author in history. You know why? I want to see the world, I want to travel. I want to come and go as I please anywhere throughout humanity. But the only way I can do that is if someone invites me in, like you did.

Gerard tried to move his fingers as they hovered motionless over the keyboard. He could not regain control.

His fingers resumed typing, and he read.

You know most books are written by demons, right? Words and music are the best way to get someone to let you directly into their head. The demon who writes for Stephen King, now that's one lucky fucker. Once people read one of his books, he's in for good - he can go right in and out of them from then on.

I wish I knew that demon's secret. I only know how to get someone to let me in if they say one of my chants out loud, and that's hard to get people to do. Dr. Seuss had it down pat, but I'm not sure I've got children's books in me. Horror is the way to go – and you helped me write my masterpiece.

Gerard's cell phone began to ring.

Answer it, his fingers typed.

He stared at the phone, motionless. His agent's New York number flashed on the caller I.D.

His fingers pounded the keys furiously: *Pick up the fucking phone!*

Before Gerard had even decided to answer, his right hand grabbed the phone, clicked the answer key, and held it up to his ear.

A man's voice was on the line.

"Hello? Hello?"

Gerard's left hand typed again.

Say hello or I will make you kill your children.

"This is Gerard," he croaked.

"Gerard, you okay?" the voice on the phone asked. "Jerry here. Got your manuscript, and I have to say...I didn't know you had it in you! That was a ballsy move, changing the whole story at the last minute, but you pulled it off!"

***

AIMLESS HOUSE PUBLISHERS loved the changes, absolutely *loved* the book, Jerry had said; but there was a tight publishing schedule.

The book would make it to press if all editing was complete tomorrow, ready for the printers. If he couldn't have it ready, kiss it good-bye until this time next year – that is, if the publishing editors still loved it as much *then* as they did *right now*.

Jerry was quite emphatic: they probably wouldn't.

Would a six-figure advance be enough motivation to have it done in the next twenty-four hours? They could always negotiate his asking price on the movie rights later, Jerry said.

The real Gerard was gone by that point in the conversation; but Maazo Maazo took over for him, finalized the details, and started to work on the requested revisions.

Sonia got home around three-thirty. She had dropped the kids off at their grandmother's house for the afternoon, eager to resume their love-making session from earlier.

She found Gerard at his desk in his study, where he was typing faster than she had ever seen him type before.

She slid a single bare leg through the doorway and wiggled it seductively, calling to him.

"Hey there, loverboy," she cooed, "the kids are at

grandma's. Can I interest you in, oh, I don't know – a little fucking-my-brains out? Please?"

He ignored her. She stuck her head into the study.

"Pretty please? I really, really need you to do me like you did before," she pleaded.

Gerard continued typing. "Get the fuck out," he said flatly.

"But Gerard, I need you so bad!" she begged.

Gerard's body stopped typing and turned to face her. His eyes were black and full of anger.

She stepped back, startled.

"Seriously, Sonia, get out," he demanded in a tone she had never heard. "Get out of the house and leave me alone. Stop wasting my time and let me finish writing my goddamn book."

Gerard's body turned away from her and began typing again.

She started to walk away, but reconsidered. She crossed her arms in defiance and dropped the sexy voice.

"You are *not* going to talk to me that way, do you understand?" she said.

"Get out," he repeated.

"I will destroy that computer *and* your stupid-ass book if you say that to me one more time. Say it - *I dare you*," she hissed.

Gerard turned and hurled his cell phone at her with all his might. It missed her head by only inches and shattered against the wall, broken pieces clattering to the floor.

That was the final straw. She was pissed.

"You want to play rough?" she screamed, and charged him. She grabbed him by the shoulder and whipped him around.

"Who do you think you are, you limp-dick, worthless fuck? The ride you gave me today is the only - and I do mean *only* - thing you've done right in your entire pointless life. You can get out of my house and out of my li..."

Her rant cut off mid-sentence. In a single fluid motion, Gerard jumped to his feet, grabbed her by the throat, and slammed her head onto the desk. The computer monitor shook as she struggled and kicked, trying to free herself from his iron grip.

He picked her head up and slammed it down again, hard, squeezing her throat harder. Her eyes bulged grotesquely as she strained to breathe.

Gerard's black eyes settled on the decorative dip pen, the gift she had given him; it lay on the desk next to her swollen face. He scooped it up and stabbed the gold-plated nib deep into her carotid, grinding it in a circular motion as deeply as he could before pulling it back out in a spray of blood.

Sonia's body went limp, and he released her. Her lifeless body slid off the desk and flopped on to the floor in a heap. He surveyed her awkward position with amusement for a moment, and then shoved her away from the desk with his foot.

He read the inscription on the pen: *"To the best man who ever wrote his way into the story of my life; make sure it has a happy ending! Love, Sonia"* Blood dripped from the nib; seeing that elicited a chuckle.

"Let me get back to writing your happy ending, my love," he whispered to the corpse on the floor.

As he turned back to his work, he noticed Gerard's face reflected on the screen. For a fleeting moment, Maazo Maazo felt a new sensation run down his spine; he suspected it was pity.

He shrugged it off and began to type.

A few hours later, Gerard's finger hit the *send* button on an e-mail, the final draft attached.

It was finished.

***

GERARD AWOKE later that day. He was in his bed, again not knowing how he had ended up there. This time, though, the linen sheets and comforter were covered in a mess of dried blood.

He found Sonia's battered body on the floor of his study, the shattered bits of his cell phone crunching underfoot.

Something inside him broke when he realized she was dead. He sat down beside her at his desk, in a state of shock.

He sat motionless - slumped over his computer, eyes staring off into space, blood-encrusted fingers perched above the keyboard - waiting for Maazo Maazo to communicate with him again, to tell him what he should do.

But his fingers never moved.

He was still there, gaunt and catatonic in front of the computer, several days later when the police broke through the front door of his home. He didn't move as they approached him, guns drawn, didn't even blink as they gingerly worked their way around the festering corpse of his wife to apprehend him.

Gerard offered no resistance as they hog-tied his hands and feet behind his back. He chanted the words "Maazo Maazo" over and over as they dragged him through the front yard to a waiting police car, while his neighbors watched with puzzled faces.

***

THE BOOK WAS PERFECTION, sent to the press just in time for an immediate release. The publishers were so impressed with the commercial possibilities of *Serenity's Termination* they doubled the size of the first edition run.

But a savvy reporter made the connection between the book and the author's arrest, and the lurid story made headlines everywhere. It was juicy news: the new novel, *Serenity's Termination*, foretold how the author killed his wife in gruesome detail.

Media outlets ran the story for days. Millions of people ran to their nearest bookstore to buy a copy of *Serenity's Termination* before it could be pulled from store shelves.

The relentless publicity helped the first edition sell out in a matter of days. After much debate, the publishers decided to keep the book in print, declaring in a public statement that it would serve as a "fine moral warning to the public" - a decision undoubtedly influenced by the fact that the book was on track to become the biggest seller in publishing history.

***

GERARD FAUST, despised wife-killer and infamous best-selling author, found himself incarcerated in a maximum security prison. Cut off from the outside world, he had no idea that his book (or as he called it, "Maazo Maazo's book") had become an international sensation.

Gerard only knew that Maazo Maazo was gone, leaving him with nothing but a dead wife, a cold prison cell, useless and ill-gotten fame, and the very real possibility of a death sentence.

Gerard passed time in his cell watching an endless procession of interchangeable guards shuffle around a desk down the cell block. The shift changed every twelve hours, but one thing stayed constant: the disgust and hatred they communicated in every glance at him. Anyone within earshot let him know the whole world wanted him to burn in hell - not only for murdering his wife, but for bragging about it in his book as well.

Death, they said, was too sweet for a demon like him.

One day several weeks after his arrest, a guard walked up to Gerard's cell and showed him the book he was reading.

Gerard was surprised to see his own name in print under the title: *Serenity's Termination*.

"I've been reading your book, you sick fuck," the guard told him matter-of-factly.

Gerard stared at him, sure that *anything* he might say would be the *wrong thing*.

"Maybe even a sick fuck like you can write one hell of book," the guard said while flipping through the pages, searching for something.

"I wanted to ask you about this part – everyone, everywhere is wondering what it means. I thought, hell, I can ask you directly."

The guard began to read aloud.

"*Mah-zoe Mah-zoe toso nimi so,*" he read, chanting.

Gerard ran to the front of the cell and grabbed the bars, shouting.

"Stop, please stop! Don't read that *out loud!*"

The guard continued reading aloud as though Gerard hadn't said a word.

"Tumay noso oolaya ma-yi
Noso olaya anona ya na-mi
Tumay noso oolaya ma-yi
Mah-zoe Mah-zoe toso nimi so."

The guard fell silent and the book dropped from his hand, falling with a dull thud onto the concrete floor. The guard stared at it, confused; then he looked at Gerard and stepped towards the cell.

Gerard backed away.

The guard smiled as he pressed his mustache against the bars, his pupils so dilated that his eyes looked black. Even from several feet away, Gerard could feel the guard's hot breath tickling the skin on his face. It was hot, too hot, almost scalding, like steam blowing from a kettle.

"You know what, boy?" the guard said, his voice surly and strange. "Your book inspired me. I think I might become a writer myself, someday."

***

This story was the opening volley of my ongoing writing adventure.

Initially published as "The Demon Writer", the original version had an added prologue & epilogue that served to add a double-twist to the story, a trick of sorts on the reader, which was removed from "Whatever Possessed You" to create a more straightforward tale.

In writing this, my goal was to employ a style that would stand nicely alongside Joe Hill's "20th Century Ghosts", one of my favorite short story collections (think 'Abraham's Sons' or 'Best New Horror').

While my writing chops are obviously still in development here, I remain proud that this story will always be my first.

GERTRUDE

"SO TELL ME about yourself," I said.

Despite his condition, the man spoke with cheerful frankness, his napkin still tucked into his shirt collar like a bib. He clutched a fork tightly in his left hand, his knuckles bone white, as though he was unable to let go of it.

"I have a symbiotic twin named Gertrude," he said, matter-of-factly. "She lives in a cavity under my ribcage, next to my spleen."

He leaned forward and continued in a whisper.

"If I lie very still in bed at night, I can hear her. I think she might be crying."

He glanced around the room nervously, as though to check if anyone were eavesdropping.

It was hard to tell from his manner of speaking that he was injured; it would have been a natural assumption that the red splatter down his front was nothing more than spilled marinara.

But the half-eaten plate of food on the table in front of him held only chicken, rice and broccoli - not a drop of red sauce in sight.

I stepped back to give the paramedic more room to work. She lifted the bottom of the man's shirt, exposing the area where his stomach should have been. The abdomen was now a tattered tangle of messy flesh, looking every bit like an exploded pot pie, all the way down to the peas and carrots.

The medic gagged as she attempted to clean the area around the gaping wound, her mind undoubtedly reeling from the impossibility of the task at hand.

I covered my face with my hand to try and shield myself from the putrid smell.

"Why did you do it?" I asked the dying man.

He carefully moved the IV tube that was taped to his forearm out of the way and leaned back a bit in his chair. He took a deep breath, a faraway look of hopelessness rising in his eyes.

Shock was setting in. I knew I didn't have much time.

"*Why did you do it?*" I asked him again, more harshly this time. My voice jarred him back into reality.

"I didn't do it. She did," he said.

"Who?"

"Gertrude."

"*This* Gertrude?" I asked sarcastically, pointing to the woman opposite him, whose body was sprawled across the table. "Are you telling me she did this to herself?"

The dead woman's face was mangled and swollen and her throat torn open, as though she had been attacked by wild animals with claws. A mass of distended blue veins bulged from the wound in her neck like wiring from a vandalized circuit box.

He shook his head from left to right.

"That's not Gertrude," he said weakly.

"Then who is she?"

"She's my girlfriend – no, my fiancé. I asked her to marry me tonight. I made her dinner," he said, the life in his voice melting away like an icicle in July.

"Then who the hell is Gertrude?" I demanded.

"I told you," he wheezed. "I have a symbiotic twin named Gertrude. She lives in a cavity under my ribcage, next to my spleen."

His sentence finished with a cough and a gurgle. Dark blood welled up in his mouth, spilling over his bottom lip, dripping down his chin. Then his eyes became fixed on some faraway spot over my left shoulder.

"If I lie very still in bed at night, I can hear her. I think she might be crying," he continued softly.

I watched the spark of life burn out at the back of his eyes.

Then, just like that, he was gone.

I motioned for the paramedic to stop fiddling with his bandages. All that was needed now was a body bag and a gurney.

Two of them, I guess.

I waited while my team marked the crime scene and taped off the front of the property so nobody could enter. With the bodies removed and sent off to the morgue we could come back tomorrow, give the scene a good combing over. No use in wasting a perfectly good evening sitting around in a slaughterhouse, when the wife had a hot meal waiting for me at home.

I hoped it wasn't pot pie.

I was the last one out of the place, I always am – as chief detective, it's procedure.

I flipped off the light in the hallway and was headed for the front door when I stopped dead in my tracks.

I had heard something, I was sure of it. I walked back into the empty hallway and listened.

There it was again.

Someone was crying.

I drew my weapon and crept stealthily down the hall, stopping in front of the laundry room door. Whoever it was, it sounded as if they were in there.

Gun at the ready, I pried the door open with my foot. There was a blood smear on the bottom half of the dryer.

I flipped on my flashlight, opened the dryer door and shined the light inside.

That's when she screamed.

I jumped back, startled, slamming into the wall on the opposite side of the hallway, knocking the wind clean out of my lungs. I tried my best to hold the light steady as it illuminated the wailing female abomination that sat, naked inside the dryer, its body covered in green slime and dried blood. It - *she* - suckled an even smaller creature that appeared to be growing out of her side, suckling contentedly on a fleshless, oozing breast.

"He was mine!" Gertrude shrieked, her eyes hot embers in the flashlight's beam. "He was my man. She had no right to take him from me! He already had a wife, already had a child!"

She pulled the horrid thing forcibly away from

her breast, and held it up in her solitary, twisted, three-fingered hand for me to see, thick pus dribbling both from her nipple and the thing's tiny mouth. It was the size of a newborn rat, but not even half as pretty.

The thing she called a child began to scream, and so did she.

And so did I.

***

I was having lunch with a group of people I didn't know and who didn't know me. Someone had the brilliantly original idea to have each person introduce themselves in turn around the table.

One person after the other said basically the same thing: "Hi everybody! I'm Bob, and I'm married, and I've got two-point-five kids who play soccer and we live in the suburbs and life is just as sweet as vanilla pudding," or something to that effect. I slipped into a semi-comatose state after the fourth repetition of the same story of life's grand adventure.

Then all eyes turned to me. I hadn't even thought about what I was going to say. My life felt messy and not easily summed up in a trite splooge of happy words.

Before I knew it, I heard myself speaking: "Well, I have a symbiotic twin named Gertrude. She lives in a cavity under my ribcage, next to my spleen," I said, surprised at the words coming out of my mouth. "If I lie very still in bed at night, I can hear her. I think she might be crying."

Everyone stared at me, speechless. After a few awkward moments, someone to my left said, "Wow. You should be a writer."

"Maybe you're right," I said as casually as possible before quickly excusing myself from the table and running for my laptop.

I didn't know where it had come from, but I had my next story.

ARBOR*EA*TUM
A NOVELLA OF HORROR

I. A Flaming Sword

Dirt is edible.

It could even be considered delicious, especially if your last meal was several days ago.

Fifteen-year-old Micah Jenkins became acutely aware of this simple fact as he lay on his belly, scooping soft gray clay from the bottom of a cool running stream as if it were ice cream.

The clay was the first thing he had found to eat since his family had run out of food three days before. There wasn't much in the way of roots or berries to forage for here in the middle of the prairie, far west of Missouri; the wild game was small and nimble, mostly a waste of ammunition to try and shoot – and a rabbit or a gopher certainly wouldn't provide enough meat to feed everyone anything close to a proper meal.

He wished that his family had stayed with the main group, but no – Lemuel's creeping mental shift had blossomed into a full-blown messianic delusion. No surprise there. He was always rambling about finding the Garden of Eden and other such nonsense.

It had all reached full boil when the family heads of the wagon train had flatly rejected his frantic demand to follow his "revelation" and veer off the established trail. That was when Lemuel had struck off on his own, dragging Micah's father Samuel and the rest of the family along.

Micah hadn't seen a trading post, another wagon, or even a halfway decent watering hole since he and his family had started travelling through this uncharted prairie. Now he was pretty sure they had fully completed the transition from *travelling through* to being *stranded in* this endless expanse of nothingness. The year eighteen thirty-nine hadn't been a good one so far, and he hoped it wouldn't end up being the one carved on his headstone.

They had passed a handful of sod huts during the previous days, but they never got within more than a hundred yards or so of any of them. Each hut featured a scrawny man or a tattered couple in front, clutching a gun and possessing a powerful case of the thousand-mile stare that suggested perhaps they had eaten some - maybe all - of their children during the winter before, and that any visitors, invited or otherwise, might end up on the menu for dinner that night.

The thought gave Micah the shivers. If ever there was a man who would gladly eat his young to save himself, it was Lemuel. He hoped they found food and shelter before Lemuel got *really* hungry.

He plunged his hand into the water and dug up a second handful of creamy clay from the streambed, sucking the goop hungrily from his fingers.

The clay had a strong mineral taste, like the medicinal tonic his father forced him to choke down whenever he got the fever; the only thing missing was the warm sting of alcohol on the back end. He also thought it tasted a little bit like blood, though that may have been from the growing number of open sores inside his mouth, Micah wasn't sure.

He stopped eating for long enough to glance at the other children, who had gathered around, watching him intently. There was a total of nine children in their wayward caravan, including himself - although he hardly considered himself a child.

He offered a forced smile to the children, clay smeared around his mouth like smudged lipstick.

Micah shoveled out another handful from the bottom, and offered it to the kids with a silent shrug, to see if anyone cared to share. He couldn't actually ask them if they wanted any, because the last mouthful had stuck to the roof of his mouth, gluing his jaws together momentarily as he struggled to swallow.

Anna frowned down at him, hands on her hips as her ankle-length dress struggled to flutter in the gentle breeze.

"No," she muttered, rejecting his offer, her voice stern but glum. Her response was only half-directed at him, more at the other children.

At sixteen, Anna was the oldest of the six girls in the group, a self-ordained authority who enjoyed pretending she was everyone's mother. Even Micah's younger sisters - Ruth, Esther and Chastity - followed

Anna around like her very own little flock of ducklings, as did her own two younger sisters, Piety and Lydia.

Anna's brothers, Jacob and Nathaniel - also younger than her and Micah - weren't quite so obedient. They looked up to Micah as their role model most of the time, not Anna.

"I've been praying, and I'm confident God will provide," Anna told the children piously, "He always does. If God had wanted us to lie on our bellies and eat mud like worms, he wouldn't have given us arms and legs in his own image."

Her proclamation dimmed the bright look of hope rising in the younger children's eyes at the prospect of having something to eat, even if it was only clay. When Anna said "no" to something, they usually listened or they ran the risk of her taking out her budding maternal instincts on them with a thin plank, when their real parents weren't looking. She had her ways of making the young ones pray forgiveness for not respecting their elders – which really meant *her*.

"I'll have some, Micah!" shouted nine-year-old Jacob, Anna's enthusiastic little brother, who thought Micah was possibly the most fascinating person on earth, and who also relished any opportunity to displease Anna.

"God made me an animal, so I've got no choice but to obey the animal urges he gave me. Gonna have me a good couple helpings," the ruddy-faced boy said mischievously, as he flopped onto his belly beside Micah. He began digging with gusto into the streambed, gobbling massive gray blobs of clay from his fingers with a hearty "mumsh mumsh mumsh" slurping sound, that he hoped was making Anna feel ill.

Micah looked up at Anna and smiled sheepishly, but she only crossed her arms and *humphed* at him. The other children took a step back quietly.

Micah knew that he and Anna had a sort of private truce between them, unspoken but always present whenever their eyes met. She had bossed him around relentlessly when they were younger, but since the unspoken agreement between them began, she hadn't given him much grief.

He liked to imagine that the truce between them was at least partly due to the fact that she genuinely liked him and respected his smarts, but deep down he really knew it was mostly because he caught her last summer, in the smokehouse, with two of her fingers buried up to the knuckle between her legs.

He still remembered the moment like it happened yesterday. She just stood there frozen when he discovered her; stood there and stared at him, fingers deep inside herself, as though not knowing what to do next. Micah had found himself frozen too, as he stared in amazement at the spectacle on display before him.

After an awkward few seconds of gawking at each other, Anna gathered her wits enough to drop her leg and skirt, and pushed her way past Micah, running from the smokehouse without saying a word.

Micah never told anyone about that day, and the two of them never spoke openly of it, not even once; but every time her gaze met his, he knew that they were both thinking of that secret moment, now shared forever between them.

Micah took a deep drink of the cool stream water

to clear his throat of the gooey muck. At any rate, he was in no mood to fight with Anna. His fighting spirit was diminished with hunger and exhaustion. The way their trip west was going so far, he figured he might end up stuck out here on the prairie with her as his only option for a wife, and there was no point in making her dislike him any more than she already did. Of course, he'd have to survive if he wanted to marry someday, and staying alive for long in their current predicament was starting to look more unlikely with each passing hour.

He sat up on the bank of the stream and smeared the clay from his hands onto his tattered trousers, giving Anna an earnest look to show that he was serious.

"Honestly, Anna, we're all very hungry," he said. "This clay might not be the best thing that the good Lord could give us, it may not be proper sustenance as such, but at least it will make our bellies *feel* full. You really should have a couple of bites, and let the others get some, too. Maybe it'll stop the cramps for a couple of hours, let us think straight. Who knows when God will provide something else fit to eat? Perhaps this *is* his provision."

Anna considered his argument for a moment and then looked towards their parents, who were busy trying to construct a makeshift bridge for the horses and oxen to cross the stream. Micah followed her gaze, and shook his head in dismay at the incompetence of the adults who had led them into this wilderness. The journey west had been one long series of disasters. If God was trying to tell them anything, it was probably that they should not go west.

Anna gazed wistfully at the arguing adults for a few seconds more, conflicted. Realizing that no guidance about eating clay was going to come from them, she turned back to Micah.

"Is it dreadful?" she asked softly.

"It's not flapjacks and molasses, but it's a ton better than sand and grass, which is likely to be the only thing we'll find to eat for the rest of the day, if we even make it past this stream before sundown," he said.

Anna pondered this, and reconsidered her previous opinion.

"Perhaps you're right and this *is* a gift from God," she conceded. "It could be that God is testing us, to see if we will accept the least of his gifts with gratitude, before he leads us to fields of plenty."

Micah said nothing, realizing anything he could say would only jeopardize the other children's chances of getting a few hours respite from the gnawing pain in their bellies.

"Just one handful," Anna said to the other children sternly. "It's God's will, I'm sure, but don't be greedy."

Within seconds all the children were digging hungrily into the clay, some shoveling it into their mouths with abandon, while others tested the taste and texture before committing themselves to the feast completely.

Micah scooped out a pristine lump of clay, not a hint of sand or rock at all, and formed it quickly into the shape of a little pie. He held it out in the palm of his hand, offering it with a wry smile to Anna.

"Imagine it's your grandma's apple pie," he said kindly.

She took it and nibbled at the imaginary crust, evaluating the taste only briefly, before spitting it out and wiping the offensive goo from her lips with the back of her hand.

She handed the mud pie back to him, as though gracefully refusing. "The Lord will provide," she stated again, though with less certainty than before.

Micah heard his father calling for him to come and pitch in with the work, so he smiled and jokingly made a curtsey to her, before running upstream to help.

It took a while, and it meant destroying one of their four remaining wagons to make a bridge strong enough for the oxen to cross, but eventually they managed it. After everything had been taken across, they loaded the remnants of the deconstructed wagon, in case they should need to use it again.

The children climbed up into the second wagon together, bellies full, quickly quieting down and falling asleep as they started forward once again, the adults happy to have respite from their grumbles, as they chased the sun on its journey west across the plain.

Lemuel sat perched atop the front of the lead wagon, resolute in his rightness. Even still, he seemed to froth to the very rim with a zealous fervor, which stewed inside him like a violent rage. He claimed that the purpose for his westward quest had been delivered to him straight from God, and so far neither Micah's father nor the wives had dared to challenge him about it.

Micah's father Samuel dutifully followed Lemuel in his wagon, his wife Rachel seated resolutely beside him, silent in rebuke, despite knowing they had long ago lost their way.

Micah brought up the rear of their tiny train, his wagon loaded with supplies, pulled by the slower but stronger oxen.

As the sun reached its highest point in the sky, a dramatic shift in the formation of the landscape presented itself in the distance ahead. The heat shimmered above the dry, stony ground, making it difficult to see clearly. However, one spot stood out strongly from the background of uniformity surrounding them in every direction, drawing them instinctively onward.

They approached the formation, a singular long rolling ridge dropped several hundred feet or so down a cliff they could not yet see. It appeared as though the ridge curved around into the distance for a mile or so, before dropping into the unending flatness of the prairie beyond, but distance was hard to gauge in the wide open spaces. As they travelled closer to the ridgeline, the ground began to slope slightly upward.

Micah heard Lemuel call the caravan to halt. He strained to see into the distance, the brilliance of the sun blinding him as he looked ahead.

Atop the edge of the ridge stood several indistinct figures, silhouetted against the sky. It was as though they had materialized out of the haze and now stood, unmoving, directly in their path.

Lemuel leapt down from the wagon. He had recently taken to wearing a long black coat, and it flowed behind him like a priest's vestal garments as he boldly strode towards the figures, his M1812 flintlock musket clamped in his hand. Micah saw his father checking the ammunition in his rifle as well, motioning to Rachel to stay put as he hurried to catch up with his trusted, lifelong friend.

Micah jumped down, bringing his own rifle along, and came to stand by the wagon where his mother stood watch with the children. He had a better view of the figures in their path now: four Indian warriors, one old and three young, with bright feathers in their headbands and war paint streaked across their faces. Micah was surprised to see them; the last of the savage native hordes had been relocated to the western reservations several years earlier, after the agreement of the tribes.

In the midst of the four warriors stood a totem of some kind, built of long upright wooden beams. Some sort of rope, dyed the color of fresh blood, was strung across the beams like a gigantic red spider web. A single human skull perched atop the construct. From a distance, it resembled a giant flaming sword.

Along the edge of the ridge, three large flat stones had been inserted into the ground in an upright fashion - like tombstones - several yards apart from each other. Odd-shaped letters, apparently derived from English, were etched on the face of each stone: O-A-N on the first, the letters A and T on the second, and C-R-O on the last. Micah wondered what they meant and thought perhaps they were markers for Indian graves.

The four Indian warriors stood in a line, unflinching as Lemuel and Sam approached. In the distance directly behind the Indians was the terrain anomaly where the families, not knowing where else to go, had been heading.

From his current vantage point, Micah could

clearly examine the landform they had been marching towards: the curved ridge of earth was shaped like an enormous open "V" lying sideways on the prairie, creating a verdant-looking, shaded valley, in which was nestled a grove of the most enormous trees Micah had ever seen.

The green valley sparkled below him like a giant emerald in the wilderness, everything about it screamed *life*. He felt like a parched castaway, stumbling upon a fresh-water lagoon on a desert island in the middle of the sea. That newfound sense of hope welled up even further as he saw three houses, clustered around the edges of the massive trees. They weren't sod huts, either, but real honest-to-goodness houses - larger than any he had seen so far on the prairie.

Micah fought the sudden urge to run straight down the ridge to the first house he could reach and bang on the door until someone let him in. He imagined the occupants serving him a welcoming feast of smoked ham and roasted chicken, pictured himself snuggling up in a plump bed, stuffed full of freshly plucked goose down, and dreamed how heavenly it would be. It had been weeks since he had slept on anything softer than dry hay.

His eyes refocused on the band of Indian warriors that stood, unmoving, between them and the newfound prairie paradise, and his daydream evaporated like dew in a desert sunrise.

"Should we go around them, Lemuel?" Micah's father, Sam, asked. "We've not got much shot, perhaps prudent to avoid confrontation."

"We will not let the children of Satan deter us from receiving this gift God has delivered unto us,"

Lemuel said as he, too, surveyed the houses in the green valley below. "These savages will either provide assistance, or step aside. They are intruders on sovereign government territory and have no right to challenge our passage here. Is your weapon at the ready, my good Samuel?"

Samuel nodded in response, but even at a distance Micah could see that his father's face held a look of deep concern.

"Then we best get this over with, Sam," Lemuel said.

"Stay with the women and children," Samuel called back to his son, his voice somber, fear painted boldly across the elder man's face. Micah knew his father was slow to anger and loathed violence, a trait that Lemuel in no way shared.

He wondered what was going on. He wanted to go with the men to speak with the Indians, but he knew his place all too well. He stood fast by the wagon as his father and Lemuel strode forward, the barrels of their rifles barely turned away as they approached the Indians. Micah had some understanding of why his mother Rachel and Lemuel's wife Sarah obediently followed their husbands wherever they went, but in his heart he wished that - just once - his father would act like a man and tell Lemuel what was what. But he never did, and that disappointed Micah immensely.

As he surveyed the developing situation, he felt Anna's warmth at his side.

"What's going on?" she asked sleepily; she had been napping with the rest of the children.

"I don't know," Micah said. "There's a settlement a bit up ahead, but some Indians are standing in the way. They haven't moved or said a word. It's an odd set of circumstances, to say the least."

The two teens watched as their fathers stopped to greet the Indians. They were too far away to be heard, so they had to settle for interpreting, solely through body language, how the conversation was proceeding.

The eldest Indian clearly shook his head "no", and pointed at the skull mounted atop the totem.

Then Lemuel began shouting, his words indistinct but nevertheless clear in their meaning, as they scattered in the dry prairie wind. He was angry.

Micah's father began to gesture urgently, clearly pleading for a peaceful resolution to the disagreement. But again the old Indian shook his head, and crossed his arms in a way that said there would be no further discussion.

That was when Lemuel brought the butt of his rifle up to his shoulder and shot the frail old man point blank in the face. His head exploded into nothingness, as the sharp report echoed across the plain.

The headless body stood its ground for several seconds more, arms still crossed, before finally collapsing onto the ground in a lifeless heap. Sam stared at Lemuel, mouth agape, but Lemuel was already busy reloading his weapon as the other three younger Indians stared in frozen shock at their fallen comrade. Micah felt his blood run cold as he realized that the Indians hadn't moved so much as a finger in a threatening manner, none had presented a weapon. He had just been witness to cold-blooded murder. Beside him, Anna let out a whimper beside and clutched his arm in fear.

Samuel spun around, waving his arms in confusion. Before he knew what was happening, a second shot rang out and a second Indian hit the deck. Then the remaining two were running, each in opposite directions, and Lemuel was screaming at the top of his lungs.

"Kill 'em, Sam, kill 'em!" he shouted, "One of them gets back to the tribe, and we're all dead."

Moments later, two final thunderclaps, one after the other, shook the stillness of the plain, and then it was just the settlers, alone on the prairie once more, with their three wagons and hungry oxen. The commotion woke the children from their slumber, and their wails carried from within the wagon as a few began to cry.

"Shut those kids up and keep 'em in the wagon," Lemuel barked at Sarah, as he strode back towards them. "Go help your father cover the bodies," he ordered Micah with a withering glare, his eyes crazed and bright with murder. "Anna, get away from that boy and tend to the children."

Anna put her head down obediently and walked away.

He's gonna kill us all before it's over with, Micah thought as he grabbed a shovel from the supply wagon to help his father tend to the bodies. He knew his father would never have killed a man in cold blood like that, not unless he had to – and now, thanks to Lemuel, he had been forced to do just that.

He toiled in sober silence with his father, piling the dead into an obscene heap, twisted carcasses tangled together. When they were finished, they covered the shredded corpses with large flat stones and spread loose dirt to cover the four separate

106

puddles of blood, trying their best to hide what had been done here. But they both knew that carrion buzzards would be circling within the hour, making it clear to anyone for miles around that death had visited this spot.

II. The Garden

IT WAS NEARLY AN HOUR before Micah and Samuel rejoined the group. They climbed down to the valley, and the houses waiting below, along a steep and winding trail that was cut into the side of the ridge. As they emerged from the dusty path onto a smooth green lawn, Micah noticed the entrance was well-marked, oddly enough, by a grotesquely shaped wooden bush, its knurled branches resembling a man with limbs tied into pretzel-like knots.

Lemuel had already brought the wagons, along with the women and children, down into the small valley. The horses and oxen were grazing contentedly as the children played, running and laughing in the soft grass carpeting beneath the canopy of the massive trees. Micah spotted two small ponds nearby, one in the midst of the grove and another, further back towards the edge of the valley, near the smallest of the three homes. Beyond the ponds stood a smokehouse - seeing it made him smile with fond memories - and a few other small wooden buildings.

Lemuel stood straight and tall, waiting for them with hands on hips, beaming with pride. "The good Lord has blessed us," his voice boomed. "He has delivered all these blessings to us, his most faithful servants!"

"What do you mean?" Samuel asked, puzzled. "Where are the owners? Are we welcome here?"

"We *are* the owners, my friend," Lemuel said with absolute certainty. "We've checked the houses and they are vacant, every one. There's no death, no disease, no sign that anyone has lived here for a very long time; yet both dwellings are furnished and tidy, the pantry fully stocked with provisions and seed, the trees above us burdened with fruit – it's as though the Lord God himself came down from heaven and prepared this garden especially for our families' blessing."

Sam gave him a dubious look, but said nothing. Lemuel, noticing his friend's skepticism, laughed heartily and slapped him on the back. The two men had been best friends since early youth, but it was clear to Micah that his father had lost faith in the soundness of Lemuel's judgment since this journey began.

"You're not fearful the Indians will return, seeking their own and thirsting for vengeance, when they discover their dead?"

"God is on our side. We will remain vigilant, and he will protect. Come, my friend," Lemuel said, gesturing to the two-story house with plank siding that he had claimed for his own. "Even now our wives are preparing the homes the Lord has given us."

Micah watched as his father followed Lemuel up onto the small porch and into the house but decided not to follow. He was having a hard time accepting the reality of everything that surrounded him; their fortunes had changed so quickly. He gazed up into the fruit-laden trees that soared above, the branches mingling so thickly. It was impossible to tell where one tree ended and the next began. He surveyed the well-built houses that stood on either side and marveled at his brothers and sisters and their friends, playing barefoot in the silken grass as if they were in the city park back home. It all seemed too good to be true. Had he died? Was this heaven?

Out of the corner of his eye, he sensed movement in the second-floor window of Lemuel's house; for a fleeting moment he thought he saw Anna between the curtains, looking out. Had she been watching him? He hoped so. Lately all he could seem to think of was the day he had found her in the smokehouse, touching herself.

He wanted to see her like that again.

***

OVER THE NEXT THREE DAYS, Micah traded shifts with Lemuel and Sam, standing watch along the ridgeline for any sign of approaching savages. The rest of the group worked hard as they unpacked the wagons to set up home in the valley, at least for a little while.

The houses, although mostly tidy, were in dire need of dusting and airing out; it was evident they had been vacant for quite some time. All the furniture and belongings of those who had lived there before, even their clothing, had been left behind. Lemuel and his family had taken over the house closest to the trail down from the ridge. Samuel and the rest of Micah's family moved into the house on the far side of the orchard. The third house was less well provisioned than the others, and they decided to leave it as it was for the time being.

The women and children worked hard to clean the houses, washing sheets and clothes in a barrel of clear water, drawn from the clear pool at the end of the valley. The pond that lay in the middle of the orchard was full of stagnant yellow water that had a sweet, syrupy aroma about it. Meanwhile, Lemuel and Sam took stock of all the supplies they could find on the premises. In the small barn by the smokehouse, they found bags and bags of dry crop seed, enough for twenty harvests, if not more, as well as enough hay to get the animals through the cold months, if they decided to winter here. There was also a small sawmill and some rough hewn lumber set up at one end of the barn. Timber for the houses had been cut from trees on the side of the ridge.

They also found a wooden shed tucked behind each house, each yielding an abundance of glass jars of preserved food. But strangely enough (and especially to young Jacob's bitter disappointment) despite the gigantic apple trees in the yard laden with fruit, there were no jars of apples to be found. There was no apple sauce, no cinnamon-sweet apple butter, and no cored apples for pie filling - only scores of glass jars, stuffed with pickled vegetables. There were turnips and squash, green beans and carrots, as well as a variety of other roots and greens that must have been grown in the now-fallow fields that lay on the plain just outside the entrance to the valley. The smokehouse was likewise delightfully stocked with smoked hams, salted and ready to eat, dried sausages and more meats hanging from its rafters.

In the evening, the children enjoyed playing underneath the branches of the mythically large apple trees; they were so enormous that Samuel joked that maybe Johnny Appleseed himself had gotten lost out on the prairie, and had died on this exact spot. "With a pocket full of seeds and a pot on his head, trees probably grew right up out of his rotting corpse," he said, laughing, taking a hard pull on his pipe and winking merrily at Lemuel. His friend, however, was too busy dictating his own version of the Scriptures to Anna to appreciate Samuel's sense of humor.

Micah sat near them at the top of the steps, whittling a stick and listening to Lemuel's nonsensical ramblings as he blathered on about new Eden and God anointing Lemuel to be his last true prophet. Every now and then he would sneak a peek at Anna, as she diligently transcribed her father's every word, a silken twirl of hair caressing her cheek.

If it weren't for her, Micah knew he would steal a horse and gallop back east on his own that very night. But he couldn't leave her. Something inside him insisted that he could never live happily without her, so he stayed, finding enjoyment in the sugary-sweetness of the cool evening air in the orchard and in his dreams of a future with Anna in his arms.

***

THE SECOND DAY IN THE VALLEY came and went with no sign of Indian scouts searching for their missing comrades. Late in the afternoon, Micah's father sent him to fetch the bodies of the four slain Indians from where they lay covered in rocks up on the ridge, lest members of their tribe eventually discover them.

Micah toiled in the hot sun, prying the stiff corpses from the ground, untangling the fetid, festering mass of decaying limbs and torsos from each other. He struggled with each unwieldy load of dead flesh, dragging the heavy bodies up into the wagon one by one. The headless old man had been drained almost entirely of blood, his figure like a piece of driftwood cast far from shore, shriveled and knurled. It reminded Micah of the twisted bush at the entrance to the trail, and he shivered at the thought.

As he was about to climb up to drive the oxen and their death-laden wagon back down into the valley, Micah stopped and looked back at the totem with the skull and the fire-red rope that stood as an ominous guard at the top end of the trail. Not wanting that reminder of murder looking accusingly down on him day after day, he tore it down, and tossed it into the cart to be disposed of with the rest of the mess.

Once back in the valley, he directed the oxen to pull the wagon alongside the smokehouse. He began to dig the graves, his shovel cutting through the soft dirt as effortlessly as a spoon through fresh chocolate cake, making much quicker work of it than he had expected.

Once he had dug four side-by-side holes, he laid the corpses on their backs in the dirt. He refilled the holes as fast as he could, to cover their shameful contents.

III. The Serpent

EVERYONE WAS JOYFUL as the sun rose on their third day. Now fully rested and restored from their stretch of hunger and the travail of their journey, the full extent of the blessing that had been bestowed upon them finally sank in.

Even Lemuel, who had shown some restraint, despite the occasional vociferous proclamation of faith in God's protection, began to let his guard down. He came striding down from his turn at watch atop the ridge with a jaunty gait, to announce that he felt that maintaining constant guard was no longer a necessity and that he intended to have a feast of celebration that very evening.

"Our wives are in the kitchen of my new home even now, preparing a feast of celebration," Lemuel told Sam as they sat in the rockers on the front porch. He was still firmly gripping his rifle, but no longer kept his finger on the trigger. "It is my pleasure to invite you and your family to dinner this evening. Tomorrow we will plan for the sowing, for the fall harvest, my friend."

Within the hour, fires were lit in the kitchen, the stoves crackling from the perfectly dried kindling the previous tenants had been gracious enough to leave stacked neatly on the porch. Dozens of full-grown chickens had been found, running wild, out back behind the house. One soon destined for the table, plucked clean and boiling in the syrupy-sweet yellow water drawn from the pond at the base of the trees.

As the women prepared the evening meal, Jacob pestered Micah relentlessly to show him the bodies of the dead Indians he had buried. Eventually Micah relented, despite his better judgment. First making sure that no one was watching, he grabbed a shovel from the tool shed and led Jacob out to where they were buried. The outlines of the freshly dug graves were clearly visible, four dark brown rectangles of upturned soil that contrasted sharply with the green grass.

Micah quickly scooped loose earth from the head of the first grave, where he knew the body of a tall, fierce-looking warrior lay, his intention only to uncover the face long enough to allow Jacob to have a quick look.

He dug gently, so as not to inadvertently damage the corpse's face. After he had dug only a foot or so into the ground his shovel struck something solid, causing the metal blade to ring. It surprised Micah so much that he jumped back alarmed.

"What is it?" Jacob asked, eyes widening.

"There's something hard, but there shouldn't be," Micah said.

"It's only the lid of the casket, right?" the young boy asked.

Micah shook his head.

"Ain't one. Put 'em straight in the dirt."

After a moment he picked up the shovel and began gently clearing the dirt from along the top of the grave to expose whatever it was he had struck.

The body was gone, replaced by a thick tree root the width and length of the hole he had dug the day before.

His mind reeled at the discovery. He hadn't

encountered a single obstruction when digging, but now this massive tendril of wood ran straight through the freshly dug grave as though it had been growing there, undisturbed, for centuries.

He brushed the loose dirt from atop the root to get a better look. The shape of it almost made it look as though a human figure was bound tightly inside it, like a snake recently gorged, its belly pregnant with food and molded to the shape of whatever poor animal it had swallowed whole.

"Get on back up to the house, boy, get," he snapped at Jacob, as an unsettling feeling gripped him. "Don't tell anyone I showed you this, or else I'll give you a beating my damn self, you hear me? I knew I shouldn't have shown you. Now I gotta go tell Pa."

Jacob readily agreed, eager to keep the trust of his hero and happy to have a secret shared between them. He ran off to the house as Micah trudged up the barn to tell his father and Lemuel of his discovery. Micah stood outside the barn a bit before entering. He listened to the men as they talked inside, trying to think of what he would tell them.

How could he possibly explain what he had found? He knew his father would listen and try to understand, and would hopefully believe him – but Lemuel? Never.

Micah put his hands on the barn door to push it open, but then hesitated.

He should go back to the graves for one last look before sharing his discovery with anyone, he decided. Perhaps he had been mistaken.

He walked back down to the smokehouse and stood by the half-covered grave.

It was empty.

No root. No dead body. Only an empty hole filled with loose dirt.

Micah grabbed the shovel and began to dig furiously into the other freshly-filled graves, frantically spooning the soil away.

All were empty. The bodies were gone, as though they had never been there at all.

A cold chill ran down Micah's spine as he pondered what to do next. Tell Lemuel? He was confused about what had happened. Had Indians come and carried their dead away? It seemed unlikely. The graves had been completely undisturbed. Why would they have taken the time to refill the holes so they would appear unmolested?

A vision flashed into Micah's mind - a giant wooden python, wrapped around a man, devouring him whole. He tried to shake it off, but still the haunting image lingered. He knew he couldn't tell anyone what he had seen. They would think he was crazy.

Shaken and no longer wanting to be alone, he quickly refilled the now-empty graves and ran back to join the others, eager to find comfort in the company of the others.

IV. THE SIN

THAT EVENING, several hours before sundown, the two families joined together for a celebration and feast at Lemuel's house. During dinner, the adults talked about their hopes and dreams for the future, about whether they should stay here permanently or press their luck by continuing the journey west.

Lemuel had become convinced that God had led them to the site of the original Garden of Eden, that it had been revealed to them at this precise time as a reward for successfully enduring the hardships that the Lord had tested them with. Lemuel said it was a sign that God had chosen him as his prophet on Earth, to lead the chosen people into the new age of Eden, a golden millennium of plenty that would last a thousand years.

Lemuel had become obsessed with the notion of starting his own "true" religion; it was all he ever talked about anymore. Micah remembered that the nonsense had first started after Lemuel had a chance encounter with a man named Hyrum Smith over a bottle of whiskey, in a Missouri saloon a few months earlier. Hyrum's tales of how he and his brother Joseph had crafted a modern religious mythology, making them wealthy and respected men as a result, had entranced Lemuel and set the wheels of his mind in motion like nothing before.

Shaking a half-eaten drumstick in one hand and a mostly empty glass of whiskey in the other, Lemuel described in glorious detail his future vision for this fertile valley in the middle of nowhere. It would become the New Jerusalem for a new Christian religion. He would be the prophet and Sam his high priest. "Bigger than the Mormons, and richer than sin," as he so eloquently put it. They would establish, right here, a new trading post for weary souls, "heavy with sin and cash, and in dire need of being unburdened of both".

"The way I see it, and please do tell if I'm missing something," Lemuel began, as the mouthful of boiled potatoes he had chewed but not swallowed bubbled out of the corners of his mouth and dripped into his ill-kept beard. "God done provided. Our bellies were empty and now our cup runneth over. Fourteen trees grow even now, laden with bushels and bushels of fruit, between the homes he has so graciously given. This place is the *"locust amoeba"* which we have sought after our entire lives," he declared in a sing-song preacher voice.

"Locus amoenus," Samuel gently corrected him.

"What?" Lemuel said. "Right, *locust amoeba*, that's what I said, Sam, listen up! These are momentous days we are living in. Mankind has waited millennia to be allowed to return to the garden, and today... well, here we are." He shoveled an oversized spoonful of pickled turnips into his mouth, as if to emphasize his point.

Sam finally felt himself being touched by the spirit as well, whether it was by the Holy Spirit or the liquid variety he wasn't sure, and he decided that it was his moment to wax philosophical while his chatty friend was momentarily rendered speechless. Sam smiled kindly upon his wife and his children, seated around the table, each of them looking clean and

EVANS LIGHT

refreshed and enjoying their first real meal in months. The whiskey was doing a nice job of clearing up any previous doubts he'd had about the whole endeavor.

"You're right, Brother Lemuel, you speak the truth," Sam said. "We have done the will of God, we have been fruitful and multiplied as the Lord hath commanded, and have even set our hand upon the unclean heathen so as to reclaim this land for the Lord and his righteous. He has seen fit to reward us, to provide us with plenty, so that we may do his will. I believe wholly, as do you, that our good fortune is a sign that God intends for us to do his work right here. Surely that is why he saw fit to lead us away from the others with whom we traveled, through trials and tribulations straight into this glorious bounty."

Micah sighed to himself. This conversation was just gearing up, he knew, and would no doubt continue deep into the night. He had heard it all before, so after listening politely for a bit, he excused himself from the table and went outside to watch the smaller kids play.

In the yard, Nathan and Jacob were throwing rocks up into the trees trying to knock loose the scarlet fruit that tantalized them from the branches high overhead - most likely apples, but so far up it was impossible to be sure. Micah was certain, at any rate, that he had never seen apple trees so large.

He joined the other boys in their efforts to knock down some dessert, but despite several direct hits, the tree stubbornly refused to yield its fruit.

He grew frustrated with the futility of his effort. He gave up, turning to go back inside.

He bumped hard into Anna, who had snuck up quietly behind him.

"Where are you off to so fast?" she asked. Her voice sounded different to him - softer, silky even.

"Back inside, I guess," he said. "Can't even knock an apple down for the kids, anyhow. It's stuck so fast to the branches that not even a strong blow with a rock may loosen it from the tree."

"But why hurry?" she asked. "It's so nice out here, and Father's just getting started, you know. He said that he thinks that hill behind us might be the very place the Bible says Jesus will return. Are you sure you want to listen to that? You know how he is when he's drinking. Please stay here with me a bit longer. Please?"

Micah had never seen her act this way. Throughout their childhood he had simply been a person for her to boss around, and more recently, someone she tried to avoid.

He stopped walking, though. Standing beside her, he turned back towards the trees, unsure what to say.

"I was watching you throwing," Anna continued. "You've gotten a lot stronger this year, haven't you? And taller," she said, as though very impressed with him.

He was surprised at how her eyes glistened so brightly in the last dying rays of the sunset. He had always thought she was pretty, but now she was beyond pretty – she was *beautiful*, he realized for the first time.

She glanced nervously back at her new house, and he looked, too. Her father had his back to the window, and was raising his freshly refilled whiskey glass as he lectured the other adults.

Anna glanced at the other children to see if they

were watching. They weren't.

Satisfied no one would see, she grabbed Micah quickly by the hand.

"Follow me," she whispered. Then she gathered her long skirt up in one hand and dragged him along behind her with the other as she ran across the yard, raven hair flowing behind her, stopping only when they were well hidden from sight behind a thick trunk of one of the gigantic trees.

She pushed him hard up against the tree. The soft bark was smooth against his back, almost like saddle leather. He felt warmth growing in his groin, and he gasped as Anna took his hands and pressed them against her breasts.

"What are you doing?" he stammered, flustered.

She didn't answer; instead, she wrapped her arms around him and kissed him, drawing his lips into her mouth, biting gently for a moment before releasing him.

He stared at her in amazement. She was panting for breath, looking as though she was a bit drunk, even though he was quite sure her father hadn't left the whiskey unattended for one moment the entire evening.

"You remember last summer, when you found me in the smokehouse?" she asked.

He blushed. It was the first time she had ever spoken of it aloud.

"Yes."

"Do you know what I was doing that day?" she asked, voice quivering with excitement.

He wasn't entirely sure how to answer the question, even though he felt he had a pretty good idea of what it was she had been doing.

"No," he said in a dry whisper.

She put her lips to his ear, so close that they brushed lightly against his flesh as she spoke.

"I was thinking of you."

He didn't know how to respond, but Anna saw a bulge rising in the front of his trousers and smiled approvingly.

"Tonight," she whispered. "Let's make it real. Meet me in the smokehouse after father passes out and everyone else is asleep. Meet me there and I'll show you where *you* should be - you know...instead of my fingers."

Micah nodded meekly in agreement. He would be there.

She slipped a small rolled-up paper into his hand and kissed him again, lightly on the cheek this time, then ran back to her house before anyone could notice she was missing.

He unrolled the paper she had given him, to see what was written there. It wasn't a note as he had suspected, but a picture. He had seen it before, a pencil sketch made by a friend of hers when she was a bit younger. It was a pretty drawing of her, he thought. The artist had done an exceptional job of capturing the fire that burned in the back of her eyes.

He rolled it back up and slipped it into his pocket, waiting behind the tree as he struggled to quash his arousal. After a while, he felt almost normal again, and went back to throwing rocks at the fruit with the children. He had noticed empty bushel baskets were stacked on the porch next to the kindling, so he assumed the fruit must ripen and fall eventually. Why else would there be baskets for collecting fruit?

But that whole evening, not a single red apple

fell.

V. THE TREE OF LIFE

LATER THAT NIGHT - long after the feast had been cleared away, the fires put out, and the children tucked up in bed - Micah lay in his room, blinking up into the darkness. It had seemed like an eternity before everyone finally settled down and went to sleep. Being the only boy - and a near-grown one at that - in a family with four sisters meant he had his own room, and he was happy for it, too. But now all he wanted was to leave it, to wrap his arms around Anna, to feel her soft lips on his once more.

Earlier, before everyone went to sleep, he had quietly prepared for his escape by prying open his bedroom window. His room overlooked the front porch, so he was confident that he could easily slip out when the time came. Getting back into the house would be a whole different challenge, but he decided to deal with that when the time came.

After waiting what seemed like years, he climbed out of bed and tiptoed to the window, where he sat and stared out across the lawn. He watched as the lanterns in Anna's house were extinguished one room after another. It had been the hardest week of his entire life. He was still exhausted, not only from the long journey and near starvation, but from the incessant gnawing of desperation, the grinding stress of not knowing if each new day on the prairie would be his last. Fatigued or not, the desire that burned inside him for Anna's touch urged him forward, prodding him awake.

As the final light in her house grew dark, he

hoped that she was still awake and eager for him, too.

For a little longer, the muffled voices of his parents bled through the thin wall from the room beside his. Then, finally, the house fell silent.

Everyone was fast asleep, but not Micah. He carefully stuck his head out his bedroom window and inhaled the cool night air deeply, feeling more exquisitely alive than he ever had before. The air was sweet with the fragrance of fruit in the trees, and it charged his senses.

Looking at Anna's house, he imagined that he saw her looking back at him from her own bedroom window across the clearing, her visage pale and beautiful in the bright moonlight. He wanted to run to her, to hold her, to take her for his own at that exact moment, but he resisted that reckless urge and waited silent and still by the window.

They would meet at the smokehouse as planned, in due time.

After a bit he heard the clock in the living room softly chiming downstairs. The moment had arrived. He quietly crawled out of the window and over the sill, planting his feet carefully on the roof of the porch so as to maintain absolute silence. The last thing he needed was for his father - or even worse, a drunken Lemuel - to mistake him for an Indian seeking revenge and pump him full of lead without a second thought. Although he was sure that Lemuel would be plenty happy to kill him intentionally, if he caught wind of the intentions Micah had for his eldest daughter tonight.

He successfully made his way to the edge of the roof, and was just about to drop down on the soft grass below when he heard something, a sound that made him stop: a soft *thump* that came from somewhere out in the yard - from where exactly, he couldn't ascertain.

Was it Anna he had heard, perhaps, leaping onto the grass?

His eyes strained in the dim moonlight to see movement around her house, but he saw nothing. All appeared to be still.

Then he heard it again, a soft *thump* somewhere in the darkness. This time the sound had been preceded by a rustling of leaves.

Thump. He heard it again.

Thump. Thump.

Indians, seeking vengeance? He wondered.

The noise continued, slowly at first, from scattered locations around the yard. Then he spied the first sign of movement in the gloom. A solitary apple rolled out from under the trees, along the ground towards him, its shiny peel glimmering blood red in the moonlight. It came to a rest on the walkway to the house, not more than a few feet from the steps that led to the porch.

At that moment, it finally occurred to him what was making the sound. He laughed quietly to himself because suddenly it seemed so obvious: the fruit was falling.

What had started out as a gentle patter quickly erupted into a downpour of fresh produce. A hailstorm of fruit poured upon the ground, thousands of apples, he guessed, if not more. The sound was like the footsteps of a hundred horses in a faraway stampede, soft and hushed, like a gentle rain, as the apples fell upon the silken grass.

The treetops shook like a wet dog drying its fur,

as falling fruit struck branches, loosening leaves that fluttered down like a million moonlit moths through the night.

It ended as suddenly as it had begun, and silence once again descended upon the valley.

Micah held his breath, listening to see if the disturbance, although gentle, had been loud enough to rouse the family and ruin his chances for a rendezvous with Anna.

He waited, full of nervous anticipation, crouched atop the front porch. But all remained dark and quiet, both at his house and Anna's. After waiting what seemed like an eternity, he felt satisfied that no one had been disturbed, so he slid down to the edge of the roof and dropped down easily onto the grass below.

Micah walked to the rim of the orchard. The thin clouds had cleared and the moon shone brightly. The apple-covered earth created a bright red reflection that shone up into the foliage. For a moment, it appeared to him as though a river of fresh blood now flowed beneath the massive trees and through the valley, dividing the houses. The thought sent a chill down his spine.

He looked towards the smokehouse; it was just visible in the moonlight. He took a few steps in that direction before pausing. He found his desire for the forbidden fruit waiting for him in the smokehouse briefly overwhelmed by his desire for the real fruit, fallen at his feet. The air was fragrant with the sweetness of it. His mouth began to water.

He plucked an apple from the ground and inspected it. It was cool, smooth to the touch. Polishing it quickly on the leg of his trousers, he brought it to his mouth, lips quivering with anticipation.

Unable to resist the intense allure of the fruit for a single second longer, he bit down hungrily. A bolt of exquisite flavor exploded into his mouth as his teeth pierced the skin. A wave of lightheadedness washed over him as he chewed the delicate, creamy flesh, sticky juice dripping from his chin.

It was delicious.

For a moment, he completely forgot about Anna and his planned meeting with her, finding himself filled instead with a powerful urge to run amongst the trees and gather as many apples as he could, to devour the heavenly fruit until his belly filled to bursting. His tongue had never tasted anything in his life as transcendentally wonderful as the rapidly diminishing apple he held in his hand. In that moment, he wanted nothing other than to keep eating them until he could eat no more.

As he nibbled the last bit of fruit down to the core, even nearly devouring the seeds, Micah noticed a pale figure standing in the clearing on the other side of the trees, skirt billowing gently in the soft breeze, watching him intently.

It was Anna, looking decadently voluptuous in the moonlight.

She turned away from him, making rapid strides towards the smokehouse, silken hair flowing across her shoulders as she went.

He let the now-slender core on which he had been gnawing fall to the ground and began to run, his desire for her once again ignited inside him. He sprinted towards the anticipated intersection of their paths near the rear of the valley, running along the edge of the tree line to avoid twisting an ankle on the fruit as he ran.

Micah caught up with her near the rear of the smokehouse, nearly tackling her to the ground as he took her in his arms, pulling her to him, pressing his lips, still sticky-sweet from the fruit, hungrily against hers.

Anna pushed him away roughly, tasting the sweetness he had left on her lips with her tongue as she did.

"What are you doing, kissing me in full view of God and man?" she protested. "I told you to meet me *inside* the smokehouse! What if Father catches us fornicating? He'll shoot you and me dead, both here on this spot."

She nervously looked towards her house to see if anyone had followed them.

Seeing her glancing back, pale skin and white dress illuminated in the dead light of the moon, caused him to think of the story of Lot's wife in the Bible - how she must have appeared as she turned into a pillar of salt after looking back towards Sodom.

"I'm sorry," he said meekly. "Let's go inside."

She ignored him.

"I think somebody saw us," she fretted. "There's somebody in the yard in front of the house. There, look - under the trees."

"Nobody saw us," he said gently, "you're imagining things." He took her hand. She pulled away from him, her agitation growing.

"We've been found out," she sobbed as she stared in horror towards the trees. "He's going to shoot our heads off our shoulders, just like he did to those Indians."

"There's nobody there," Micah insisted, and

turned to point at the empty yard spread out under the trees, eager to soothe her anxiety and get her into the smokehouse. But there *was* someone there, a few hundred yards or so away - someone moving rapidly across the yard from Anna's house and heading towards his.

Alarmed by this discovery, he grabbed Anna and quickly forced her down onto her knees in the tall grass so they wouldn't be spotted.

Crouched low, they watched as the silhouetted figure disappeared onto the porch of Micah's house. Across the valley, the windows of Lemuel's house remained dark, as did the windows in Micah's house.

"Look!' Anna said, pointing.

In the middle of the cluster of trees other people were moving about – two, no, three of them - small people walking and stopping, ducking down and standing back up. Some were toting something along in front of them, something big and wide, nearly as large as the little people themselves. Hidden in the shadows of the trees as they were, it was impossible to say what it was they were carrying.

Micah and Anna began to creep through the grass towards them to get a better look, doing their best to stay hidden behind the massive tree trunks as they moved quietly forward. As they approached the strange creatures, they began to hear the sound of whispers and soft laughter, stifled squeals of delight.

At the top of the steps to Micah's house, which thankfully remained dark and quiet, the figure that had disappeared there moments before returned to the top of the steps, motioning to someone hidden in the dark shadows of the porch. Facing the moon, Micah and Anna were able to see, finally, who - *or what* - the creature was.

It was Anna's younger brother, Nathan, smiling from ear to ear as he gestured enthusiastically for someone to come into the yard. They both let out a sigh of relief.

As Nathan marched back down the steps and into the orchard, other small figures emerged from the shadows. Following behind him, Micah's three sisters, each carrying an empty bushel basket with them. They joined Nathan and the other small folk, whom Micah had by now identified as Anna's other brother and her two younger sisters. Once together, the children began to work in earnest to fill the baskets with as much freshly fallen fruit as they could manage, chattering softly amongst themselves as they plucked the apples from the ground.

The two would-be lovers regretfully separated, Micah approaching the children to distract them, while Anna crept unnoticed through the deep shadows back to her house.

VI. The Tree of Knowledge of Good and Evil

"What do you think you're doing?" Micah asked in a deep voice, startling the children as he stepped from the darkness.

Nathan was the first to answer, confident that he had the best shot at winning Micah over to their plan.

"The fruit fell, Micah," he said, gesturing excitedly at the ground around him as though the carpet of apples wasn't already obvious to anyone with a working eyeball. "We thought it would be a great surprise for our parents, a very nice surprise indeed, to have these bushel baskets full and waiting for them in the morning. Don't you think so, too?" he asked, his face bright and expectant of praise.

Micah glanced towards Anna's house and thought once again of her warm lips, of her silken inner thighs, of her full breasts that he was unlikely to see this evening, not now, with kids loose and prowling in the dark.

He let out a long sigh of despair at the thought. Nathan, assuming it was a sign of disapproval, looked crushed.

Micah's youngest sister, Chastity, strolled happily through the shadows to where he and Nathan faced each other, each boy frowning for his own reasons. The little girl was oblivious to anything other than the magical wonder of a fragrant summer night. The full moon was bright on her innocent face, full of joy. She hugged Micah hard, looking up at him with love.

"Eat an apple, big brother," she said with

concern, her four-year-old voice as adorably high-pitched and squeaky as a little mouse. "It'll make you feel better," she insisted. "Let me find you a good one."

She scanned the ground, searching for an apple for her big brother, the best she could find. There were so many to choose from, almost all perfect specimens. Finally she spotted the perfect one to cheer her brother up, about fifteen yards away near the trunk, and she scampered off into the darkness to fetch it.

Micah turned wistfully back towards Anna's house, scanning for any sign that she might still be waiting for him in the darkness. Perhaps if he got the kids settled down and back in bed - maybe, just maybe -they could salvage their plans for each other this evening. But the darkness held no trace of her, no promise of her desire for him waiting to be fulfilled.

At that moment a piercing cry shattered the night - a howl of fear melting into agony. It cut off mid-shriek, as though a hand had been clamped over the screaming mouth to silence it.

Chastity, Micah thought, and his heart seized with panic. He knew his baby sister's voice anywhere. It had always sickened him to hear her cry. He bolted towards the place he had last seen her, frantically scouring the gloom as he ran beneath the trees. She had gone for an apple. She hadn't gone far, but now she was nowhere to be found. The scent of fresh soil hung thick in the air, nearly choking him with its dank, peaty fragrance.

"Chastity!" he yelled, desperately spinning about on the spot where she had been only moments before.

"Chastity, where are you?" His words cracked

under the weight of the panic they carried. He turned back to Nathan with questioning eyes.

Nathan stood frozen, his mouth agape and arm outstretched as he pointed a single shaking finger towards where Chastity had last been. His lower jaw was moving up and down slightly, as though trying to say something but unable to get his lips to cooperate long enough to form a single word.

Micah grabbed him by the shoulders, shaking him, shouting.

"Where'd she go? Where is she? What happened?"

Nathan found his voice after a few seconds and began to stammer, as though decades had passed since he last uttered a word.

"I don't know...she disappeared. She bent down to pick up an apple, screamed - and then she was *gone*, like that," he said, his words coming in short bursts, "like she was sucked straight down into the ground."

Micah felt as though the world was swimming around him, and he placed a hand on Nathan's shoulder to steady himself. The other children, still lost in their joy of collecting apples, hadn't even noticed the commotion. In his peripheral vision, Micah saw lights flicker to life in Lemuel's house.

He had to help his little sister. He had to find Chastity. He knew he needed to gather his wits about him and quick. Everything happening around him suddenly seemed surreal. The other children floated through the darkness around him, collecting fruit like ghosts at a Halloween harvest.

Piety, the older of Anna's two sisters, blissfully strolled up, as Micah searched desperately for the missing girl. She sat her basket of fruit down on the ground beside him as she reached for an enormous apple. He absently stepped back to give her room, wondering if perhaps Chastity was playing tricks on him in the darkness. He wasn't in the mood for hide and seek.

Micah watched as Piety wrapped her tiny fingers around the enormous piece of fruit she had found for him. She struggled to pick it up from the ground, but it was too heavy for her. She tried using two hands, pulling with all her might, but still it resisted.

Piety resembled Anna. She was almost a miniature version, had the same long black hair and china-pale skin, but for some reason Micah thought her nowhere nearly as beautiful. She was missing something, the thing that made Anna so irresistible to him, that fire in her eyes, the fighting spirit, that inner strength that made Anna carry herself as though she were the only perfect creature in an otherwise tragically flawed world.

The girl refused to give up her prize and dug her fingernails into the skin of the fruit. Finally, she managed to lift it. She hadn't moved it more than an inch or two off the ground when the apple split open with a harsh clicking noise. Sharp wooden appendages shot out from it, stabbing deep into the young girl's delicate palms. The skin on the back of her hands ripped open, the protrusions making a wet slurp as they pierced upwards through her flesh and bone, finally clamping themselves tightly about her wrists like long claws.

Piety looked up at Micah, stunned, her wide eyes filled to the brim with confusion. The sight of her tiny mangled hands, blood throbbing from her wrists in silky crimson ribbons, caused Micah's mind to recoil in his skull. Hot vomit pushed hard at the back of his throat as he tried to process what was happening.

In the blink of an eye, before Piety could manage a single whimper of pain or fear, the apple, the *thing* that had sewn itself into her flesh, yanked her wounded hands violently downward, and pulled both of her arms completely underneath the ground up to her shoulders. Her china-doll face hit the soft dirt with so much force that her head snapped back -- - *too* far back. The rear of her skull struck her spine hard, Micah heard a shrill, cracking sound, like a walnut being shattered in a vice.

Piety's head and shoulders were stuck for a moment as she was being pulled under, chin now planted in the dirt, head canted back at a ninety-degree angle, her glassy unblinking eyes staring upwards towards the night sky. Before Micah could take a step forward to help, she was yanked down again, and again, and then she was gone – vanished, head-first, like a shoelace pulled deftly through an eyelet. A small puff of dust and two empty shoes were the only remaining evidence that she had even existed.

Micah and Nathan stumbled backwards away from the small hole Piety had left in the earth, stunned. Anna's youngest sister, Lydia, joined them, unaware of what had just happened to her sister and curious to see what the commotion was about. Micah hastily scooped the girl up in his arms and began to back away from the trees, careful not to step on any of the apples.

In the distance, from inside one of the houses, he heard a man shouting urgently. Lemuel was awake, he realized through his panic, probably stumbling around in the darkness looking for a lantern and his gun. This thought brought Micah back to his senses and out of this upside-down world for a moment. For a single split second, he felt a brief sense of clarity about what was happening and about what he must do.

Before that impending clarity could develop completely, chaos erupted around him, exploding on every side, and the understanding that had nearly been within his grasp exploded along with it. He spun about, bewildered.

Everywhere around him, children were screaming. Some were desperately trying to pull their hands away from the ground. Others tried to run but were unable to move, as though their feet were staked to the ground.

"Get away from the trees!" Micah screamed. "Get to the house! Make haste!" he commanded, but it was too late.

In the darkness around him, children began to vanish, one after the other, their fragile bodies ripping and contorting. Shrill screams were choked silent with a mouthful of dirt and a gurgle of blood, as tiny guts squeezed up and out of their mouths, their bodies dragged underground. Overhead, the prodigious branches rattled and shook as though buffeted by a fierce storm. But the sky was clear and the wind was still.

Micah continued his retreat out of the orchard, carrying Lydia high up off the ground as he went. But Nathan stood frozen on the spot, paralyzed with fear. A ring of bright red apples popped out of the earth around Nathan, circling him.

"Don't move! Don't touch them," Micah instructed, but the boy panicked. Nathan took a step forward, as if to run, and in the process stepped directly atop one of the apples. A brilliant crimson stain splattered up the leg of his beige canvas pants, as the top of his leather shoe burst open. He tried to pull his foot back, but it was stuck firmly in place. He looked to Micah, desperate for help as thick rivulets of blood began to pulse out of his shoe. The expression on his face told Micah it was already too late.

Nathan's body jerked downward into the ground up to his kneecaps, the bone and muscle of his legs yielding skin, like fresh bark stripped from a tree.

Micah set Lydia down and ran to where Nathan struggled to pry himself from the ground. Micah grabbed hold of the boy's wrists, latching onto him with all his might, determined to win this game of tug-of-war that was quickly devouring his young friend.

But his efforts were futile. The force that pulled the boy downward was stronger than he could withstand. He felt the bones of Nathan's fingers slipping out of their skin like a hand being pulled from a glove. Yet he held on, clinging to the husk of the boy's body until the last bits of juicy insides were sucked away with a soggy, slurping gasp.

Micah continued clutching the limp, empty shell of skin for a moment. It was heavy, like a wet blanket. He finally let the formless, squishy-soft fingers slip from his hands.

The blanket of skin, still dressed in the clothes Nathan had been wearing, fell to the ground, folding over on top of itself like a peeled banana. It settled into a bloody and quivering heap, the empty eye sockets of the mask-like face filling with red mush above the toothless and gaping mouth hole. A messy shock of hair crowned the vile display.

Micah snatched Lydia back up into his arms, away from the hostile earth. He ran, his legs shoving the traitorous ground away with all the force he could muster. He nimbly dodged every assassin apple that littered the ground, each now squirming, as though filled to bursting with a million busy maggots, feasting on the rotten flesh of the demon fruit.

He finally made it to the outskirts of the orchard, to the steps of his home, stopping to catch his breath and gather his sanity. It was only then that he realized that the screams had grown silent, the voice of every child, his brothers and sisters, had been extinguished underneath the fetid earth. The sudden stillness of the night pierced his heart as he realized what it meant, and he began to weep.

The solitude of his mourning was shattered as Lemuel burst forth from his house, like a general striding into battle. The drunken, self-ordained prophet staggered brazenly into the orchard, gun in hand and wife Sarah in tow, shouting as he walked, bobbing the small light through the darkness as he went.

Anna ran along behind Lemuel, almost lost in the shadows as she tried to keep pace with her father.

"Don't come any closer!" Micah shouted desperately. "Stay out of the orchard! It's not safe." He clutched Lydia tightly to him, as though he was the last line of defense between her life and hell.

Lemuel ignored him, and closed the gap between them in what seemed like an impossibly short time.

To Micah's surprise, the group traversed the orchard without incident. He was sure that at any moment the ground would come to life and devour them whole. Yet the night remained still, the air breathless.

"What in the devil is going on, Micah? Where are the children? What kind of game are you playing?" Lemuel rattled off the litany of accusatory questions at Micah like verbal buckshot. It then occurred to him that Micah was clutching his youngest daughter in his arms, the two of them alone in the night. Lemuel lowered the barrel of his rifle until he was almost, but not quite, aiming at the boy.

"I sense the devil at work here. Unhand my daughter, swine," he growled at Micah through a clenched mouthful of half-rotten teeth.

Micah nodded wordlessly in agreement, and gently set Lydia down. The little girl ran to her mother, clutching Sarah's long skirt as she sobbed against her leg.

"Is it the Rapture?" Lemuel's wife screeched. She was an anxious woman, easily alarmed, and the thought of being left behind in a world of the wicked etched her face with horror in the dim light.

Lemuel appeared as though he would strike her for her insolence in suggesting that the good Lord would pay the Earth a visit and leave him, of all people, behind. But before he could act on the impulse, he was distracted by the door on the porch of Micah's house slamming open.

Sleepy and disheveled, Samuel and Rachel emerged from the shadows, rushing past Micah to meet Lemuel on the lawn. After a moment of heated discussion and exchanged accusations, they fell silent and everyone turned to face Micah, faces full of bewilderment, unsure whether to feel sorrow, anger, or fear.

Micah's eyes darted from person to person. He was uncertain of what to say, not knowing himself what was happening, or what to do about it. On each parent's face he saw a mirror image of the same confusion he himself was experiencing. When he looked into Anna's worried eyes, he wanted nothing more than to bury himself in her arms, to bathe her in his tears.

The twilight engulfed them like a swaddled tomb, a silence so profound it was almost tangible; it could be felt, cool to the touch, like glass on skin. Micah took a deep breath to speak, doubtful he could even manage to find the words to say. He had seen his sisters die, and Anna's siblings as well. Except for Lydia, all of them had been destroyed right before his very eyes – but *how* it had happened, he could not say. How could he explain what he had seen? How would they believe what they had not seen for themselves, when he -who *had* seen it - could not believe it? His body grew cold at the thought, a numbness rising up from his feet and his fingers, clawing its way into his core.

Before his lips parted to say the first word, a disturbance in the treetops broke the stillness, drawing attention away from Micah and his attempted explanation. The group turned to confront the orchard, all faces turned skyward, to see what was happening in the branches overhead.

VII.   THE TREE OF DEATH

IT BEGAN AS A RUSTLING of branches at first, here and there among the treetops, the source of the commotion hidden behind a dark veil of shadows. A few leaves had been shaken loose, and the bewildered settlers watched as the green teardrops gently fluttered to the ground.

The earth began to tremble beneath their feet, softly at first, like a train approaching. But the vibration grew stronger. Before long, the massive trunks began to shake as though quivering with cold, deep wooden fibers cracking, audibly groaning as the ancient canopy convulsed, like a an old hound dog shaking itself awake from a nap by the fireside.

Without warning, a deep guttural roar bellowed into the night across the valley, a rolling tidal wave of sound that stripped the stillness from every nook and cranny as it screamed past, drowning everything and everyone in a painful flood of noise. The force of it drove all thoughts of missing children, the devil and the rapture from their minds as Micah, Lemuel and the rest clamped hands to their ears in a futile attempt to defend themselves from the unrelenting assault on their senses.

As the thunderous roar subsided, a torrential outpour of objects was ejaculated out of the treetop, a glistening white arc in the bright moonlight, like snowflakes carved from white stone. The objects rained down upon them.

As the plummeting debris pelted the group,

Lemuel grabbed Sarah, Lydia and Anna, pulling them under him to shield them like a mother hen protecting its chicks during a hailstorm. Samuel tried to huddle over Sarah and Micah in a like manner, but the discharge of objects still struck Micah painfully on his head and along his back.

The trees convulsed three more times, each contraction following immediately after the other, each occurrence accompanied by the deafening roar and a streaming emission of objects.

Then, at last, tranquility descended once more upon the orchard.

The group crouched together, heads covered, for a few moments longer, unsure if the barrage from the treetops would commence again, fearful to believe that the abrupt disturbance had truly ended. Micah glanced around the moonlit orchard. The ground glittered with the reflection of the fallen objects that lay scattered on the grass, an odd assortment of irregularly shaped sticks and stones, all painted white.

Micah picked one of the stones that had landed nearby. He rolled it in the palm of his hand, feeling the weight of it, and the texture. It reminded him of the piece of coral that his grandfather had shown him as a young boy, supposedly brought back from an expedition to Florida. He held the white stone up to the moonlight to better examine its shape. Light shone straight through the middle of the stone, as though a hole had been drilled through its center.

Lemuel also began to examine one of the strange objects, selecting a longer, stick-shaped piece of debris from the hundreds on the ground. He ran his fingers along the length of it, feeling the slickness, the smoothness of it, a slight look of recognition dawning in his eyes. Then he stuck the end of it into his mouth and tasted it. A sudden awareness lit up his face.

"It's a bone, a rib bone," Lemuel said, his voice hollow and strangely devoid of his typical macho bluster and fury.

Micah looked down at the small white stone in his own hand.

A tiny vertebra. From a child, maybe his own kin.

He tossed it away from him as though diseased. His mother Rachel began to weep uncontrollably as she began to understand the meaning of this discovery, falling so hard on Samuel that she nearly took him to the ground with her.

Lemuel's wife, slower in understanding what he meant, finally caught on to the implication. It struck her hard. She didn't look to Lemuel for comfort. Instead she turned to her only living children, to Anna and Lydia, for sympathy.

"Oh Anna," she sobbed, "my babies, my babies!"

Anna took her mother into her arms, holding her tightly, patting her on the back as though comforting an infant. She glared stoically at Micah from over her mother's shoulder.

A few feet away, Lemuel still clutched the rib bone. It was clear from the look on his face that his rage was fast regaining its footing, fury glowing bright as embers under bellows in his eyes.

He jabbed the pointy bone through the air at Micah like an oversized accusatory finger.

"Speak, boy," he snarled, baring incisors that gleamed like tiny eggs rolled together in the nest of his beard. "What evil have you wrought upon us?"

Everyone turned once more to look at Micah,

their eyes now brimming with a mixture of shock at what had happened and an insatiable longing for an explanation to somehow make sense of it all. Even Samuel, his own father, stared at him as though he was a stranger caught trespassing.

"It was the apples," Micah stammered, "the kids were out gathering apples...something grabbed them...they're...they're gone."

He knew what he was saying was true, that it had happened just as he said it had, but even his own words rang false in his ears. What he was saying, what he saw, wasn't possible. He was trapped in a nightmare from which he couldn't wake.

Lemuel cast his gaze once again about the ground. Although the earth was still blanketed with scattered bones, there was not a single apple in sight. He looked back at Micah, cocking back the hammer on his rifle. The sharp click of metal on metal said everything that needed to be said.

"There *were* apples, apples on the ground everywhere," Micah pleaded. "Anna, you saw them, tell them – tell them I had nothing to do with this. Tell them that there were apples – please tell them!"

He turned towards Anna, who was still comforting her mother, hoping to beseech her to intercede on his behalf. He knew there was nothing they could do now for the dead children. The realization suddenly struck him that they should be focusing on saving themselves from the same fate, not arguing about who was at fault.

In his peripheral vision, he noticed something moving towards his face at an incredible rate of speed. Before he could react, it struck him hard in the head, and he found himself falling. His body hit the ground with the force of a blacksmith's hammer against an anvil, an explosion of brightly colored sparks lit up the inside of his mind.

As he lay staring at the muddy toe of Lemuel's boot, he felt the grit of dirt on his lips and the metallic taste of blood in his mouth. It reminded him of eating clay from the streambed, and for a moment he felt himself starting to drift away to a far off place that was bright and warm. He wanted to go there more than anything.

A swift kick to his shoulder brought him back to the orchard with a flash of pain, the force of it rolling him halfway onto his side. Through blurred eyes, he saw Lemuel looming at the far end of the barrel of his gun like a bearded demon, grinning with excitement at the evil he was about to do.

"Murderous Cain! Treacherous Iscariot!" Lemuel raged, jamming the barrel fiercely into Micah's ribs. "I wish I had just one single apple, so I could ram it into your lying mouth before I roast you alive for this evil you've brought upon us."

Micah heard his father's deep voice rumble to life.

"Leave him alone."

Micah felt as though the ground was swaying back and forth underneath him like ocean waves, making him seasick. Although his line of sight was partially obstructed by Lemuel's boots, he saw his mother fall to her knees, as Samuel let her go and squared off with his son's attacker.

There was a brief scuffle in the darkness, accompanied by the sounds of a struggle. Then the night was illuminated briefly with a flash of fire accompanied by the sound of thunder and the screams of women. Gunpowder and sulfur stung his nostrils as Micah peered through the settling cloud of smoke. Then he realized that he had been joined in his repose by another man lying on the ground only a few feet away, knees bent, legs askew. Micah's mother crawled across the ground and fell on top of the man, her body shaking with uncontrollable grief.

Bright squiggles swam along the edges of Micah's eyelids, and he closed his eyes for a moment to clear them. When he opened them again, he was startled to find Lemuel crouched over him, eyes maniacal, breath fetid with the stench of chicken and whiskey.

"You're of the devil, the whole lot of you" Lemuel slurred, working his fingers into Micah's thick hair and pinning his head to the ground so hard it felt as though his scalp might rip off. "All against me, tried to keep me out of the Garden of Eden where the Lord has led me, defiled the tree of the life with the blood of my own children."

He lay his gun on the ground by his knee, and withdrew a large hunting knife from its sheath hidden inside his coat.

In an instant Anna lunged at her father, grabbing his arm, trying to pull the knife away.

"Father, stop it! Why are you doing this?" Anna screamed.

Lemuel was not deterred. He grabbed his daughter by her slender throat, shoving her roughly away from him. He studied her with cold eyes, like a cat with its prey.

He released his hold on Anna's throat after a moment, and began to turn away – but then spun about, striking her hard in the face, knife still clenched tightly in his fist. The blow knocked her clean off her feet, and she hit the ground forehead-first, emitting a moan of anguish, muffled by a mouthful of dirt.

Micah tried to crawl away, but Lemuel was back on him in a flash, yanking his head back roughly, exposing his neck to the long sharp blade, as he breathed curses into his face.

"I'm going to gut you like the pig you are," he seethed. "Going to slice you and your dead old man there, Judas and Brutus the lot of you, right down the middle – going to hang your carcasses in the smokehouse, feed your flesh to that stupid sow that bore you, while she repays me by bearing me twofold the children you stole from me today."

Out of the corner of his eye, Micah saw movement on the ground, inches from his face. A bright red apple now rested where none had been before. Lemuel noticed it, too.

"Well ain't that nice," Lemuel sneered. "There's that apple I needed. Can't roast a piggy without a shiny apple stuffed into its lying mouth, now can we?" he said, setting his knife down to grab the fruit.

The second his fingers touched it, the fruit split open, sharp wooden appendages piercing and twisting their way through Lemuel's hand, wrapping around his wrist, slicing into his skin. He stared at his mutilated hand in shock, shaking loose his grip on Micah's scalp to pick up his knife. He stabbed at the fruit that was devouring his hand, ignoring the injuries he was inflicting to himself in the process.

His blade found the center of the fruit, piercing it to the core. As the knife stabbed through into the apple, the entire earth began to quake beneath them. A guttural roar tore through the night again, an enormous growl of pain.

Micah scuttled away from Lemuel towards where Anna lay, stunned. He pulled her to him, shaking her gently. Blood poured from her nose into her mouth.

"Anna, we've got to run," he pleaded, pulling her upright.

Lemuel frantically used his knife, sawing away at the root that attached the apple to ground. The sharp appendages of the fruit flailed wildly like the legs of an overturned crab, where they jutted through the backside of his hand.

Behind Lemuel, in the dark shadows of the orchard, Micah saw the entire trunk of one of the trees lift up from out of the ground, roots dangling beneath it as though it was a mere weed pulled from the garden. The tree hovered a few feet in the air for a moment before slamming back down to earth, sending shockwaves reverberating along the ground. The tree beside it followed suit, pulling itself into the air as roots ripped from the soil, the trunk moving forward briefly before pounding back into the earth.

Then the entire orchard was alive and moving, and Micah realized that the trees were not separate trees at all – they were connected, two sets of four thick trunks moving in unison across the ground like legs, another tree raised in front as a long neck or head, and another swinging along behind like a tail. The orchard had uprooted itself, separating into two sets of trees - two gargantuan beasts - stomping towards them through the darkness.

The horrific sight brought Anna back to her senses, and Micah pulled her to her feet. Hand in hand they began to run towards the mouth of the valley. The earth shook underfoot as the creatures took chase. He hoped they could make it to the open plain before the beasts picked up a full head of steam.

Still unaware of the orchard on the move behind him, Lemuel pried the last bit of apple from his mangled hand and tossed it away in disgust. He snatched his gun from the ground with his uninjured hand, clutching it between his knees to reload the chamber.

He glanced about for his wife and daughters in the darkness, and realized that they, too, had abandoned him. A hot breeze blew down onto the top of his head, accompanied by a rustling flurry of leaves.

Lemuel looked up just as the creatures closed in on him. To Micah looking back, it looked as if Lemuel were Ramses swallowed whole by the Red Sea. The massive trunk-legs of the behemoths slammed together as they simultaneously lunged for him, tree branches bristling along their spines like quills on a porcupine's back.

As Micah continued his flight with Anna towards the open prairie, he heard the thunder-crack of a single gunshot pierce the night amidst the bedlam, followed by a man's brief yet piercing scream. He glanced quickly over his shoulder to see if the creatures were still occupied in the valley, and was dismayed to find the titans already cantering towards them, slowly at first but clearly gaining momentum, working up a full head of steam.

The realization settled upon him that he and Anna had no chance of outrunning them on the flat open plain, especially if they continued their straight-ahead trajectory. But the beasts, though clearly enormous and powerful, also seemed stiff and clumsy; perhaps it would be difficult for them to follow up the steep ridge. Micah made the split-second decision to head for higher ground, for the trail that led up and out of the valley. It lay to their left, about a hundred yards away. If they made a sudden break for it now, they could make it.

"Anna, this way," he yelled, pointing to where he knew the entrance to the trail lay hidden in the thin brush that lined the hillside. He pulled her towards it as he cut a sharp left. "Follow me!"

As they changed course to flee for the hilltop, he saw the blur of the beasts as they bore down on them, massive dark shadows in the moonlight. He suddenly felt like a newborn lamb, still stumbling on feeble legs, as he fled across the valley. Anna clutched her long dress to her waist, blood still trickling from her nose down her neck and onto her breasts, the flesh of her bare feet shredding away as she ran across the coarse gravel that littered the ground where the lush grass gave way to rugged mountainside.

Micah heard her labored breathing over the splintiferous sound of timber thundering after them. He prayed she could make it. Just a few more steps and they would be climbing up the mountainside. Whether or not the beasts could follow them, he did not know, but he was determined to survive this madness and to bring Anna through it with him. His own lungs were screaming, each breath a chest full of fire as he ran. Bright lights blossomed in his eyes as adrenaline surged through him, turning the night sky into a swirling galaxy of stars, decorated with constellations of fear.

He scanned the murky gloom of the brush for the path to the top of the ridge, their last chance for salvation. His senses were blinded by panic. The trail was lost in the darkness. His eyes tracked back and forth across the hillside, searching for any sign of it. He could see where the trail led halfway up the ridge, tracing a pale serpentine path up to the top of the ridge, the packed dirt reflecting an ashen glow back into the night sky.

The beasts were almost upon them. A maelstrom of timber would collapse on top of them at any moment, a swirling roar of rushing leaves, with ten thousand pounds of murderous, stabbing boughs lusting after their blood and flesh.

The scent of their ancient hunger filled his nostrils, and Micah, still running, still searching as he dragged Anna along behind him, tasted the sweetness of forbidden fruit upon his tongue again, the flavor of the frothing drool of the beasts in pursuit misting the air. They were close, the end was near, and the trail…the trail…where was the god-damned trail?

Then – there, in the same abominable darkness that greedily swallowed his chances of salvation - a blossom of orange and red erupted in the shadows, sparks briefly illuminating a group of men, huddled together and gesturing for him to run to them, their faces etched with both fear and hope in the blinking flashes of light as flint struck stone, again and again, signaling their location.

Micah's heart seized with joy as he recognized, lit up in the flash of light, the twisted human pretzel of the bush that marked the entrance to the ridge trail. He pulled Anna towards it, his conscious mind briefly overpowered by animal instinct, as he fought for survival, his hand clasped over hers with a grip that nothing less than death could pry loose. The sparks flashed again, then again. *Life, here,* they seemed to say. They were almost there, just a few more steps, so close now.

So close.

Then all the earth was thrown to the sky as Micah was ripped away from the prairie floor, his feet continuing to pedal frantically as he soared upwards into the air. Hope still surged through him as he clutched onto Anna with a death-grip, even as he felt her hand go limp in his.

The shower of sparks fluttered again. But this time the sparks were below his feet, not in front. He realized that he was no longer running towards safety, but being dragged away from it. His mind struggled to compute his spatial relationship with the world, and when it did so, he realized Anna was now above him, not behind him, and that he was dangling twenty feet or so in the air from the end of her arm.

Micah looked up along the path formed by his arm, across the bridge of his hand linked with Anna's. His eyes slid along the porcelain skin of her slender arm until they met her dark eyes just beyond. Once beautiful orbs, they now bulged from their sockets, brimming with pain and the hell of the creature that was devouring her. A dark mouth was hidden in the cluster of tangled branches, with rows of piercing, stabbing wooden teeth that pulled her legs mercilessly into its hungry maw.

Her body vanished up to her knees, then to her waist, as it greedily gobbled her down.

Then she was gone. The bright light of her spirit was snuffed out in an instant. Micah was sure he was gone, too, as he felt himself falling into a dark abyss, plunging into nothingness as he fell, the world around him a blur as it receded away in his vision.

The only comfort he still had was holding Anna's hand in his, and he thought that enough. If they could not be together in life, then together in death would have to suffice.

He clenched her lifeless hand even more tightly as he braced himself for the end.

Micah collided with the hard prairie floor, landing flat on his back, the wind knocked from his lungs in a single bone-shattering blow. He saw blurry shapes of swooning trees towering over him, silhouetted in the night sky, branches interlocked with each other in battle over the tasty morsel each desired. Then he felt himself being pulled along the earth, dragged across the ground by his feet. The world around him was going dark fast. Disoriented, he clutched Anna's severed arm close to him for comfort, feeling for the rest of her and not finding it. He was confused.

He felt the sensation of many hands hoisting him into the air, carrying him away.

Then, he felt nothing at all.

VIII. CRO-AT-OAN

TWO DAYS. That was how long they said he slept, in their broken English. When he finally awoke, with an old Indian chieftain who had skin as rough as dried snake hide hunching over him, he at first thought he had been dead and come back to life.

He was injured; not fatally, but enough to make even the slightest movement excruciating. It took time for him to heal, but his saviors were patient and the compassion he saw in their eyes told him they were no savages, that they understood that there were some wounds that would never heal, no matter how much time passed. Losing Anna and his family would be a scar he would carry on his heart forever, they said. Their spirits lived on in him, now.

He asked about the trees.

Cro at Oan, the ancient chief said, in a hushed whisper drenched in a millennia's worth of fear and respect.

Ancient beast, oldest of all earth creatures, he said. *Here long time before sky gods brought our people to this world, to the first garden. First father and first mother disobey sky gods. They ate of tree, then tree ate of people. Cover their nakedness with leaves to hide from tree.*

Micah asked them how the trees came to be here.

Sky people move people from the garden, across the big sea. Our tribe left to guard Cro at Oan, to make safe the world, to give sacrifice of single body every forty seasons to stop the hunt, to make no breed. But children of first people come back across the ocean and no listen to warning. We tell them, "Stay away from the Roaming Oak," as we call the place in your language. But like your fathers, they not listen, they not understand. They laugh and call their village "Roa-noke," they build houses under the branches and eat of Cro at Oan fruit on the island by the sea. Then Cro at Oan awaken and eat all the first people. They breed, they come here and we follow until they rest.

Micah asked them if the creatures could be killed.

Skin like stone, blood like fire. Only after certain seasons pass do they feed, they move, under the big moon – unless sacrifice be made. Then they eat only sacrifice and sleep, bellies full, till certain seasons more.

Once he was able to walk on his own, one of the scouts led Micah to an outcrop that overlooked a well-used trail. They camped there for several days, until finally a rising cloud of dust on the horizon signaled the approach of a wagon train headed west, Micah's ticket out of the prairie and into his future.

IX. A Sacrifice is Required, Sayeth the Lord

Time does heal wounds, despite opinions to the contrary - or in Micah's case, time at the very least thickened the scars to the point that he could no longer believe his own memories. He wasn't even convinced he had once been part of a family traveling across the prairie. He wasn't sure if anything he remembered happening really *had* happened.

As he aged, he felt somewhat certain that during his childhood he had, in fact, eaten some sort of poisoned apple - or whatever kind of fruit it had been – but beyond that a feeling settled upon him that his other memories and recollection were nothing more than hallucinations - the whole thing, his childhood, a fairy tale. He became convinced that he had spent his entire youth lost, running around madly in a delirium, that everything before he finally became lucid again in San Francisco was but a fever dream.

Deep down, however, his subconscious mind stewed and festered. Even after he became an old man with his life behind him, dying in California, a small part of him always wondered if his family - his beautiful Anna (who still visited him in his dreams) - were still living somewhere out on the prairie, in the little houses under the big trees.

Eventually the lurking thought of it bothered him so much that, despite his better judgment and the certainty that he was acting out of nothing more than the dementia that came with old age, Micah found himself at a train station. He bought himself a ticket on an east-bound train. He boarded the train and, guided by nothing but instinct, he scanned the distant horizon for hours, as it crept along the tracks laid across the land.

As soon as his eyes lit upon the ridge, he knew it was the place where his life had very nearly met its end so many years ago.

He disembarked at the next station and hired a carriage to drive him out past the small town that had sprung up around the railroad station. Distance was hard to gauge in the wide open spaces, and Micah watched the buildings of the town thin out into nothingness. He crossed empty miles onto the open prairie, as he directed the driver towards the ridge he had recognized from the train.

Eventually, the horses slowed to a stop in the valley that nestled in the curve of the ridgeline. He instantly recognized the houses there as those from the fever dream of his youth. They slumped on their foundations, empty and decrepit, and he felt happiness for a moment that the town nearby had chosen not to settle in this evil place.

Micah lightly climbed the dry-rotted steps of the first house, the one he remembered from his dreams, where he had lived with the family he couldn't possibly have had. The front door was unlocked, though he could have easily pushed it in, even at his age. The house was still furnished exactly as he remembered – it was all coming back to him now, becoming real as he searched through it. In abandoned dressers he found the dusty tattered remains of his family's clothing.

In the upstairs bedroom, underneath the dry-rotted mattress, now barely more than a collection of rusted springs, he found the old faded drawing of Anna he had hidden there so long ago, her piercing eyes gazing at him from the past. He brushed a hot tear aside as he looked out the window towards the orchard, and a cold fear filled his heart as he realized what he saw there. Nothing.

The trees were gone. No stumps, no piles of decaying wood, no sign of any kind that they had ever been there. The verdant, green lawn that had once carpeted the valley below was also gone, he realized, as was the pool of clear water at the end of the valley, and the thick cesspool, too – both now dry as a bone.

He slipped the drawing of Anna into his pocket and headed back to the waiting carriage, the thick ache of forgotten fear welling up inside of him. As he left that cursed valley he knew the nightmares of his imagined childhood *were* real, and that his attempt to forget what had happened here as an adult, was, in reality, the childish dream.

The carriage bumped its way along the rough road, it headed back into town and Micah spied the tall white spire of a church piercing the sky in the center of town, framed on each side by an impossibly enormous green canopy of trees, looming above the town.

After certain seasons pass - the words of the old Indian Chief rose up in Micah's mind. The last great beasts of hell were well equipped to wait, he remembered, and like every living organism regardless of size, to adapt.

He leaned over the front seat and asked the driver to head into the center of town. As the carriage rolled to a stop near a curb by the church, bathed in the cool shade of the massive trees, Micah spotted a child's tricycle a few feet from the gargantuan trunk. It was overturned and deserted, front tire still spinning. On the ground beside the tricycle rested a single, impossibly red apple, shiny and delicious. From down the street he heard a mother's panicked cry approaching.

The *Cro at Oan* had survived. Now they stood before him, hiding in plain sight – the monsters of his childhood made flesh and blood, drawn from the faded memories of days long past and suddenly thrust into the vivid realness of now - patiently waiting to feed.

God had cast mankind from the Garden of Eden for a reason - for their own protection - but now the garden had found man again. The ancient guardians were gone, rounded up and herded off to the reservations. There would be hell to pay for this town, without a sacrifice.

Micah opened the carriage door and stepped onto the curb, pulling his wallet from his pocket to pay the driver. He started to pull out several bills, then thought better of it and handed over his entire wallet to the driver instead, waving aside protestations.

He walked over to the tricycle, stopping the spinning wheel gently with his shoe before reaching down to pick up the apple. As he felt the warm pulse of the fruit's flesh in his hand, he closed his eyes and smiled.

***

The novella ARBOREATUM had been simmering since the summer of 2008, when I awoke at dawn one morning from an incredibly lucid dream. I ran to my desk to jot out a five page outline of the story before it slipped from my mind.

I shouldn't have worried. Bits and pieces of this strange tale have been bubbling up for the last three or four years - a bit here, a bit there - and I dutifully added each new piece to the tale as it came to me. I hoped I would be able to recognize when it was finished.

Over time this tale (that I originally envisioned as a 20-30 page short story) continued to grow and grow, until the revelations about it finally stopped coming towards the end of 2012 and I knew at long last it was time to polish it up and release it into the wild.

This is one of those stories that came to me from some unknown place that exists apart from conscious thought (CURTAINS FOR LOVE is another). The setting and the themes are definitely not ones that I would have purposely written. I secretly like to imagine that this story is true, but don't tell anyone I said that, okay?

NOSE HEARS

GEORGE LAY DOWN to take a nap. He was always tired on Saturday afternoons, after mowing the lawn and trimming the hedges; a couple hours on the couch helped to refresh him.

But this Saturday, something strange happened.

Just as he was about to fall asleep, he heard the murmur of soft voices, the sound of whispered words that rose and fell with each breath he took.

George sat up in bed, holding his breath, listening; but the voices were gone.

Finally content that what he had heard was nothing more than his imagination, he lay back down and tried, once again, to fall asleep. As his breathing settled back into a steady rhythm, the soft voices started up again, indistinct words spoken so faintly that he could not quite tell what they were saying.

George was sure that the source of the whispering had to be close by; it sounded as though it was almost in his ear.

He held his breath again to listen and again the voices stopped.

It was becoming frustrating, he really needed his nap.

A realization settled upon him: the sound he was hearing was nothing more than his own breathing, air passing through his nostrils, and vibrating in his nose hairs.

Now fully aware of it, the noise in his nostrils began to drive him crazy. It was as if a muffled conversation was constantly taking place inside his nose, as though the two sides of his nostrils were talking to each other.

Day after day it continued. He was afraid he might be going insane, and decided it would be best not to tell anyone else about the voices in his nose.

Two days later, George was working at his desk. His eyes were drawn to the computer microphone there. It gave him an idea.

He checked to make sure nobody in the house was paying attention to what he was doing and turned the volume of his computer speakers up, then inserted the tip of the microphone into his left nostril.

A booming voice burst forth from the computer speakers, clear as day. The voice was deep and mature, like a radio announcer, rambling on in excruciating detail about the news of the day, the weather in Topeka, what the neighbors next door were having for dinner tonight.

George was relieved at finally being able to hear what the voices in his nose were saying.

He put the microphone into his right nostril to see if it yielded the same result.

It, too, was talking, but in a slightly different-sounding voice, a running commentary that responded to the factoids coming from the left nostril, adding its own observations, tossing out humorous quips.

Completely blown away by his discovery, George grabbed the microphone and jumped into his car, eager to show his best friend, the only person he trusted not to lock him in an asylum if it turned out the voices were really only in his head.

He had to know if other people were able to hear the voices in his nose, too.

It would prove that he wasn't crazy.

Once at his friend's house, he eagerly plugged the microphone into the speakers and stuck it up his nose, into his left nostril.

His friend played along with him, laughing heartily at his silliness.

George cranked up the volume and sure enough, the voice in his nose came booming out of the speakers, discussing this and that: polling results in Des Moines, the weekend-only sale at Dillard.

The friend was incredulous, and thought the whole thing was somehow a prank. He laughed and asked George how he did it, how he made the voices come out of his nose.

George held out his hands, palms up, insisting it was real, but at the same time, he was unable to explain it, either. To prove his point, he pulled the microphone from his nose and slipped it into the right nostril.

A different voice started talking through the speakers, just as it had before; but this time, instead of talking about random current events, it started talking about the very friend who sat beside George.

It started telling its audience about all the horrible things the friend had done, of the secret wrongs he had committed against those who loved him, about how he had even betrayed his best friend who sat there, even now, with a microphone up his nose.

Vile, terrible betrayals, things he wouldn't even have believed true of his worst enemy.

George turned pale as a ghost as he listened, the microphone still nestled inside his nostril. He stared, mouth agape in horror, at the man he had thought was his friend.

He wanted to ask if the things his nose said were true; but he could tell by the look on his friend's face that they were. No other answer was needed.

Then the voice in his nose fell silent.

George dropped the microphone to the floor and gave his former friend one final look of disgust before walking away, never to return.

The voices in his nose never spoke again, but George didn't mind.

He figured he nose enough already.

***

Part of this story really happened.
The rest of it I made up.
I'll leave it to you to guess which part is which.

THE MOLE PEOPLE
BENEATH THE CITY

THE 50TH STREET station was practically empty, rare in New York City at any time of year.

The train was still nowhere in sight. The air in the station was suffocating us, the stench of stale diesel making the wait almost unbearable.

I pulled my daughter closer to me. You have to be careful with those you cherish, especially in a city this big.

Sometimes it eats people, I thought.

This city had taken my wife long ago. The three of us had been so happy once, but the memory of those times now seemed like a dream, fast fading away. Kat was all I had left in this world and I wasn't about to lose her, too - not now, not before all her hopes and dreams had been realized.

I peeked around a pillar at the security camera, nestled close to the ceiling near the stairs.

What good would that do anyone? For every camera, malintent hands were still lurking in a thousand dark corners, waiting to snatch the unsuspecting from here to the wherever, in the blink of an eye.

Soon, we would travel into a dark gaping maw; the subway tunnel lay off to our right, indifferent, not imposing. It reminded me of a lazy dog on a hot day with its mouth hanging open, the empty tracks lolling out of the darkness like a tongue.

No more than a dozen late night revelers occupied the stop with us; their conversations mingled as they echoed off the curved ceiling overhead. Whatever energy they had generated earlier at one club or the other was waning fast in the stifling heat and the fluorescent glare.

Standing off a bit from the ebullient youngsters was an old Chinese woman, clutching a stack of crumpled newspapers with claw-like hands. She was hunched and wrinkled, her dark eyes peering through such thin slits that it was impossible to tell if they were open or closed.

I checked my watch for the fourth time in two minutes.

It was one-thirty in the morning and I didn't like being here. I was ready to get this whole thing over with and go home. I loosened my collar and felt hot sweat trickle down my back.

Where the hell is the train? It should have been here by now.

My Baby Kat, my pride and joy, looked up at me. Beads of sweat glistened on her forehead, above the rim of her pink Hello Kitty sunglasses.

She loved those glasses, refused to take them off

whenever we came up to the city; though I knew why, I still thought it a shame. The dark lenses covered up her most beautiful feature: her wide, glowing eyes, pools of molten steel so deep they appeared bottomless.

She squeezed my hand tightly. I knew she was wondering where the train was too.

I took a handkerchief from my pocket and dabbed at the perspiration on her brow. I wondered if she was anxious or simply hot. It was no secret; we both knew how much was riding on tonight. I gave her my most convincing smile, hoping she would buy it.

She cast a wary glance towards the intoxicated merrymakers that shared the platform with us. They were getting louder, laughing stupidly. Any native New Yorker would peg them immediately as a nuisance of the worst sort: out-of-towners.

"It's going to be okay," I told Baby Kat as reassurance, whether she needed it or not. Maybe I was only comforting myself.

"We'll be home soon enough, little one." I promised.

One of the young men standing nearby pushed his friend playfully towards the edge of the platform, causing him to stumble and almost fall. "Watch out for the third rail!" he shouted.

Morons, I thought. *But good enough.*

"Touch me again and I'll stick *my* third rail straight up your ass," the shoved friend retorted, the word *ass* slurred so that it sounded like *ash.*

The girls nearby tittered at their rough horseplay. I wondered if they had met them at the club or brought them into the city with them - not that it mattered.

I counted them.

Four girls.

They were pretty enough, but despite their flashy dresses and gaudy makeup I was sure they were nothing more than run-of-the-mill girl next door types. That was okay. Two blondes, a brunette and a red head; I suspected that a closer inspection would reveal they were, in fact, three brunettes and a redhead - but I'd been wrong before.

Five guys.

The jackass doing the shoving was undoubtedly so drunk he would pass out as soon as he sat down on the train. He was certainly the third wheel of the group, the dateless wonder. He probably hoped his sorry display of machismo would entice one of the girls into his empty, pathetic arms. He was oblivious, but it was clear to me that his antics were backfiring.

Except for this wise-ass, I thought everyone in the station seemed harmless enough. Now if the train would just arrive, everything would be fine.

Finally, a cool wind began to sweep across the platform. You can always feel the wind just before the train arrives, before the ground begins to vibrate underfoot, even before the first faint rumble of rushing steel can be heard. The breeze that heralded the approaching train swirled into the station like cool summer rain, even before the first flickers of light emerged from the darkness.

Everyone in the station instinctively turned to face the flowing coolness, drawing in thirsty gulps as it whispered invisibly by - cooling hot sweat, filling oxygen-starved lungs.

"Is this our train, Daddy?" Baby Kat asked softly.

I nodded.

The group beside us became hushed, sensing the change in the atmosphere.

The train was coming. It was late.

A flash of light illuminated the darkness inside the tunnel briefly.

Baby Kat saw something there, raised a trembling finger towards the tunnel and screamed like a kitten dipped in boiling oil.

Everyone in the station spun around to face us, startled by the unexpected howl – everyone except the old Chinese woman. She stood without flinching, unblinking, like one of the wax statues at Madame Toussaud's.

I dropped to my knees beside Baby Kat and pulled her into my arms.

"What's wrong, my baby?" I asked as I took her little hands into mine.

"I saw them, Daddy, I saw them. In the tunnel," she cried.

"Saw what?"

"People, Daddy, there were people in there. I saw them, down in the tunnel on the tracks," she whimpered. "It's the mole people coming for us. I'm scared. I want to go home."

I took her into my arms and held her tight as she sobbed on my shoulder. Several sets of eyes bored into us. "It's okay, baby girl," I reassured her. "There's no such thing as 'mole people'. It's just a fairy tale. Don't worry, we'll be safe at home soon."

I scooped her up and she wrapped herself tightly around me, her head heavy and sweaty on my shoulder. I cast an apologetic glance at the group of people who now surrounded us. Their doe eyes ran over Baby Kat and me, their sympathy evident.

The train burst into the station, a horizontal steel tornado. The force of it growled up through my soles and vibrated into every square inch of my body.

It felt good.

It felt like home.

The brakes screeched on the tracks as the last uptown express of the night slowed to a halt. We had waited for this exact train tonight, since it would pass uninterrupted through multiple stations during its trip through the subterranean darkness towards home.

We were waiting at the near end of the station and the last car on the train finally shuddered to a stop beside us, the doors sliding open with a soft hiss and a beep.

It was empty.

Excellent.

"Is she okay?" one of the group, the red-haired girl, asked as we boarded the car, her emerald eyes sparkling with concern.

"She'll be fine," I said. "Just gets scared in the subway - especially at night. She heard some crazy story from a friend of mine and now it's all she can think about every time we take the train."

Baby Kat perked up when I said that.

"But daddy, the mole people *are* real!" she protested indignantly, fresh tears streaming down her cheeks from under her pink sunglasses. "I saw them!"

"There, there," I told her as we shuffled aboard. Everyone took a seat near each other in the back of the car by the door, except for the old Chinese woman. She sat by herself at the other end of the car, a mirthful smile playing about her lips.

The doors slid closed and the train crept out of

the station into the tunnel. It grunted and lurched with a labored, oil-choked wheeze, until it finally picked up a full head of speed, eventually settling into a soothingly hypnotic click-clack rhythm.

I peeked at Baby Kat, her head still resting on my shoulder. Within seconds she was fast asleep. I set her down gently in the seat beside me so she could snuggle up more comfortably, my arm wrapped protectively around her.

Her eyes popped open and for a second, she smiled at me before lying back on the seat, her arms crossed over her little chest.

The young people seated around us began to quiet down as we traveled north through the night. I couldn't make out their conversations over the soft din of the train.

"She asleep?" one of the young men asked, nodding towards Baby Kat.

"Yes, poor thing," I replied, trying to be friendly. "Riding on the subway knocks her out cold every time - especially this late."

"You from here?" he asked.

"*New Yawka* my whole my life, born and bred," I said. "How about you? First time in the city?"

"How'd you know? We're from Indiana," he said, gesturing to the brunette beside him. "Came to visit over winter break, you know?" he drawled.

He had a strong, lean physique, but for some reason struck me as the type who'd piss himself in the face of confrontation. He'd probably be good at following orders, though - a real workhorse.

Just the kind of person our world needs.

The guy's girlfriend whispered something into his ear. Watching from behind dark lenses made it easier to pretend I hadn't noticed.

The young man nodded in agreement, and then turned back to me.

"Mind if I ask what your little girl was going on about?" he said.

I furrowed my brow, and gave him an uncertain look.

"Back at the station, right before the train pulled in - she said something about 'the mole people'," he said. "What was she talking about?"

As soon as he said the words *mole people*, everyone in the train suddenly became interested in our conversation; every eyeball - save for the Chinese lady's – was fixated on me, anticipating my explanation. The Chinese woman sat there, the smile still on her face, as though laughing at a joke no one else had heard.

"Ah, yes…that," I replied.

I waited a moment before continuing, taking in the steady *clack-clack-clack* of the steel track that echoed in the darkness as it chased us through the tunnel. I glanced out of the window as we passed through an off-duty station at 96th Street, a half-dozen empty cars sitting on the switch, like an armada of sunken ships.

I checked my watch. It was 1:50 am.

Four minutes, thirty seconds to go.

I returned my attention to the crowd of eager youngsters that had gathered around me.

"The mole people. It's an old urban legend," I said. "People tell stories about a secret world that lies beneath the city, where hundreds, maybe thousands, of down-on-their-luck people have abandoned life on the surface for one below. Supposedly, they live in a

Swiss cheese maze of abandoned subway tunnels, dark cathedrals of massive underground government projects that lost funding and shut down before they ever amounted to anything. Some people say the city goes a half-mile down in some spots - room enough for thousands and thousands. Or so they say."

"Is it true? Do people really live underground?" the man asked, his eyes as wide as spotlights.

"Depends who you ask," I said. "Jerry Springer got a lot of people believing it, even did a television special back in the nineties where he went down into a tunnel in Central Park with some guy who showed him where he lived. Said hundreds of people had given up on the world and were creating a new life, down here in the tunnels."

"So it is real?"

"I dunno. Do you believe Jerry Springer?" I asked, smiling coyly.

I noticed the redhead trying hard not to put her three cents in. Finally she couldn't stand it anymore and jumped headfirst into the middle of our conversation.

"No, really - it *is* true," she said eagerly. "I saw a Geraldo special about it on YouTube, it was really scary. There were people living in boxes, eating garbage like rats," An earnest tear glistened in the corner of her eye. "It was terrible," she said, wiping her eyes with the back of a delicate hand, smearing dark eyeliner across her pale cheek in the process.

I glanced at my watch again. Three minutes left to go. I tapped Baby Kat's shoulder.

"You live here, you ever seen anybody coming up out of the tunnels?" the redhead asked me.

"I've never seen anybody crawling out of

anything, myself," I said, "but you know - I *have* heard things. Not sure if I believe them, though."

"Heard things? Like what?" One of the other guys asked, hugging his girlfriend closer.

"Well, I don't want to spread rumors and scare the tourist business away," I admit, I was having fun with them. They wanted a good story. "Fine. If you insist," I said, huffing slightly as though relenting only with great hesitation. They hung on my every word.

I savored that moment – and still do, looking back on it. I knew even then that they, too, would remember that moment for the rest of their lives.

"Some say that there's more people living underground than anybody knows about – a lot more," I began. "The rumor is that some of them have been living down here a lot longer than anyone could imagine. Did you know that the very first New York City subway tunnel was dug all the way back in 1869? Most people don't realize it's so old. Lots of abandoned lines since then, lots of upgrades," I said. "Some people I've talked to, people who claim to know someone who lived in the tunnels, said that the mole people have created a whole separate society, an underground country of sorts, with its own laws and ways. It's hard to imagine a scenario like that, sitting here in a modern molded plastic seat on a high-tech subway train, hard to imagine that we might be passing right through the middle of that other world right now – nothing but concrete and dirt separating us."

"You don't think it's true?" the redhead asked, her trust in Geraldo's integrity clearly diminished now that she had given the matter further thought.

"I doubt it – but I've heard stuff that made me wonder," I said.

"Like what?"

"Well, a couple of weeks ago, a subway train stopped dead on the tracks for no good reason at all," I said mysteriously. "It was an express train, late at night and the lights went out all of a sudden - both on the train and in the tunnel - then a few seconds later, the train screeched to a halt."

"What does that have to do with mole people?"

"Well, that's just the thing. Some folks on the train that night said they saw people outside in the tunnel, moving in the darkness - a whole group of 'em, lit up by the sparks emitted from the brakes."

"Mole people?"

I shrugged. "That's what some of them said the next day. One guy in the last car all by himself swore it was mole people that done it, said they were testing the system. Said they popped open the doors and boarded the car he was riding in. Said they told him they needed fresh bodies to keep their population healthy, get some fresh breeders into their society."

"If that was true, why didn't they take him, or any of the other people for that matter? Was there anybody missing?" she asked, skeptical.

"No," I replied, "and nobody else on the train saw anybody come on board, either - just a few witnesses saying they thought they saw people in the shadows. The news said that the train was stopped for less than sixty seconds before the lights came back on, and that it was able to make it into the next station just fine. The transportation authority never did say what happened exactly, just explained the whole thing away as a 'mechanical anomaly'."

The redhead cocked her eyebrow at me. It was clear that she thought I was shoveling bullshit.

"So reports about the mole people are kind of like UFO sightings," she said. "Lots of people see *something,* but nobody can ever *prove* anything - what about the security cameras on board? Couldn't they tell from the video if the man who said mole people boarded the train was lying?"

"Funny you mention that," I said, cocking my head to one side. I'd have to remember her later; she seemed more intelligent than I had first supposed.

"Funny? Why?" she asked.

"Because the article I read mentioned that the on-board security cameras have backup batteries that can run for hours. even in the event of total power failure," I said.

"So did they see something on the film?" she asked, her green eyes glowing in the fluorescent light.

"No," I said, trying to appear disenchanted. "They didn't – or couldn't, rather. The article said that someone had put a big yellow smiley face sticker over the camera lens and blocked the view. Ironic, don't you think? That the only camera on the whole train that didn't work that night was the one on the last car – which coincidentally was the only car anyone claimed had been boarded by mole people."

"That seems like a pretty big red flag to me. I wouldn't be surprised if that guy put the sticker there himself."

Most of the other people in the car had lost interest in our conversation by now and were talking quietly to each other, or playing with their phones. A couple had nodded off, like Baby Kat.

I checked my watch. Twenty seconds remaining.

"Speaking of coincidences," I said in a low voice, to draw the redhead closer from her seat across the aisle, "did you notice that we happen to be in the last car on this train, too?"

She turned and looked out the back window at the dimly lit track as it receded into the darkness behind us. Her eyes widened.

"That's not the only similarity," I continued. "We also happen to be riding in the last car on the same route on the *same* day of the week at the same *exact* time as that other train," I told her in an icy tone.

A look of alarm crossed over her face for a second, and then she laughed – a bright shiny laughter, a kind of laughter I had not heard for years - and have never heard since, no matter how much I have tried to coax it forth.

"You really had me going there, mister," she said. "Now what would've really scared me is if I would've looked at the camera on the ceiling and it was covered up with a…"

She fell silent, her smile falling away as she turned to point at the camera. I followed her gaze.

A big yellow smile looked down upon us.

She turned back to me, speechless.

I took off my sunglasses and showed her my eyes.

I shouldn't have. The brilliance was painful. I grabbed the steel grip bar beside me as tightly as I could with one hand, and clutched Baby Kat close to me with the other. She was wide awake.

The lights went out. The laughter that I had heard just seconds before from the girl in the seat across from me was replaced with a scream; the same scream that I have heard many times since, so much easier to draw from her than giggles.

In the darkness they waited. I knew as surely as anything I've known in my whole life that they had waited and plotted and planned this whole thing, down to the millisecond. Measured response times, practiced backup plans. Even stopped a train - *this train* - once before, just to see if it could be done.

It could.

They had suffered one casualty during the practice run. A piece of equipment in the makeshift track jam had come loose and impaled one of them, but they had accomplished their mission, stopped the train smoothly and gotten on board.

Then they had gotten back off, gathered their equipment and their dead friend and had gone back underground.

No one had ever suspected it was more than an accident, an isolated technical malfunction, except for that one man in the last car of the train.

Me.

I felt the train shudder as its front end caught on the track jam. Strong vibrations from the sudden loss of speed rattled down the entire length of the train, like shivers down a spine, to where we sat.

"Oh my god, what's happening?" someone yelled, their voice only one of many in an erupting cacophony of distress. The pretty redhead screamed again as she suddenly hurtled towards the front of the car along with all the others.

Despite the sudden force of stopping, I held onto my seat. The *clack-clack* that had droned in the background was gone and I knew that the train had come to a complete stop.

The sharp end of a crowbar stabbed into the car through the seam of the doors across from me.

Fingers appeared – pulling, prying at the doors.

They yielded and popped open with a loud hiss, revealing a crowd of people standing in the darkness of the tunnel, their eyes glowing.

They flowed onto the train like flood waters breaching a levee, filling every empty space and drowning their unsuspecting victims in a sea of their clutching, grabbing hands, dragging them under, holding them down.

The mole people invaded the car through every entrance – ten, twenty of them at least – it was hard to tell exactly, after having polluted my eyes with the blinding fluorescent glare in which the train had been awash until only seconds before.

They moved through the darkness silently, with military precision. I moved my feet aside so as not to interfere with them.

Then Baby Kat was on her feet and in motion, leaving her pink sunglasses on the seat beside me as she joined the dark tattered crowd.

She whirled amongst the now helpless passengers as they were grabbed from the floor, their screaming mouths sealed with duct tape, nylon sacks pulled over their heads as they were stripped of their clothes, of their phones – of everything but the shock and horror of what was happening to them.

Baby Kat spun about the car with the cords she had been given, binding, tying and knotting as she went, with the grace of a master seamstress.

I beamed with pride; she really was something to behold.

In the light of day my daughter wilted like a cut rose tossed on scorched desert; but in the darkness she thrived, she was the best of her kind. In the darkness she was a steel-cable strong vine in the rainforest, pulsing upwards to greet the faint moonlight with bright glowing eyes, a tiny, thirty-year-old viper of death.

Only half a minute had passed, yet the dark intruders had successfully managed to restrain, muzzle and render immobile every passenger in the car. It was an impressive display, a silent ballet of overwhelming force.

Thirty seconds down, thirty seconds to go.

In the crisp darkness I watched, as the nine bound passengers were hoisted from the floor and passed from one person to the next like freshly stripped logs at a sawmill. Headfirst out the door and into the darkness of the tunnel they went, one after the other, until the train car was empty of everyone except Baby Kat, the old Chinese woman and me.

Baby Kat handed me a satchel containing all the cell phones that had been collected from the passengers we had taken. Those phones had to leave the train, be taken from the subway at its final station and be spread out across the city, tossed into dark corners or sold on the street. No one could ever connect this stopped train to anyone's disappearance.

Our entire way of life depended on it.

I turned to face the old Chinese woman. She still sat clutching her bale of newspapers, staring ahead into the darkness. She looked up at me slowly, careful to avert her eyes from mine as I handed her the bag. She, too, had once been one of us, had lived in the darkness beneath and we had shown her great kindness. Now she lived on the surface, providing assistance to us, from time to time.

"As we agreed," I said and she nodded, her

wrinkled old face as vacant as space itself. She lifted the top half of the stack of newspapers and hid the satchel inside.

A city this big...sometimes it eats people, I thought. *You gotta be careful.*

Then Baby Kat and I climbed from the train into the tunnel, running alongside the tracks to join our family and friends, who had begun to drop into a small square hole, disappearing one after the other into the ground between the tracks, behind the train.

The equipment used to jam the track had already been gathered up and stowed, as had the new people we had collected for our tribe – nine captive souls, bound like mummies, each dropped into the hole for our people to catch below.

It was fitting, I thought, that we wrapped them like mummies as they left this world for ours; for it was just as the ancient Egyptians had believed – they, like the Pharaohs of old, had now passed from this life and into the next, into the underworld.

Five seconds remained. Baby Kat and I were the last ones standing on the tracks by the hole. She took her *Hello Kitty* sunglasses from my outstretched hand, then turned and jumped into the hole like a little rabbit, disappearing from sight.

I hesitated for one last moment and turned to look back at the train. Against the windows of the forward cars I saw the outlines of pressed faces, blind eyes wide with fear of the darkness.

For a moment I wondered if they could see me, but I knew they couldn't; it had taken several generations before the first earth dwellers were born with eyes like mine, eyes that could truly see.

As I turned away from the blind faces on the

train, I almost felt sorry for them, for their misfortune to be trapped in the blinding light and withering glare of the miserable surface world. They would never know the joy of living below – that is, unless they happened to ride the last car on the right train on just the right night.

I lowered myself down into the hole and closed it up behind me, taking care in the process to conceal its existence from the surface world.

Baby Kat waited for me in the tunnel that led towards home, where we would take stock of our catch. Some of the captives, those who possessed the proper traits, would become family – maybe we had found a suitable husband for my daughter, and a new red-haired wife for me. Others, those unlikely to adapt, would have to be hobbled and blinded, to be used as livestock. For the most desperately unfortunate, however, an altogether different fate awaited.

Baby Kat took me by the hand, and together we walked through the dark corridor as we followed our brethren and the captives they carried to the glorious city we had built below.

***

THE MOLE PEOPLE was my attempt at delivering a tightly-written thriller in a similar vein as Richard Matheson. Realism was a goal, as well as giving the reader very few clues as to where the story was headed. This is one of only a couple of stories that I've written straight through with little revision. It felt like it ended up being the perfect length.

A direct sequel to this story has been outlined, and I also have some ideas for creating a book based on the 'mole people' underworld that was introduced in this story. I envision a format similar to Ray Bradbury's MARTIAN CHRONICLES, where the story is told through a series of interrelated but not directly connected tales told from various viewpoints. It would be interesting to explore this world not only through the eyes of different mole people characters, but also from the perspective of the victims and of their families who try to find out exactly what happened to their missing loved ones.

Writing this story was a lot of fun. I love it when I sit down at the keyboard, my fingers start dancing, and then the world melts away. Several hours later I come back from an adventure in my head and there's a story about it finished and sitting on my desk. It's the closest thing to real magic I know of.

PAY BACK

I REMEMBER IT all so clearly, sitting here now - every detail, every word, every smell. That day keeps playing over and over again in my mind.

I keep trying to forget about it, to erase the memory of how I got here; but even a random event, a simple word or noise, will trigger a memory and then all of a sudden it's like I'm really there, like I'm back in my bedroom at the start of that fateful day.

Before I know it, it's all happening again and there's nothing I can do to stop it.

Now, I'm there again.

It was a Saturday in late spring, exactly shit-thirty A.M. when the beating on my bedroom door started.

Goddamn it, Mom, I'm going to have to kill you one of these days, you fuckin' bitch, I remember thinking.

Mom had locked herself into her room earlier than usual that evening, had made the excuse that she was feeling poorly. Unless "Poorly" was the name she had given to her vibrator, I knew she was full of shit. She was up to something, I could tell by the look on her face. I should have known.

BANG. BANG. BANG.

I peeled my pillow off my face; it was soaked with warm slobber. I stared daggers at the door through bloodshot eyes.

"Mom! Leave me the fuck alone!" I yelled. I was so tired it hurt to talk.

BANG. BANG. BANG.

"I said, go away!"

There was a half-eaten slice of sausage pizza on a paper plate next to my head. I threw it at the door. It stuck there for a second before slowly peeling off and falling onto the rest of the shit on the floor with a greasy plop.

I squinted at my R2-D2 alarm clock on the dresser.

Nine-freaking-thirty in the morning and that bitch was already harassing me? I *never* got up before eleven. It was my religion. If the house was on fire or something, she'd better go get a hose and put it out. I needed my rest.

"It's not your mom," a deep voice came through the door. I wasn't expecting that. Mom hasn't had a man in this house since dad left and I was only six years old back then. I think that was the year her pussy finally rotted all the way off.

I sat up and rubbed my aching forehead. I needed to lay off the Mountain Dew. Then I remembered: it was Saturday, the first in May. That could only mean one thing.

The Nard was here.

He knocked again.

"Come on Stephen, open up. We're going to be late."

I pictured him standing there, all sorts of shits and giggles excited about his big day with a friend at the amusement park, holding himself and doing the pee-pee dance. There was probably already a dark stain around his crotch, from dribbling on himself with anticipation.

As usual, I couldn't resist fucking with him. I spoke in my most serious voice.

"Nard, you know I can't open the door to just anyone. There are security measures in place, you know that. For all I know, you might be some crazy person with an axe holding my mom's severed head in your hand," I said. God, I almost wished that were true.

"Come on, Stephen, just open the door," he said.

"You know the procedure," I said. "No pass code, no enter."

"Fine. You are so retarded," he huffed, and then knocked the secret code I had made up for him. I didn't need him walking into my room while I was beating off to a sexy spread of Princess Peach in my old Nintendo Power magazine.

Knock.

Knock-Knock.

Knock-Knock-Knock.

I unlocked the door, waiting a second before opening it, savoring the moment. It was all about the timing.

Then I swung it open to find the Nard standing there, looking surprisingly dapper, wearing a neatly pressed golf shirt tucked into olive green khakis. His hair was still wet and neatly combed, like he had just gotten out of the shower. He smelled like he was wearing my mom's perfume; he probably did wear women's perfume - probably douched, too.

Time for the punch line.

"Why hello, Joe Peeing-ping-pong! You have lovely knockers, has anybody ever told you that?" I said.

He just stared at me.

"Come on, I'm joking- no wait, *you're* Joe King!" I said, and laughed loud and long. It was really the only thing the Nard was good for – a good laugh and I had developed this annual ritual of ours into an art form. I knew he loved it, he had to.

I'm sure I was the only friend the poor guy had.

"It just gets funnier every time," the Nard said dryly as I let him into my room – nay, my abode. He was the only person to ever actually be allowed inside, except for my mom, I mean – but she's my maid, so that doesn't really count, does it?

He managed to step right onto the piece of pizza I had thrown at the door; it squished out from underneath his shoe like roadkill. A disgusted look crossed his face as he looked around my room.

I guess my room *was* a little disgusting; after all, it's the same crap hole I've been forced to live in since I was little. The room stank like the sideways smile between the legs of a dead hooker on the floor of a Chinese brothel in the back of a condemned seafood shop. It's a bunch of crap. I mean, come on – I'm twenty-one, I'm the man of this house now. Mom should have let me have the master bedroom years ago and moved her fat ass in here. She's always bitching about how dirty my room is. Maybe us trading rooms would give her something to do: she could clean all this shit up.

"What the hell, Nard?" I yelled. "I let you in my abode as a special guest and the first thing you do is step on my food? What the hell kind of manners is that?"

I loved calling him Nard. It was a very clever name I made up that described him perfectly. It was a combination of the words "nerd" and "retard". I think he thought it meant something awesome.

His real name was Joe King, but the way he said it sounded like "Joe Ping", or "Joe Peeing", which had inspired a lot of funny names since we first met, in second grade. On his first day in class, one of the kids heard his mom tell the teacher that he had Ass-booger syndrome, and we called him "Ass Booger" until they made us quit.

"How do you stand living like this?" the Nard said, looking around my room with a disgusted look on his face.

Jealous.

"You mean, how do I stand all this awesomeness?" I asked, as I proudly surveyed the fine assortment of rare collectibles that I had been lucky enough to stash away over the years. Star Wars action figures, vintage. Transformers, original series – none of that new Michael Bay bullshit. Every issue of Nintendo Power magazine since it started publishing. There were cheat codes in those that weren't even on the internet.

And in the middle of the room, under my primo thirteen-inch color television, was my baby: my Super Nintendo with the Super Mario All-Stars cartridge in it.

The Nard tried to act as though he was

unimpressed, but he didn't fool me.

"I thought you were going to move, now that you've got a job?" he asked.

"Are you kidding?" I said, and laughed as I started digging through a pile of my clothes in the corner, looking for something to wear.

I smelled them to see what I could stand wearing all day. That was a mistake. The first shirt I picked up smelled like vomit. God damn it, my mom is lazy. She needs to get her fat ass in here and wash this shit.

"Why would I want to move? I've got it made here," I explained. "Besides, I'm so close to getting a world record on beating Super Mario Brothers - including the lost levels. Do you even realize how much practice I've put into this? I'm scared if I moved it would mess up my mojo."

"You're still playing Super Mario Brothers? Why don't you go get an XBOX 360 or a Playstation 3 like everybody else, now that you've got a job?" he asked. God, what a dumb question; but that was why he was the Nard.

I finally found a shirt that didn't smell too bad and pulled it on.

"Well, Nard, for one thing, I don't have a job anymore, I lost it over complete bullshit; and second, they call the Super Nintendo Entertainment System a classic for a reason: it's a classic. It's the pinnacle of gaming."

"Okay, fine. I didn't mean to get you started on *that* subject again," he said, looking at his watch, impatient. He was always such a baby about getting there right at opening time. I started digging through the Taco Bell wrappers under the bed looking for my shoes. *God, mom needs to clean this place up.*

"How'd you lose your job?" he asked. "I thought you were doing well."

I finally found my shoes. One of them was full of the new dippable ketchup packs I had been collecting from Chick-Fil-A.

"I was, man, I was real good at my job. But them fuckers were paranoid," I told him. It was the truth.

"What happened?"

"They set up a sting operation on me, all secret spy stuff and shit. I could have sued, but I didn't want to screw up my Mario-jo with legal bullshit," I said.

"I have no idea what you are talking about," the Nard said, "what happened?"

"I had it down to a science. It was completely undetectable," I explained. "I figured out exactly how much of the toppings I could eat off a pizza without anybody noticing. It was a victimless crime. I got to eat some toppings while delivering pizzas and nobody, I mean *nobody*, could tell they had been touched. How is that a big deal?"

"So did somebody complain?"

"No man, I am *sure* nobody ever called and complained. Like I said, I knew exactly how to do it, it was undetectable," I told him. "It was a trap those fuckers set on me. The manager made a pepperoni pizza for me to deliver, must've been made special for one of his friends to check up on me. He actually counted the number of slices of pepperoni he put on it and had the person call and tell him how many were on it when I delivered it. How paranoid is that, right?"

"So you got fired when you got back?" the Nard asked.

"Yeah man, it was all kinds of screwed up. It was a medium pizza, it had twenty-five pieces of pepperoni on it and medium pizzas *never* have more than twenty unless the order is for extra pepperoni – and this pizza *wasn't* extra pep. As long as a medium pizza had fifteen slices of pepperoni on it no one will notice the difference. I only ate five off that pizza – *only five* – and that fucker fired me! Can you believe that shit?"

The Nard shrugged. "Yeah, that sucks. I know your mom had to be disappointed. I remember her telling me how excited she was that you had a job and would be moving out," he said, like he and my mom were all best buddies or something.

He wishes.

I think he's always had a thing for my mom. Every time she walks by he stares at her ass the way an Ethiopian looks at a chicken.

My mom's desperate, but I'm pretty sure even she draws the line at *ass-boogers*.

Speak of the devil. Just then she poked her head through the doorway, a shit eating grin on her face. "You boys ready to get your picture together?" she said, waggling her piece of shit Digimax camera around like it was worth something.

She always looked at the Nard like he was so amazing; there was this shining look of love whenever she saw him. Sometimes I almost wonder if she wished the Nard was her son, instead of me. I guess an idiot like her *would* prefer an imbecile for a son, instead of someone as brilliant as me. I probably make her feel stupid a lot.

"God damn it, mom! Can't I ever just take Joe for his big day out without you making us pose like it's the prom?" I asked.

"Stephen, I've gotten a picture of us all together every year since you boys were little. You never know when something's going to be your last time doing it. I still remember the last time your dad and you and me had dinner together as a family," she blabbered.

Oh god, not this shit. Here we go again.

"If I had known then, that it would be the last time the three of us would be sitting around a dinner table as a family, I would have made something nice. Do you know, after he left, I looked through all our pictures and the last time we had taken a picture together as a family was two years before?"

I couldn't let her get started down this road or else we would die of old age and boredom before she was finished.

"Fine, mom. Whatever. Take the stupid picture so we can hurry up and get the fuck out of this shithole," I said.

We went into the hallway. Mom sat the camera down on the little table by the front door and set the timer, before jumping into the picture with us, wrapping an arm around each of our necks just as the camera flashed.

God she was an embarrassment. I honestly couldn't wait to bury her.

I finished getting my shit together and we were out the door. Normally, I wouldn't hurry on purpose, just to fuck with *Joe-peeing*, but it *was* pretty sweet being one of the first people to get into King's Gardens. They had a new coaster this year, the longest and fastest in the southeast or some shit, and I intended on taming that bitch three or four times before the line got so long I'd die of old age waiting.

The Nard was driving us today, he's so retarded I'm surprised anyone gave him a license, but my car is in the shop and mom won't let me use hers anymore. It's not my fault someone hit me last time I used it. They saw that I was going for it when the light was changing and they decided to try and beat me anyway.

Assholes.

"Be careful with the door," the Nard said as he clicked the car unlocked, "It's close to the curb and I don't want to mess it up."

"Holy shit, Joe, how'd you get a Maserati? You win the lottery?" I asked.

"No, I bought it, Stephen. Remember I told you I sold my nanotech patents to the JPL last year for a bundle?" he said.

"I thought you were just making up stuff to impress me," I told him. "A little monkey like you should be pretty good at ba-nano-tech for the Junior Pussy Lickers, though," I laughed. He just stared at me. How he did not find a classic joke like that funny? I had no idea.

"No, I really do have a job and make money, Stephen. You should try it," he said.

"Don't get all high and mighty on me, *Joe-peeing.* You're still a Nard, and no money in the world can change that," I told him, and that really shut him up. Sometimes you just gotta put stupid people in their place, whether they're driving a car with real leather seats or not. When my name's at the top of the Nintendo Power high score world rankings, I'm gonna buy two cars like it.

Joe has always been a dork. Taking him to the amusement park one day a year was my way of contributing to society, my charity work, if you will. Besides, it's the only thing Mom will pay for me to do anymore, the cunt. I don't care if I am twenty-one, I'm still her son and a guy needs to have fun once in a while. I work very hard on my Super Mario drills and sometimes it's nice just to go blow off some steam, even if it's with a Nard like Joe.

As we pulled into the parking lot, I could feel my excitement growing. The new coaster, the Dominator, loomed over the parking lot like a giant red snake, just waiting to devour anyone who got too close. I couldn't wait. I hoped Joe didn't make us go on the Scrambler fifteen times in a row again this year. The guy had a fucktard obsession with that stupid ride.

We parked and headed for the gate. There weren't many people in line yet, so that was good – maybe we could actually ride something without waiting in line.

"What time is it, Joe?" I asked as we got in line for tickets. I was ready to ride that coaster this instant.

He checked his watch. It looked really expensive, one bad-ass piece of arm-candy.

"Ten till ten," he said.

"What kind of watch is that?" I asked. "I need to get me one of those."

"Oh, this?" he said, holding it up so I could see. "You can't buy this watch anywhere – I made it."

"Bullshit," I told him.

"No really, man, I did. I didn't go to MIT for nothing," he said.

"No, you went to MIT because *Monkeys In Training* is the only college that will let a primate like you go," I told him.

I loved that joke. I must've said it a hundred

times, when they kicked him out of high school at sixteen to go there. It must be a special school for special kids. If he was really smart, he would have gone to State. I felt a little bad for teasing him about being sent away to a special school, but not much.

"Check it out," Joe said, showing me his watch up close. "I programmed it to play the original Super Mario Brothers using the original code. It even has the secret levels glitch."

He pressed a few buttons on the watch and the Super Mario intro screen popped up on a mini high-res color screen as the theme song started playing. *In stereo.*

That watch was possibly the coolest thing I had ever seen in my entire life. I would have traded him my left nut for it, in an instant.

"It's okay, I guess," I said. I didn't want to let on that I was impressed, even though the watch had to be the coolest invention the Nard had ever made in his entire life, by far – and he had made a lot over the years. It was at least ten trillion times better than the assortment of stupid gadgets he usually brought with us to King's Gardens: wind speed testers, accelerometers, laser distance calculators, and other retarded geek shit like that. Having the coolest watch in the world strapped to his arm was proof that even a blind squirrel can find an acorn in the woods from time to time.

"So you don't like it," he said, looking disappointed. He reached into his pocket and pulled out a second watch, identical to the one he was wearing.

"Then I guess you probably don't want the one I made for you?" he said sadly.

I couldn't keep up the act anymore. I was about to crap my bloomers.

"Are you shitting me?" I said. I still couldn't believe it. "I'll take it, definitely. This watch is just like that one?"

"Well, I made it especially for you, so there is one little difference from mine," he said as he handed me the watch. "Look on the back."

I flipped it over and holy shit - etched perfectly into the metal on the back was the Transformers logo, the original one, too – not that stupid Michael Bay bullshit.

I didn't know what to say. I felt a little bad for treating him like a 'tard, even though he was one.

"Thanks Joe," I told him.

"You're welcome, Stephen. Try it on," he said, and smiled so big I thought for a second that his head would split open.

I slipped my hand through the smooth metal wristband, and as I did it made a whirring sound, automatically tightening itself around my wrist.

"That is so bad ass," I said. "We can go ride the Scrambler first again, if you want to," I told him. I felt like I owed him that much.

"No, it's okay. I want to save the Scrambler for last this time," he said. No figuring out that fucker.

Just then, the gates opened and we pushed our way through with everyone else. It was a bright sunny day, not hot, but perfect, with just the right amount of cool spring breeze blowing. I loved the smells of King's Gardens more than just about anything and the air was full of them today: deep-fried elephant ears covered with cinnamon-sugar, roasted turkey legs, cotton candy, french fries – it was enough to give my tongue a hard-on just thinking about it.

It suddenly occurred to me that this was the first time I'd been out of the house since I got fired. That had been a month ago. It felt good to be outdoors, in the fresh air and away from Mom's relentless bitching and groaning.

I played Mario on the watch the Nard had given me while we waited in the short line. It worked perfectly. I had never seen anything like it in my life.

And the Nard seemed to enjoy watching me play with it. In fact, he seemed happier than I had ever seen him in our entire lives, smiling and whistling like he had a corn dog with mustard up his ass or something.

I couldn't believe that he actually rode the Dominator roller coaster. I figured he'd duck out at the last second, but he rode it with me - not just once, but three times in a row.

You gotta understand, this guy hasn't ridden a real roller coaster since I tricked him into getting onto the Gunner Barrel triple-looper back when we were in fifth grade.

That had been the first time our parents had let us come here by ourselves. He looked like he was going to kill me when we got off of it, he had no idea what he was getting himself into with that one. His pants were a dripping mess after I tricked him into getting on that one; he pissed all over himself on that one. I almost died laughing that day, seriously, no joke – I almost blacked out I laughed so hard.

He hadn't ridden a single roller coaster on all of our trips here together since then, just the pussy baby rides. I didn't care; the single rider lines always went faster on the coasters, anyway; and besides, I didn't want the Nard pissing all over me.

But today, the Nard seemed like he was up for anything.

While we were waiting to get on the bumper cars, I saw him checking out a woman's ass while she was buckling her kid up.

"So when you gonna get your cherry popped, Joe? You're old enough to drive, old enough to vote, old enough to drink – so when are you gonna grow yourself a pair and get some? 'Fraid it'll have teeth and bite off your teenie weenie?" I asked him.

He looked at me like he wanted to kill me. For a minute, I almost thought he might take a swing at me. Instead, he took a deep breath and let it out slowly.

"Maybe I have, Stephen. Maybe I have a girlfriend and we have sex a lot. Maybe I had sex with her last night. How would you know?"

I thought about this. It didn't take long.

"Well, Joe, I know because you are a nard, and nards don't have sex with anyone but themselves and other nards. It's like a law of nature, or something," I said. "And besides, your shoe is untied."

He didn't even bother to look. I had probably pulled that trick on him one time too many.

"I don't think sex is the most important thing, Stephen. It's whether or not you love someone, whether or not you find them smart and stimulating, someone who gives you a reason to get up every day. I think that's what's most important," Joe said, sounding like a total idiot, as usual.

"Smart girls? Really, Joe-peeing?" I said. "*Smart girl* usually means 'ugly girl', in my experience. Myself, I prefer dumb girls. Their expectations are lower because of their limited imaginations. Also, they're easier to manipulate so I can control the relationship, which feeds my ego and makes me feel like God."

"Well if you're such an expert, maybe you could tell me about the last time you slept with a woman? Perhaps I could learn something," Joe said, and crossed his arms waiting for me to answer, challenging me.

Really? The Nard is questioning my sexuality? I'm sure crossing a black cat's path was the closest this guy has ever gotten to a real pussy.

It *had* been a long time since I had got me some snatch myself, come to think of it, but I couldn't let him know that. In fact, the last time I even got stinkfinger was tenth grade when Jesse May, a chick with Downs or something, maybe just inbred, made the mistake of sitting next to me on the back of the bus. They said she was retarded, but those titties weren't retarded, that's for sure.

I tried to think up a story real quick, about me banging some snootch that would sound remotely plausible, but I'd been so tied up with my game practice the only pink I'd seen lately were porno cartoons of princess Zelda.

The Nard realized that I was stalling, so I decided to deflect him with a joke.

"Your mama," I said. "I fucked her last night while you were in your bedroom beating off to magazines. You didn't hear us? I'm surprised, because only a total dick-for-brains wouldn't have heard their mom getting reamed five ways to Friday last night."

I think that must have really gotten to him,

because he turned pale when I told him I fucked his mama. He choked on his coke and a little bit dripped out of his nose as he sputtered it up.

He turned away so I couldn't see the embarrassed look on his face. He was so short bus he probably thought it was true, that I really was banging his mom. God, what a moron. It's hard to believe anyone could really be so oblivious.

We didn't talk for a while after that.

After riding roller coasters for almost four hours straight, we finally worked our way around to the side of the park where his beloved Scrambler was. I couldn't believe Joe hadn't begged to come here sooner. Usually it was the first place we came, he always insisted on it. I wondered why today was different. Maybe his testicles had finally dropped.

When I say the Nard was obsessed with the Scrambler, I mean really *obsessed*. Not just liked, but Charlie Sheen levels of crazy for it.

He had been eaten up with his love for the Scrambler since the first time we rode it, when we were seven years old and our parents had brought us to King's Gardens together for the first time, hoping it would help us get along, after I called him an *assbooger* and everybody made fun of him.

I'm not sure what it was about the ride that made him so head over heels for it, exactly; it was a lame ride, probably the lamest ride in the whole park except for the merry-go-round. All you did was sit in a long seat while the whole thing went around in circles, and each of the four arms of the ride held for seats that also went around and around, faster and faster until the person stupid enough to have sat on the outside seat got squished so bad by everybody else that they couldn't breathe.

I guess it was *okay* when we were little, but there was something about that ride that Joe was fixated on in his own *ass-booger* kind of way. He would watch it for hours if I let him, and he always jabbered on like Rain Man while he watched - about velocity and orbit and trajectories, inconstant variables and long-range, pin-point precision target odds ratios – total *ass-booger* shit.

And it wasn't just the ride that had Joe fixated; it was the outside seat in chair number twelve that was the precise focus of his obsession. That exact seat was the one we always had to sit in when we rode it, even if that meant we had to wait for the next time loading to get it.

His fixation on the Scrambler got worse with every passing year. He started bringing equipment with him to the park – laser-pointers, wind socks, scientific calculators. He would write down ridiculous-looking formulas and equations in a little notebook, while he watched the ride go round and round.

To this day I have no idea what he was trying to accomplish. Whenever I'd ask him what he was trying to figure out, he would just mumble a bunch of garble-dee-gook. I think the Scrambler had scrambled his already fragile mind. He even kept track in his notebook of where every security camera was around the ride, and would update it meticulously if anything changed.

One time he even rode the ride while wearing a hat that had one of his gadgets hooked to the top of it. He said it was a device to measure wind speed.

Another time, he pestered me into riding it while

I wore a dorky looking pair of sunglasses he had made. They were all flat and shiny and mirrored, and the left lens had a little target reticule drawn on it like a gun scope. The glasses looked so stupid I wasn't going to do it at first, but he promised to me an elephant ear with extra cherry topping, so I rode the ride and wore his stupid sunglasses while he stood by the exit and shot a laser pointer at me, taking notes in his nardbook.

He would get back in line and ride it over and over again, and always in seat number twelve. Sometimes as he rode, he would peck away furiously at his calculator, other times he would just stare off into space, like he was in a trance.

The one thing that never changed, was that I'd eventually have to drag him away from the Scrambler. Every single year.

As we got older, the gadgets he created to do experiments on the Scrambler got fancier and fancier. Who knew what stupid shit he would do this year? I was almost excited to see, but he always made it so embarrassing. The worst year was when we were in tenth grade, the year before they sent him away to the special Monkeys-In-Training school in Massahackie.

That year he had broken down and literally cried when he found out that they had replaced the engine that turned the ride. He collapsed onto the pavement and curled up into a ball crying like a baby. He said years of his planning and research had been destroyed, that his equations would all have to be redone. He finally got to talk to the mechanic who had replaced the engine, even got him to open up the housing and show him the guts, that seemed to make him feel a little better, but the whole Rain Man episode was majorly embarrassing.

As we walked up to the Scrambler, I glanced at Joe. I was surprised to see he wasn't shaking with his usual excitement yet, but it was obvious he was having to work hard to control himself. The look in his eye told me he was still about to lose his shit.

Next to the Scrambler was a concession stand that sold pizza, corndogs and beer. Evidently it hadn't been a very good combination for somebody, because the air around it reeked of vomit. The day had really started to heat up, and stink fumes quivered above the asphalt walkways like stench from a dead man's armpits.

Joe was making a bee-line for his beloved Scrambler, ass cheeks clenched tightly as he walked. Even from behind he looked like a total nard.

I couldn't resist anymore. I *had* to fuck with him. He had been trying to play it cool all day, trying to act like he didn't give a fuck about the Scrambler, but he wasn't fooling me, wasn't fooling anybody but himself.

I grabbed his shoulder just as he was about to get in line.

"Hey Joe, I'm hungry. Let's get a bite to eat. Those corn dogs sure do smell good!" I said and pretended to sniff the air.

Joe followed my example, as I figured he would, and took a big whiff, expecting to smell something delicious. He scrunched his face up in disgust when he got a nose full of the hot vomit smell instead.

"Mmmm, Mmmm," I said, rubbing my stomach and laughing at him.

I could tell it was killing him to have to wait. I'm sure his pockets were full of the new dorky scientific

Boy Scout badge shit he had made up, festering to do his egghead experiments on that stupid ride again.

And he expected me to believe that he worked for NASA. Yeah, right. He probably bought that Maserati with a disability check for being a retard, the fucker.

But he played it cool, I'll give him that.

"Fine, Stephen," he said. "I think I'm going to have a corn dog. Fudge it all – let's celebrate! I'm going to have a corn dog *and* a beer. What do you want?"

I pulled out my wallet. It was empty except for some papers with cheat codes for Donkey Kong Country 3 on them. Mom didn't even remember to give me lunch money, goddamn it! That whore knows I got shit-canned in an illegal bullshit sting operation. Does she want me to starve to death?

Joe pulled out his wallet to pay for his food. It was stuffed with green bills, and one of them was a hundred.

"Hey Joe," I said, holding my wallet open so he could see it was empty. "You mind picking up my lunch? I appear to be having a cash flow crisis at the moment."

"No problem Stephen, what do you want? Anything for you, buddy," he said.

Damn. That was easy. I should have had this fool buying my food sooner. I'm sure all that money in his wallet came from my hard earned taxes from when I was working, anyway. Fucking welfare leech was probably pulling in a mint with his disability.

"Yeah, Nard, thanks," I told him. "Gimme two corn dogs, and a beer. No, make that two beers. I'll get you back for it later."

Like fuck I would.

When he pulled some cash out of his wallet to pay for the food and drinks a little card fell out, but he didn't notice. He started fumbling with a packet of sugar or sweetener or something, and stirred it into his beer. *Ass-booger brew*, I thought.

I grabbed the card that had fallen out of his wallet off the ground real quick while he wasn't paying attention. I was hoping it was a credit card. There was some stuff I needed on eBay for my game collection.

It wasn't a credit card, though; it was the picture mom took from last year when we went to King's Gardens, only I wasn't in it. It was just a picture of the Nard all snuggled up with my mom, a big shit-eating grin on his face like they were a couple or something. He had cut me clean out. I could only see part of my shoulder in the picture in front of mom.

"What the fuck is this shit?" I asked and shoved the picture in his face when he turned around. He almost dropped the three beers he was trying hard to balance.

"You got the hots for my mom and her saggy ass titties or something?" I demanded to know.

Joe took the picture from me, his face turning red. He slipped it quickly back into his wallet like it was a winning lottery ticket or something. I was feeling angry, but first I grabbed my corn dogs and beers away from him, and chugged one down.

"You better take it slow on the beer, Stephen," he said, trying to speak in what I'm sure he thought was a calming manner, but it just pissed me off even more. "You don't want to puke on the Scrambler."

I wiped off the beer that dripped down my chin and slammed the cup down on the table.

"Fuck you, Joe. Fuck you and your stupid

Scramburgler," I told him. I wanted to punch the stupid fuck right in his stupid fuck face.

"Come on, Stephen," he said, "don't get mad at me. We've been having a good day together. Let's not ruin it now."

"I didn't ruin shit, Nard – you did," I told him, and I meant it. I can only put up with his donkey-ass dumb shit so far, and this crossed the line.

"How can I hang out with you, knowing you're running around with a picture of my mom in your pocket?" I asked. "You beat off to that picture, Joe-peeing? You think about my ugly-ass mom while you play with your wee-wee?"

"You should show some respect to your mother, Stephen," the Nard said. He looked like he was starting to get his dander up. "She's a very smart and beautiful woman and she has taken good care of you your whole life. Show her some respect."

That was it. It was game on. I had treated the Nard with kid gloves for years, had made him my special charity case, taken him out in public for a day of fun every year, despite the hit I had to take to my reputation for being seen in public with him, and now he's going to lecture me?

I don't think so.

"Let's get something straight right now, Nard," I said and took a long pull of my second beer. "You are not my daddy. Just because you got a picture with my mom and cut me out of it does not give you the right to lecture me. Is this how you treat your only friend? Like a punk? Huh, retard? Speak up. I can't hear you."

Joe started to take a sip of his beer, but stopped as he thought of how to respond. For a second, he almost looked normal. I fully expected him to try and change the subject, to start spouting off Scrambler-related scientific nonsense.

Instead, he sat up straight and looked me dead in the eye.

"Stephen, there's a few things I think we need to get straight between us," he said calmly, wearing an expression as serious as a hot iron poker in the ass, and sat his beer back down on the table.

"Oh yeah, you can bet your dick there is," I said trying to remain in control of the situation, but I was feeling uncomfortable. Suddenly he didn't seem so retarded anymore. He was acting like a counselor, or a police officer, or something; like *he* had authority.

I didn't like it.

"Look Stephen, I don't like you. I never have. You've always been a stupid, selfish, mean-spirited, petulant little prick," he said. "You tell me that *I* should be kind to you because *you're* my only friend? Maybe you should take a look in the mirror, Stephen, because the last time I checked it seemed like I was *your* only friend. I've got lots of friends."

I couldn't believe my ears: the Nard biting the hand that fed him? I would never have expected this. Talk about deluded. This guy took the cake.

"Bullshit, Joe. You were so stupid they had to send you away to the defective baby school in eleventh grade. They didn't even let you stay in the special classes you were so malfunctive. They didn't have jars of paste big enough to feed people your size," I told him. That should put him back in his place, where he belonged.

He didn't even blink.

"See Stephen? That's what I'm talking about.

You're so dense you never have a clue about anything that's going on around you," he said. "You're not stupid, you're just willfully *ignorant*. If you had paid even the slightest bit of attention to what people were saying about me going to college in the eleventh grade, even read a newspaper even once, you would have known that I wasn't going to MIT at the age of sixteen as a student. I went there to teach."

I just sat there looking at him, blinking. I could feel the beer kicking in. It was giving me a pretty righteous buzz. I finished off the dregs as I tried to come up with an appropriate response.

Then it came to me. The perfect response.

BUUURRRRRPPP!

I let it slide out of my throat slowly, like a big ol' bullfrog singing a mating call. I could feel the grease of the corndog all slippery in the back of my throat as I blew my belch in the Nard's direction.

"Nice, Stephen. Real nice," he mumbled. "Here I am – a person who has created self-sustainable nano-propulsion systems, engineered indestructible bonds within subatomic chains, patented self-replicating organic materials production techniques, devised a method for conducting electricity across hundreds of thousands of miles without the need for rare or precious metals. Hell, Stephen, I've single-handedly created a way to turn a single small rock into an unbreakable atomic chain that could reach from here to the moon, did you know that? And yet here I sit, breathing in the corn dog breath of the world's most obtuse, narcissistic, completely non-self-aware numbskull, on an otherwise glorious afternoon. I'm talking about you, do you comprehend anything that I'm saying, or is it all just eight-bit bleeps inside that thick head of yours?"

I took another bite of my corn dog, listening. Fascinated, even. This was the most I had ever heard an ass-booger speak at one time, and the extent of his delusion was amazing to me. The words he was saying almost sounded like he was making sense, but then you try to put them all together and it was easy to realize he was just gabbling nonsense, like a parrot that's been stuck in a room with the Discovery Channel on TV for too long.

I glanced at the game watch he had given me. The park would be closing in an hour.

The Nard pushed his beer aside and leaned in towards me, narrowing his beady eyes, examining me. My second beer was empty, so I grabbed his and took a long pull. The world around us was starting to spin a little. I kinda felt like we were riding the Scrambler already.

"But you know what, Stephen?" he whispered. "Sitting here, thinking about it now - I wouldn't change a thing. All these years I've resented that my mom kept making me bring you here, year after year, being nice to you when all you'd do is torture and belittle me."

"It feels strange to say," the Nard continued blathering, "but looking back at it now the truth is if it wasn't for you being such an asshole to me when we were little, then I would never have accomplished so much. I honestly have to say that my entire course in life - all my scientific discoveries, almost everything I've ever done - was initially inspired by you."

He paused and cast a wistful look at the Scrambler spinning behind us.

"Yep, you inspired me all right," he said, pointing

a finger at the ride, "and so did that."

It was clear to me that the Nard had now gone completely crazy. I took another long chug from his beer and it foamed up, dripping all over the front of my shirt.

"You know what, Joe-peeing?" I said, trying not to slur my words. The beer seemed stronger than usual. "I don't like you. I've never liked you. I've only ever taken you here every year to be nice and let you have a day out with normal people, to try to make you feel like a normal person. But you just showed me that you think you're so much better than everybody, but you're sick, Joe-peeing, you're real sick, and you need help. I don't want to ever see you again. Don't bother coming to my house next year, begging for me to take you to King's Gardens again. We're done, you got it?"

I guzzled down the rest of the beer, waiting for his crying and whining to start. The Nard lived for this day, for the single chance each year to get to ride his beloved Scrambler. There was no way he was going to let me go home without promising to bring him back next year. I'd undoubtedly be dragging him along on the ground behind me as I tried to walk away, him clutching my ankle with both hands, blubbering and snotting everywhere, begging for me to forgive his insolence.

But I meant it. I was done with this imbecile.

I was surprised when, instead of freaking out like I expected, the Nard just smiled.

"You're right, Stephen. This *is* going to be our last time coming here together. And I want to say, I'm sorry."

Ahh, there it was. I knew he would be begging for

forgiveness.

"I'm sorry for acting so pompous today," he continued. "I'm just a stupid retard and I make up stupid shit, and I'm really just jealous because you're so good at Super Mario Brothers and you have an awesome room and an awesome life and I'm just an ass-booger and I got sent away to a school for retards and they make me wear a helmet so I won't hurt myself," he said.

Jealous! I knew it! He was so envious of how cool and talented I was that I hadn't realized how hard he had been working to make up stuff about himself, just to impress me. I almost felt a little sorry for the loser. Not much, but a little. I still was done with him, don't get me wrong; I wasn't going to bring him back here, ever - but I didn't want the last fun day of his entire life to end badly. That would just be mean.

I knew exactly what would cheer him up.

"What do you say we go ride the Scrambler right now?" I said. "One last time for old times' sakes?"

"You mean it? Really? That would be swell, Stephen," he said. His eyes lit up like a little monkey who found a cat turd while digging in the litter box.

We went and got in line for the ride together. It was a short line; like I said, the ride was lame.

When it was our turn to get on, some bunch of assholes got into Joe's favorite seat, seat number twelve. I told them that they had to get off and let us have it, that I was Tom Cruise and my friend was Dustin Hoffman and if they didn't, he would piss himself and scream Judge Wapner until they did.

They didn't argue.

I offered Joe the outside squish seat, his favorite, and he took it. I kept waiting for him to whip out some gadgets, to get out his pen and notebook, to strap on a windmill hat or shoot a laser pointer at something; but he didn't, even when the ride started.

We sat there together in silence and the ride started moving, turning, spinning - slowly at first, but then faster and faster, two grown men who had once been little boys sitting in these same seats every year for the last decade and a half. Even though so much time had passed, I was still smart and the Nard was still, well, the Nard. Not much had changed, I guessed; not much but the size of our shoes.

The ride started really picking up speed. It felt like we were chocolate chips, being whipped into cookie batter by a monster-sized blender. I could feel the corn dogs paddling for their lives in the swimming pool of beer that was sloshing inside my stomach, churning, foaming, building up pressure like a hot two-liter of soda, shaken up and ready to explode.

I fought back the urge to spew all over Joe as the ride flew, spinning past the other cars, smiling faces of other riders rushing at me and then shooting away just as we were about to collide, over and over, the metal sound of the gears grinding in a steam engine din, behind the sounds of laughter and the diesel engine that powered the whole thing.

The pressure of the ride squeezed me up against Joe so hard I couldn't pull myself away from him. We weren't so little anymore, and I had packed on a few extra pounds during the winter. I wondered if I was crushing him to death.

If I was, you wouldn't have known from the look on his face. I had never seen him look so happy before, so joyous, rapturous even. Usually he was so uptight, always busy working on something, even while riding rides he was always calculating, experimenting, taking notes. But not today. Today he was simply riding the ride, eyes closed, his hair buffeting back and forth in the breeze, a wide smile of pure bliss spreading across his face in the warm sunshine, like melted butter on pancakes. He looked happier in that instant than I could ever remember being in my whole entire life.

Ignorance is bliss, they say. I figured if that was true, then it stood to reason that Joe should be just about the happiest man in the whole universe.

After the ride slowed down and finally came to a stop, Joe and I got off and walked through the exit gate, where we stood and looked at each other with our hands in our pockets for a minute, not sure what to say, not sure how to end it, whatever *it* was – friendship wasn't the right word. Maybe fifteen-year-long play date was more like it.

"Well, Joe," I said after a bit, "It's been fun. Be good."

I offered him my hand.

"Thanks, Stephen," he said, taking my hand. "Thanks for being my friend."

"I'm not your friend, Nard. I never was," I said. I just wanted him to be clear on this point, so he wouldn't be bugging me for the rest of his life whenever he got lonely.

He held onto my hand for a moment, silent, looking at the watch on my arm that he had given me. His palm was sweaty and he looked nervous, though fuck knows why. For a second I thought he was going to ask me to give it back. Fat chance of that happening; there would be no Indian-givers on my

216

watch, pun intended.

"Ok Stephen," he said, finally dropping my hand. I wiped it on my jeans to get rid of the sweat-slime he had left there. "But there's one last surprise I have for you, before we say good-bye," he said.

"I'm not doing any more stupid experiments for you on the Scrambler, Joe. You're a grown man, go do them yourself."

"This has nothing to do with that, Stephen, I swear," he said, suddenly seeming very earnest. "This has to do with you achieving your life's full potential. Are you interested?"

What does this moron know about my potential? Honestly?

Achieving my life's full potential could only mean one thing: the highest score on Super Mario Brothers *in the world*. The top of the Nintendo leader board, baby.

"What could you possibly know about *that*," I asked with as much sneer as I could pack into my voice. "Have you ever even picked up a controller in your life?"

"Let's just say, for arguments sake, that I could upload a program to the watch I gave you. If that program could show you the fastest possible solution to Super Mario Brothers, based on years of research and reverse engineering, would you be interested in seeing it?"

"Does a bear stick his dick into the honey twat?"

"That's what I thought," Joe said. "Let's just say that this is my good-bye gift to you Stephen, my final way of saying 'thank-you' for so many years of fake friendship."

I started punching buttons on the watch, but

nothing happened.

"How do I make it show me the fastest route?" I asked.

He shook his head left to right slowly and smiled.

"It's not on the watch yet, Stephen. It has to be uploaded," he said. "Remember that spot where I used to stand with the laser measuring tape? Walk over there and look for a small white 'X' painted on the ground. Last year, I embedded a small transmitter into the asphalt there. Go stand on the 'X' and hold your arm with the watch straight out in front of you towards the ride and then count to sixty. The transmitter has a sensor that will detect the watch and automatically begin uploading the file to the watch. Don't move until the watch begins to beep, or else the file will be corrupted. It's programmed to only send the code once, so make sure you don't screw it up."

Typical Nard: always finding a way to make something simple into something excruciatingly complicated. But if he had found a shortcut that I could use to get to the top of the leader board faster, I was happy to take it. The sooner I was world champ for Super Mario Brothers, the sooner I could get started on the original Tomb Raider.

He pointed in the general direction of where he used to stand with his laser pointer and I headed towards it, scanning the ground for an 'X'. Sure enough, there it was, just on the other side the rails where people lined up next to the entrance.

I stepped directly on top of the X. I looked back at the Nard to make sure I was in the right place, but he was already talking excitedly to a couple of park employees, no doubt about what kind of paint they used to paint the stripes on the Scrambler this year or some other dumb shit.

The ride was beginning to load, and people were pushing their way through the gate towards the pathetic ride like people on welfare jostling for free cheese. I decided to wait until the ride was fully loaded so no one would accidentally bump me and mess up my upload.

I touched the watch on my right wrist. The metal felt so heavy and solid, cool and smooth to the touch. I looked over to the Nard's favorite car, the ever-amazing seat number twelve. A lanky redneck man with scraggly muttonchops and a camouflage t-shirt had made the poor decision to plop himself down in the squish seat between his four-hundred pound wife and hard steel.

Good luck surviving the ride with Roseanne Barr crushing you to death, I thought.

The ride began to move, and I held my arm straight out in front of me towards it as the Nard had instructed. It suddenly occurred to me that maybe he was tricking me into helping him with one last experiment. It better not be, or else I would cram this watch down his throat, I decided. If this would help me achieve my goal of becoming the Mario World Champion, it was worth a shot, I figured.

The watch started to beep. On the display the words COUNTDOWN COMMENCING flashed briefly, and then the numbers *60, 59, 58, 57* began ticking off.

I held my arm out as steady as a rock, just beyond my open palm I watched as the Scrambler began to hit full speed, the screams of riders growing loud in my ears just before they shot away again, leaving a blast of hot wind in their wake.

I glanced at the Nard and was surprised to see that he was now surrounded by several security guards. He must have been asking too many specific questions about the ride's motor, I guessed. I hoped they'd arrest him as a possible terrorist and ship him off to Guantanamo, it would serve him right. The Nard was gesturing urgently, and then he pointed to me. The security guards all turned and looked straight at me.

What the hell is going on? I thought.

I checked the time remaining on the watch. At the exact moment the watch hit thirty seconds remaining, I saw, in perfect focus just over the end of my outstretched arm, the redneck in car number twelve flash by. It was like a moment frozen in time, as his bloodshot squinty eyes gazed into mine, our lines of sight locked into each other's for just the slightest fraction of a second before the ride yanked him away, his swine-sized wife squealing and oinking in delight as she crushed his ribs into the steel frame of the car.

At the exact instant the redneck lined up with me, the watch stopped beeping and let out a long high-pitched tone, like a heart-monitor alarm when a patient has flat-lined.

A pinprick of hot white heat flashed on my wrist underneath the watch and surged up my arm to my armpit. I tried to yank my arm back, but it was locked at the elbow, stuck straight out.

The events that happened next occurred undoubtedly in the blink of an eye, but to me it seemed as though everything happened in slow motion. The watch began to open itself up like a flower with thin shiny metal petals unfurling on a summer morning. The metal shifted and turned, like a densely-packed puzzle rearranging itself. In less than a second the watch on my arm had become what looked like a small gun in my hand.

The son of a bitch; the watch really *was* a transformer.

And then, it fired itself. A projectile exited the barrel with an odd-sounding whoosh and a small burst of smoke.

I heard someone shouting, "He's got a gun!"

In my peripheral vision I saw dark shapes running towards me from all directions.

It's hard to believe, I know, but I watched the projectile as it flew from the end of the gun. Maybe it was from my adrenaline surging, maybe it was the stuff the watch had stuck in me, but everything was in slow-mo – *Matrix-time* – whatever you want to call it, and the thing that came out of that gun was no bullet.

I watched the small object as it hurtled away from me and towards the ride, small plumes of flames burning blue at its tail end before little bits fell away from it. Then it stretched out like a spring, about the size of the spring inside a click-pen, and then fell back into itself, then stretched out again picking up steam.

I watched hopelessly as the tiny thing chased the twirling ride, glinting in the bright sun as it expanded and collapsed, going faster and faster.

Then I saw the redneck flash by me again, just a blur in my vision, a snapshot of his face red and straining against the crushing heft of his marital sow.

Then I saw the projectile do the impossible. Instead of flying past the right side of the ride in a straight line like a normal bullet, it shifted course. I saw it shoot to the left and then back towards me, then it shot off to the right again only ten feet or so in front of my face, expanding and collapsing, pulsing as though it was gaining momentum from its own movements.

The men in uniform were getting closer.

"Drop the weapon," I heard one of them shouting, but I was mesmerized.

The projectile still flew, around and around the ride, darting this way and that through the spinning arms and cars and screaming heads, like a silver wasp, chasing its prey.

Car number twelve swung back into view again, the redneck's eyes bulging as he strained to draw oxygen into his compressed lungs, his wife still laughing and snorting like the prize pig at the county fair.

Then the minuscule metal hunter stung.

The projectile straightened out into a single sliver of metal, sliding straight into the redneck's left eyeball, like a pin through a pin cushion, and his entire eyeball disappeared in a spray of blood and viscous fluid, as the ride snatched car number twelve out of sight again.

I felt the gun disintegrate into hot particles in my hand. The gritty bits of it blew away like ash in the wind as they fell through my fingers.

"Hands in the air," an angry voice screamed, and then a sharp blow to the back of my legs caused the asphalt to rush towards my face. The next thing I knew, I was being tasered from all sides, on my throat, my back, my arms.

The last thing I heard was the Nard's whiny voice, gurgling and crying. "He told me he was going to do it, but I thought he was joking."

I've been here ever since, that day replaying over and over in my mind, wondering what the hell happened, what I could have done differently.

The trial was a joke, there wasn't even a gun and the redneck guy didn't die. I told them over and over that the Nard gave me a watch that was a transformer and that it had turned into a gun; but all I got for trying to defend myself was to be declared incompetent and my bitch of a mom ended up being made my guardian.

I told the judge that my mom was a bitch and that there was no way in hell that a walking, talking twat was going to speak for me; they could all go to hell if they thought I would let her. But the fat fucker in the black robe had me ball-gagged and dragged out of the courtroom.

I was found guilty, based purely on a single photograph of me holding what looked a gun, pointed at the ride. Purely circumstantial, if you ask me, but nobody did. The police did a piss test on my urine, too. I peed into the cup willingly; I had nothing to worry about, I've never done drugs in my life. I've wanted to, but I couldn't afford to. The report that came back from the lab said I had cocaine, heroin and meth in my blood, which is totally false. I was framed, pure and simple. There's no other way to explain it.

Now I guess the rest of my life is going to be wasted, rotting away here in the state forensic prison with a bunch of Gumps. Every time I try to explain to anyone what really happened to me, they strap me down and dope me up until I pass out.

Now I just keep my mouth shut.

There's nothing to do now but sit here and remember that god-damned day, over and over.

BANG. BANG. BANG.

Here we go again.

I closed my eyes, and leaned back against the white cinderblock wall; before I know it I'm back in my old bedroom, the wet pillow, the pizza, the Nard, the watch – well, you know the story.

The banging stopped. I opened my eyes. Then the door to my cell swung open and a guard poked his head in.

"Stop daydreaming about the mushroom princess, limp dick," he said. "Let's go. You got visitors, sugarplum."

He pushed me down the cellblock corridor to the visiting area, where there was a long line of windows and phones, and a bunch of folding chairs lined up in a row. I've been locked up for over a year now, but I'd never seen this area before; no need to, I guess, I've never had a visitor.

I like to imagine the reason Mom has never come to visit me is that she killed herself after I got sent away, overcome with grief and unwilling to go on. I always knew she was on the road to going completely bat-shit insane from her ongoing total lack of dick, and this happening to me probably pushed her over the edge.

The guard shoved me into the metal chair so hard that my butt bone made it ring like a bell. He handed me a phone so I could talk to my visitor. I began to complain, but then I saw who was sitting on the other side of the glass.

"Mom?"

I couldn't believe my eyes. She beamed at me, a big cheese-eating grin plastered on her face; I almost didn't recognize her. She looked years younger, slim, her hair styled, her teeth whitened; she almost looked *pretty*.

Then I realized who was sitting next to her.

"Why is the Nard with you?" I said into the receiver.

She turned and gave the Nard a look of such love and lust that I almost puked chunks, right then and there. Then she kissed him, right on the mouth.

"Oh Stephen, I'm so happy," she began to blather. "Joe and I got married last month," she said, holding up a finger with a big rock on it. "He's so wonderful. I wanted you to know that he's taking good care of me, which I need, especially after all you put me through, with your drugs and your murder and your porn. I think it's good that you're locked up, I just didn't want you to be worrying about me."

I stared at her in disgust. I didn't have anything else to say to that bitch, not now, not ever.

"Guard, I'm done here," I called, and dropped the phone back into the receiver.

The Nard leaned towards the glass and held up a magazine, smiling and pointing for me to look at it.

It was the latest issue of Nintendo Power. I couldn't resist. I would have given anything to have a copy of Nintendo Power to read in my cell. Hell, even a single page torn out of it would help to relieve the crushing boredom of nothing but four white walls.

The Nard held up his index finger, giving me a "wait a minute" gesture; then he began flipping through the pages.

When he found the page he was looking for, he pressed the magazine against the glass so I could see.

It was the Nintendo High Score World Rankings. He pointed to the top of the list. It read: *Joe King,*

Super Mario Brothers, World Champion.

He pointed to the words printed underneath his name.

Perfect Score. Unbeatable.

Then he took my mom into his arms and sucked her mouth into his. I could see his thick tongue as it stabbed at her lips. She closed her eyes in disgusting bliss as Short Bus munched away at her wrinkled pie hole. The bastard actually flipped me off while he kissed her, behind her back where she couldn't see what he was doing.

There wasn't much to say after that - not that they stuck around much longer, anyway. They probably got a room at the Motel 6 on the way home so Mom could stick her rotten clam chowder in his mouth. I hope the Nard chokes to death on it.

Goddamn it, Mom - if they ever let me out of here, it's gonna be pay back, I promise.

I'm going to kill you one of these days, you fuckin' bitch.

***

"PAY BACK" was originally titled "ME & THE NARD" upon release, but the brightly colored cover art and odd title kept sales low.

After changing the title and updating the cover art, sales took off and feedback started rolling in. The polarization of reader response to this story was amazing to behold; either people realized that the story was tongue-in-cheek humor and loved it, or they thought the pigheaded outlook of the narrator was shared by the author and were outraged by it.

Love it or hate it, it was a fucking blast to write. You can't please everybody all the time.

CURTAINS FOR LOVE

"PROMISE ME you'll take good care of her."

The old man leaned forward as he spoke, concern etched around the corners of his eyes. His wife, a frail woman, equally advanced in years, placed her hand reassuringly on his shoulder.

"George Hill, now really," she protested gently. "He's a good boy! You'll care for her, won't you James?"

She smiled at the well-groomed, youthful, thirty-year-old from across the small kitchen of the new retirement village apartment. His face shone brightly with excitement underneath a shock of thick dark hair.

James glanced at the real estate attorney sitting across from him, a frowning man, with an angular face, who tapped his fingers tersely atop the papers that needed to be signed. It was clear from his expression that he thought the deal was going south.

"It's important, Helen! You know how she is," the

old man snapped.

James decided it was time to get things back under control. He took the old man's hand into his own and gave it a gentle yet businesslike shake.

"I take my obligations very seriously, Mr. Hill," he said as his eyes met the old man's withering glare with unwavering confidence. "You have my word. I will uphold our agreement."

"And the curtains in the tower room?" the old man asked, for the third time in as many minutes. His voice was thick with skepticism.

"Not to be touched. Understood."

"Young man, those curtains are not to be taken down, not altered, not covered - nothing - or else the deal is off," Mr. Hill said stridently. "The maintenance company will be checking."

"I'm sure I wouldn't want to take them down even if I could," James said. "You made them yourself, didn't you Mrs. Hill?"

As the elderly wife nodded in reply, the old man's expression softened and he settled back into his seat with a palpable air of resignation.

"Let's get it signed," he mumbled.

Hearing this, the attorney perked up and quickly spread the papers out across the table.

"This is an incredible deal, Mr. Hill," James asked as he picked up the pen. "Are you sure you're okay with selling your house to me? I hope I'm not taking advantage."

"The truth is, James, we don't live there anymore and there's no one else we'd let have it. We'd give the house to you straight out if we could afford it," the old man said.

"She needs you James," Mrs. Hill agreed, "we

should have let you have her a long time ago. We were afraid that after all this time, you wouldn't want her anymore."

"Are you kidding?" James protested. "I've loved your house since I was little! I used to feel like I was in a magic castle whenever I came to play with Sophie."

A look of sadness passed over Mrs. Hill's face, as her daughter's name was spoken.

"Sophie wanted to marry you when she grew up - did you know that? She was so devastated when you moved away," Mrs. Hill said.

James shifted uncomfortably in his seat and let out a nervous little laugh, unsure of how he should respond.

Mr. Hill interrupted before he could speak.

"Martha, we don't need to talk about this," he said, taking his wife's hand. "You're going to scare him away, dear."

He turned to James.

"She's emotional in her old age, James, she doesn't mean any harm by it," he said apologetically.

"Your first love, your *true* love," Mrs. Hill mumbled, and a confused look clouded her eyes as she spoke. "If you'll excuse me, I think I'm going to make some tea now," she said, and stumbled away to rummage through the pantry.

"The stress of moving has been hard for her James, but we'll manage," Mr. Hill said sadly. "It's good that Martha and I can finally be alone. We've taken care of her for so long, but she's gotten older and has needs we can't tend to. I imagine taking care of her should come naturally, for a strong young man like you."

***

JAMES TOOK A LEFT onto Downing Avenue as he drove towards his new home. It was a quiet neighborhood, just a few blocks removed from the old Main Street of the small Ohio River town.

The area had an eclectic stew of homes – big and small, old and new – that ranged from century-old masterpieces to freshly built faux-vintage facsimiles, slapped up by repatriated suburbanites, during the building boom a couple of years earlier.

James pulled up in front of 1517 Downing Avenue, the grand-pappy of them all. It dominated the landscape with quiet stateliness.

His girlfriend Claire, a beautiful young woman with raven hair that glistened in the sunlight, was already waiting for him in the front yard. Even from a distance he could see excitement glimmering in her cinnamon eyes.

As he drank in her beauty, it suddenly occurred to him how much Claire reminded him of Sophie at that moment – that was, if Sophie had lived to see adulthood. He was surprised he had never noticed the similarity before. Maybe it was just seeing Claire waiting for him - there in the exact same spot that Sophie used to wait patiently when they were children - that made the resemblance so pronounced, he wasn't sure. But at that moment the only thing that kept Claire from looking exactly like a grown-up version of Sophie was the difference in their eyes: Claire's were dark reddish-brown, while Sophie's had been brilliant sapphire-blue.

The massive, Victorian-style, Queen Anne

loomed behind Claire, and made her seem very small by comparison. Its elegant three-story-tall tower culminated in a spire that soared into the sky, as though the house was giving a middle-finger salute to the inferior homes that surrounded it. The windows that circled the top floor of the tower were open and long cream-colored curtains streamed from them, flowing gently in a spring breeze.

James shut off the engine, and glanced across the street to a different, less proud abode, the house he had lived in for a time as a child.

That house was nothing like the one he had just bought. It was a rather depressing, dilapidated ranch with weathered white plank siding and crooked black shutters. Its weed-ridden lawn was a stark contrast to the manicured yard of the house he now owned.

The grass really is greener on the other side, he thought, *even though the little house has the better view.*

***

CLAIRE HAD BEEN WAITING nervously for him to get there for almost an hour. She couldn't believe that this was happening, that he had asked her to move in with him, that she had accepted instantly, without even thinking about it.

She wondered if a proposal could be far away. She hoped not. She had never met a man half as wonderful as James in her entire life. They had been dating for almost two years now, and if he didn't propose soon she was afraid she was going to be the one getting down on one knee and asking *him* to marry *her*.

She hoped it didn't come to that.

He had been sitting in the car for a few minutes, and he was already an hour late. Claire hoped he didn't have bad news about getting the house, or even worse - cold feet about her moving in with him.

Just when she couldn't stand the suspense any longer, James popped out of the car, triumphantly holding up a key for her to see.

"We got it!" he announced with his kind smile beaming broadly as she ran up and gave him a hug.

"Did you tell them I was going to be moving in with you or did you chicken out?" she asked.

"I might have fibbed a little," he said. "They're old and peculiar, and they still think of me as the little kid who lives across the street. They probably don't want any fornication going on inside their precious house – but I figure what they don't know, won't hurt them," he said, and smacked her lightly on the bottom.

"Cool it, lover boy," Claire said in a fake stern voice, laughing. "Race you to the porch!"

They dashed through the soft grass, stopping when they reached the front door to catch their breath as they admired the ornate trim work on the central tower, high above.

"Wow, look at my arm," she whispered. "I've got actual goose bumps. You did good, James, real good."

"Wait until you see inside," he said, slipping a thick old key into the door. It unlocked with a metallic pop.

Without warning, James scooped her up in his arms and carried her over the threshold into the house, setting her down on the mosaic tile in the oversized portico. They spun about like amazed children, the sound of their delight echoing among intricate arches high above. The painted ceiling of the living room to their right soared three stories high; a massive fireplace with an elegant mahogany mantle served as the imposing centerpiece.

"Can you believe this place?" Claire asked breathlessly.

"I told you it was amazing," James said. "Come on, let's look around."

They were off, drifting from one room to the next in a slipstream of excitement. They explored the expansive kitchen and the stately dining room, before chasing each other up the grand staircase that curved along the portico wall to the second floor.

At the top of the stairs, there was a walkway across a balcony that overlooked the entrance. That, in turn, led to an alcove, in the center of which rose an ornate wrought-iron spiral staircase; and just beyond that, a long hallway lined with bedrooms on either side.

Claire strode past the spiral staircase into the hall, glancing into the bedrooms on either side, as she went. One of the rooms caught her eye, and she stepped inside to take a look.

It was a spacious bedroom, if a bit old fashioned. Two large windows allowed plenty of sunlight to illuminate the sheen of the polished wood floor; cloth wall coverings muted the sound of her footsteps, making it rather cozy.

She thought it was perfect.

"Hey James, I think I found our master bedroom," she said.

"Oh yeah? Be there in a sec," he called from somewhere down the hall.

Claire walked to one of the windows and

admired the view of the gorgeous front yard. It was lushly planted with flowering bushes, many already in full bloom.

A rusted iron cross, about two feet tall, jutted from the ground near the base of the tower. It struck her as odd, and seemed out of place in the otherwise well-groomed yard.

"Hey James, come take a look at this," she called.

He didn't answer.

"James?" she called again. Her voice sounded small in her ears, as though the words were being consumed by the empty house the instant they slipped from her lips. A profound stillness settled upon the hall and she suddenly felt uncomfortable.

Feeling anxious, but unsure why, Claire ran into the hallway, hoping to find James in one of the other bedrooms, but they were all empty. She ran down the hall, back to the alcove where she had last seen him, the emptiness of the house seeming to grow more oppressive with each step she took.

She stopped at the base of the spiral staircase and looked up to the top, calling for James again; still no reply.

Not wanting to be alone any longer, Claire bounded up the stairs, her throbbing heart beating loudly in her ears as she went. It was a sound that was alive, a sound she was extraordinarily delighted to hear.

When she reached the top of the stairs, she found herself confronted by a closed door. A soft wind whistled through the narrow slit between the bottom of the door and the floor. It occurred to her that this was the door to the room at the top of the tower, where the windows had been open and the curtains billowing in the breeze.

The door creaked loudly on its hinges as she turned the handle and pushed it inwards.

"James?" Claire whispered as she entered the room.

He was there, standing by an enormous window, eyes closed as though in a state of bliss. The sweet mingled scents of jasmine and honeysuckle found their way into the room through the open windows, the sweetest fragrance she had ever smelled.

In the middle of the room, silken curtains floated upwards, gently brushing against James. The curtains flowed around his body, almost sensual in their caress.

James took one of the curtains in his hand and began to absently rub it against his face, moaning softly as it touched his skin. As the warm air rustled through the sheer fabric, it made a sound that was almost like a sigh of pleasure in response.

"What the hell are you doing?" Claire asked sharply. Her voice startled James, interrupting his reverie. He released the curtain he had been holding and as it fell away the breeze died with it.

"Sorry," James said sheepishly as he took her hand. "I think I drifted off for a minute."

The tower room was gorgeous, ringed with five enormous windows that rose from the floor to the ceiling. The front-facing window was emblazoned with a single, crimson, stained-glass heart in its center.

The ceiling came to a pointed peak about twenty-five feet above them, the steepest point supported by intricately carved arches. The walls were painted in a soft pastel pink, trimmed in glossy cream.

Claire thought it would be the perfect room for a little girl, a place to pretend to be a princess, locked away in a castle.

The resplendent curtains that graced each window were the room's most striking feature by far, however. They were beautiful, each of the five panels unique and gorgeous in its own way. The curtains were an elaborate patchwork, composed of a variety of different fabrics mingled with cream-colored silk and lace embroidery with bits of iridescent pearl inlay, which flowed gracefully as they shimmered, sensually dancing in the sunlight.

One of the curtains even had two round beads of sapphire-blue glass set into the fabric, and these jewel-like baubles cast thin strips of blue-tinted refracted sunlight across the polished floor.

Four parallel grooves had been worn into the hardwood floor by the front window, and James thought of Mr. and Mrs. Hill in their rocking chairs at the retirement condo.

They must have rocked away at that window for years, he thought to himself.

From the driveway below came a long, loud honk. The moving truck had arrived.

Claire poked her head out of the window.

"Be right down," she yelled to the movers.

"Come on James, time to get to work," she said and ran out of the room, the sound of her rapid footsteps fading away as she descended the spiral staircase.

James took one last look out of the window, past the red stained-glass heart at the street he had grown up on as a boy. It was hard for him to believe so much time had passed, that he was already a man, the owner of the incredible house he had admired so much as a child.

The soothing spring breeze had not returned and without it the old curtains lay lifeless and unmoving. The silk fabric looked worn and the lace faded, not nearly as beautiful as they had seemed moments before.

Claire poked her head back into the room.

"You coming or not?" she asked impatiently. "The movers need to know where you want them to put stuff."

James took her hand and followed her down the stairs.

***

HOURS LATER, darkness descended on 1517 Downing Avenue. The movers had littered the rooms with a maze of boxes and scattered pieces of furniture. Unplugged floor lamps congregated in dark corners like department store mannequins after closing time.

In the master bedroom, a mattress on the floor had been the best they could manage for their first night in the house. Claire patted an empty spot beside her as James walked into the room, carrying three precariously stacked boxes.

"Come to bed," she said. "We can finish tomorrow. We've got all weekend to unpack, and I'm cold – come warm me up," she purred.

James sat the boxes down carefully and massaged his lower back as he straightened back up. He cast a longing glance at the mattress, where Claire waited for him.

"Are you sure? It doesn't feel like we've gotten

anything done."

"Just come lay with me," she said, stroking her fingertips softly along the sheets on his side of the bed.

"Okay, but just for a minute," James said, slipping off his shoes. He plopped onto the mattress beside her and let out a loud sigh of relief.

"Oh my god, this feels so good," he moaned. "I'm not sure I'll be able to get back up again."

Claire gently pulled his face towards hers and kissed him.

"Oh no, you've uncovered my evil master plan," she laughed and started unbuttoning his shirt. She kissed him again, harder this time.

He pretended to struggle to get away and she jumped on top of him, pinning him down to the bed by his wrists.

"You're not going anywhere, mister," she breathed into his ear as she nibbled down the side of his neck.

He felt a burst of energy surge through him. He wrestled her onto her back before kissing her deeply - tasting her lips, feeling her tongue on his. She arched her back, pushing herself towards him as he worked on slipping her blouse off over her head.

A loud knocking sound from somewhere outside the bedroom broke the mood. Claire jolted up, alarmed.

"Did you hear that?" she asked James. "I think somebody's at the door."

He moaned softly and continued kissing down the side of her breast, ignoring her.

"James, stop!" She shoved him away with her feet to get his attention.

"What?" he said.

"I think somebody's at the door."

"I didn't hear anything."

Just then the knocking began again, harder than before; after a few seconds, it stopped.

"There. See?" Claire said.

"So what? I don't want to answer it."

She crossed her arms and frowned at him.

"Please go see who it is – what if it's important?" she said earnestly.

The knocking resumed, this time so loudly it sounded like someone was trying to break the door in. Claire shoved him hard towards the edge of the bed with her feet, eyes wide as saucers.

"Okay, fine, I'll go," he grumbled as he slipped on a pair of jeans. "It had better be Ed McMahon with a giant million dollar check, though, or I'm going to be pissed."

The knocking continued unabated as he ran into the dark hallway barefoot, zipping his pants as he went.

"I'm coming, hold on a minute," he yelled down the stairs, and the knocking stopped, mercifully.

He ran down the curved grand staircase into the foyer, flipped on the porch light and opened the door. He stuck his head out into the night, fully expecting to find an overeager neighbor clutching a fruitcake, but the front porch was empty.

"Hello?" he called into the darkness.

Then the knocking began anew, furious and violent. It was coming from somewhere in the house, somewhere behind him.

Upstairs, he thought.

He slammed the front door closed with his foot

and raced back up the stairs, stopping when he reached the alcove by the spiral staircase to listen. The knocking was coming from up there - the tower room – and it was urgent, insistent.

He grabbed the handrail and sprinted up the stairs, the banging sound growing louder with each step. The door to the tower room stood open wide.

Inside, the large windows had all been flung open wide, except for the one with the stained glass heart in the middle. The long curtains sparkled, iridescent with ghastly beauty in the moonlight, and swirled in the gale wind that howled through the window, as though straining to break free from the rods that held them captive.

In the dim light, James spotted the source of the racket. It was a solitary picture frame that smacked loudly back and forth against the wall as it was buffeted by the breeze.

James pushed his way through the tangle of flying curtains to close the windows, hoping to shut out the wind and silence the din. The curtains assaulted him from all sides, wrapping around his arms, brushing his legs, the silky softness of fabric sliding against his skin. The cloth was smooth, sensual as it caressed him, embraced him.

As he reached up to close the first window a strangely warm gust of spring air scented with jasmine and honeysuckle rushed in, tousling his hair. He thought he heard his name softly spoken, almost imperceptible, as the wind whistled in his ears. He hesitated before closing the window.

"Jamie," the wind seemed to say in an ethereal voice as light and wispy as the curtains themselves. He hadn't heard that name since he was a child, not

since he moved away and insisted new friends address him as "James", which was much more grown-up.

The curtains billowed around him like whirling dervishes in the wind, the picture frame loud and unrelenting in its pounding against the wall.

He felt a presence behind him, moving stealthily into the room in the darkness behind him, and he spun around to find a dark silhouette framed in the tower room doorway.

"James!" the shadowy figure shouted, and in that instant a light fixture burst into brilliant bloom overhead, revealing a panicked Claire panting in the doorway. James jumped back, startled, the back of his knees slamming against the window sill. His legs buckled under him, causing him to pitch backwards, out of the open window. He grabbed onto the side of the frame just in time to stop himself from falling three stories to the lawn below.

"Dammit, Claire, you almost killed me!" he gasped as he pulled himself carefully back into the room. He stepped away from the open window and let out a loud sigh of relief.

"You didn't come back and I was worried," Claire said. "Are you okay?"

The instant she spoke, the wind that had been howling through the room died away, and the flowing curtains fell sullenly into place over the windows.

The picture frame that had been causing the commotion smacked loudly against the wall one final time and came to rest. For a moment, everything in the room was quiet and still.

"Is that where the knocking was coming from?"

Claire asked, pointing at the framed photo. James nodded in silent agreement.

"I must have forgotten to close the windows," he said, shaking his head in bewilderment. "I could have sworn I closed them," he said as he shut and locked the windows one by one.

As he slid the last window closed, the picture on the wall behind him broke free from its hook and fell to the floor, breaking the silence of the tower room as it landed with a shattering crash.

Claire jumped into James' arms for comfort, both of them still jittery from the unexpected commotion.

They both stared, wide-eyed and incredulous for a moment, at the frame that lay face-down on the floor, before looking at each other and laughing.

Claire turned the fallen picture over carefully. Behind jagged lines of freshly shattered glass was a faded photograph, two children - a freckled boy with thick messy hair, and a smiling girl with dark raven hair and bright blue eyes. In one hand, the girl grasped a bouquet of wildflowers and with the other she clutched the boy's hand. She wore a ring of daisies in her hair.

Claire held up the picture for him to see, careful not to knock the glass out of the frame.

"Aren't they cute?" she exclaimed, "I wonder who they are?"

James examined the picture for a moment.

"That's me, when I was a boy," he said. "I'm surprised I didn't notice that picture when we were up here earlier."

"That's you? Really? You were a handsome little devil," Claire said. "A hit with the ladies, too, if the crush in that little girl's eyes is any indication. She looks like she's head over heels in love with my man. Do I need to find her grown-up self and kick her ass?" Claire asked jokingly.

"No, I don't think any grudge matches will be needed," he said with a wink. "I haven't seen her for years. That little girl lived here a long time ago, back when I lived across the street. I moved away not long after this picture was taken, actually – I'm sure she's long gone as well."

"Well you better keep it that way, mister," Claire laughed. "I don't need some long lost love of yours trying to steal you away, now that you're back in the old neighborhood."

"Well, nobody could ever steal me away from you," James said, as he pulled her body tightly against his, kissing her deeply.

***

A LITTLE LATER THAT EVENING, James finally fell asleep, with Claire snuggled against him, her head resting on his chest.

Long moonbeams streamed through the windows, stretching like ghostly arms through the darkness to the dresser across from the mattress where they slept. James had placed the faded photo from the tower room there, and the moonlight bathed it in a pale glow, illuminating the young faces, captured as they smiled through the cracked glass, frozen in a state of eternal childhood bliss.

Then James began to dream.

In his dream he was ten years old again, living across the street in the run-down single story ranch. He was walking out the front door of his old house, down the sidewalk, heading towards the big house at 1517 Downing Street.

His dream was like an old home movie; the colors were faded, the picture was a little warped, but it felt real. The afternoon sun was hot on his skin as it browned his freckles.

In the dream, James looked across the street and saw Sophie, waiting for him in her front yard. The colors of everything around her were washed out like an old photo, but she radiated light - especially her eyes. They burned brilliant and blue.

Sophie looked sad.

He waved to her and she waved back, her expression brightening when she saw him. Her beauty was so stunning it made him dizzy. He felt a longing rise inside him that he didn't understand, perhaps the gentle tug of prepubescent lust, a vague desire to hold her, to have her.

He waited for a shiny new El Camino to pass before he crossed the street to where Sophie waited for him.

"Where have you been, Jamie? I've been so lonely," Sophie said as he ran up to her. He was confused.

"What do you mean? I haven't been anywhere," he said.

"I've been waiting for you for so long," she said, with a plaintive sigh. "For a while I thought maybe you were never coming back."

"I don't know what you're talking about," he said. "I've just been at my house. Come on, let's go play."

He nodded towards her back yard, but she had more questions.

"Who was that girl with you? Do you have family visiting?" she asked.

Ten-year-old James turned and looked at his house across the street. He scrunched his face up, still confused.

"Are you going cuckoo?" he asked playfully. "There's no girl at my house except for my mom."

She smiled and stuck her tongue out at him like he was a meanie.

"I missed you, Jamie," she said and took his hand in hers. Her touch caused his heart to start pounding. "You better never leave me again."

She smiled at him so sweetly it made him want to kiss her right there and then, but he didn't.

"Come on, I want to show you something," Sophie said, tugging his arm eagerly.

Laughing, they ran through his dream world, hand in hand; around the big house to the back yard they went, through rows of trellised ivy and her father's neatly manicured garden. They ran all the way to the woods at the edge of the yard, where the lush green grass gave way to fallen pine needles and scrub.

Sophie led James along a footpath that wound through the woods. It was a path they had worn into the soft peat with thousands of footfalls, as they had run through the trees and underbrush, playing.

At the end of the path stood the playhouse they had built, the summer before, using discarded pieces of plywood and fallen branches. They had furnished it with stools and overturned buckets, and created a thatched roof with thick layers of pine straw. It was a little house, nestled in the woods, just for them.

Its appearance had changed from the way James

remembered it. Its roof was decorated with dozens of brilliantly colored flowers. Pine cones had been lined up in two neat parallel rows, creating a walkway that led up to a cloth door made of red gingham, remnants of a baby blanket, tattered from years of being cherished.

Sophie led him to a spot she had chosen in front of the playhouse, then stopped and turned to face him. James noticed that they were standing in the middle of a ring of white stones, arranged around them in the shape of a heart on the ground.

She took his hands in hers and looked up at him, her bright blue eyes shining with love.

"Jamie, will you marry me?" she asked. Nervousness crackled in the edges of her voice.

James was unprepared for this question, and he simply stared at her for a moment without saying a word, stunned. He could feel love radiating from her, like prickly heat on his skin. It felt so good that he thought he might die happy, right there and then.

"Of course I would marry you," he said.

"I love you so much, Jamie!" she squealed and kissed him.

Like any ten-year-old boy, he reflexively wiped the kiss away, but she kissed him again. This time he returned it, putting his arms around her, pulling her close.

"Promise you'll never leave me again?" she whispered.

"Promise," he swore.

In his dream they spent an imaginary afternoon lying about in the sun, wondering about their future, talking how they would raise a family together in her big house someday, laughing about what names they would give their children.

Later, Sophie sang a lullaby to her baby doll while Jamie braided a ring of daisies for her. After a while, tired from playing, they curled up together in a cozy corner of the playhouse, her head nestled in the crook of his arm.

Then James fell even deeper into sleep, into that dark place where dreams dare not follow.

***

IN THE MORNING James was awakened by Claire, who was calling him from somewhere in the house.

He didn't want to get up and instead covered his eyes with his arm and groaned. He felt like he hadn't slept a bit. The mattress was hard as a rock and he was freezing cold.

He tugged at the thin blanket to try and better cover himself, but it was stuck. He grudgingly opened his eyes to the bright sunlight and sat up to face the day.

As his sleepy eyes began to focus, a woozy feeling of disorientation washed over him. He was in the tower room, the bottom edge of a long curtain draped across him. His mind reeled as he tried to imagine how he could have gotten there in his sleep. He clearly remembered falling asleep in the bedroom downstairs the night before.

Claire called again. He tossed the curtain aside and got to his feet.

"I'm upstairs," he called back. Within seconds she was making her way up the iron staircase, her footsteps clanging loudly with each step.

James quickly started opening the windows, as

though that was what he had been doing all along.

Claire took one look at his puffy face and wrinkled clothes and frowned.

"You look like hell. What are you doing?"

"Cleaning up from last night," he lied. "I'm going to take a shower and go pick up some things for the house. You okay by yourself for a little while?"

Claire shrugged.

"The next door neighbor stopped by. She said the 'welcoming committee' is coming by to get acquainted."

"You want me here for that?" James asked.

"Seriously? If I were you, I'd get out of the hen house fast. Neighborhood gossip, nosy housewives poking through our house looking for hidden dark secrets," she laughed. "Why would you want to miss that?"

***

AN HOUR LATER, Claire was sitting in the kitchen surrounded by a dozen women, the assortment of baked goods they'd brought spread out before her. A peace offering from the natives, she thought, as she eyed them warily. She had never trusted women that ran in packs.

"I can't believe the Hills actually sold this house and moved out," said a plump lady, with a nest of bleached blonde hair and a questionable sense of fashion to match. "I always figured they would die here and nobody would find their bodies until months later."

"I know!" chimed in another woman with knee-high leather boots and earrings so long they touched her shoulders. "They were so weird!" she exclaimed, touching Claire on the thigh.

"Honestly, I don't know them at all," Claire said. "They called James out of the blue and asked if he wanted to buy their house. I don't think he had spoken to them since he was a boy. He used to live in the house across the street, you know."

"How strange!" the women grew hushed and leaned in to learn more.

"James always loved this house when he was a kid, but never dreamed he would be able to buy it someday. But they made him an offer he just couldn't refuse," Claire continued.

"Why did they want him to have the house? I'm sure they could have sold this place for a mint," blonde fashion disaster said.

A lady decked out in a hot pink spandex workout suit with black stripes spoke up. "I saw the old curtains still up in the tower," she said. "Are you planning to change them?"

Claire gave her a look.

"It's funny that you ask. That was the one condition made when we bought the house, to agree never to take down those curtains," she said. "They're actually paying someone to check up on us to make sure we don't take them down? It's bizarre."

The lady with the boots seemed excited to have an excuse to put her hand on Claire's leg again, and she took full advantage of it.

"Nobody told you?" she said sympathetically, as she stroked Claire's knee.

"Told me what?" Claire asked as she tried to scoot away.

"About those curtains…and the little girl," Touchy

Boots said and gave Pink Spandex a knowing look. "Should I tell her, or do you want to?"

"You tell her," Pink Spandex said.

A hush fell over the room as the women leaned forward to watch Claire's expression as she heard the tale.

"All right, I'll tell you what I know," said Touchy Boots mysteriously. She rubbed Claire's inner thigh reassuringly, until Claire scooted away.

"The people that lived in this house were very successful in life and they had waited until they were fairly advanced in age to have a child, a little girl. Her name was Sophie. They cherished her. "

"I saw a photo of her," Claire said. "James said they were friends when he was little."

"Best friends. Inseparable," Touchy Boots clarified. "They used to go around telling everyone they were married when they were only like in the third grade, or something."

The women tittered as Boots announced that.

"Sophie loved to spend time up in the tower room. When I was younger, I would see her there, dancing and spinning next to the big glass windows."

Boots paused dramatically, letting the story sink in before continuing.

"Mrs. Hill made special curtains for the tower room as a surprise for her daughter. She showed them off to everyone while she was making them."

"So what's the big deal about the curtains, anyway?" Claire said, eager to get to the point.

"Well, this is where the story gets weird," Touchy Boots said. "One day, before the curtains were finished, Sophie was dancing in the tower room, spinning around. She tripped over a doll and smashed through the front window. She fell three stories to the ground. Died instantly in the front yard. There's a rusty cross that still marks the exact spot."

Claire shuddered. "That's terrible," she said. "James never told me any of this."

"He probably thought you'd freak out and he had the deal of a lifetime on his dream house," Fashion Disaster speculated.

Boots continued.

"You know the stained glass heart? Sophie fell through that very window," Boots said. "After she died Mr. and Mrs. Hill became total recluses. They sat rocking in their chairs staring out that window day after day, year after year. They never got over it."

A large woman in beige pants and a golf shirt, who had sat in silence until now, decided to chime in.

"I don't think they ever accepted the fact that their little girl was dead," she said. "I used to see Mr. Hill carrying toys into the house from time to time."

"What does any of this have to do with the curtains?" Claire asked impatiently.

"Oh yeah, the curtains - that's where the story goes from weird to downright bizarre," Boots replied. "Mrs. Hill kept working on those curtains after Sophie died, adding on to them, making them longer, more ornate. A lot of rumors are floating around about those curtains, but nobody knows for sure what's true or not."

"Like what?" Claire asked.

"Well," Boots continued, "I heard that Mrs. Hill used cloth from the dress Sophie died in to make them, for one thing."

"I heard that Sophie's head was shaved before the burial and Mrs. Hill braided her hair into the trimming," Pink Spandex said.

Fashion Disaster perked up, eager to add to the tale. "I heard Mrs. Hill had the funeral home pull off Sophie's fingernails and toenails and save them for her. She polished them up and used them as mother-of-pearl inlay on one of the curtains."

Claire gave everyone a skeptical look, then burst out laughing.

"You guys had me going for a minute," she laughed, looking around the room hopefully, for signs of jest. "You don't believe any of that stuff, do you?" she laughed.

But the women only stared back at her in solemn silence.

"Honestly - you ladies really believe those stories?" Claire said. "I'm sorry, but to me it sounds like an absurd urban legend, foisted on two old people who led a very tragic life."

"I hope you're right," Touchy Boots said as she gave Claire's leg a final squeeze.

"Come on ladies, we've wasted enough of Claire's time with our silly stories. I'm sure you need to get back to your unpacking, dear. If you need anything – *anything*," she said with a knowing wink, "Please let *me* be the first to know."

***

WHEN JAMES GOT BACK from the store, Claire was waiting for him on the front porch, arms crossed. She glared at him while he retrieved the groceries from the back seat.

"You weren't going to tell me?" she said, following him as he carried the bags into the kitchen.

"Tell you what?"

"That a little girl *died in this house*?"

James sighed with relief.

"Claire, that was a long time ago - and it wasn't *inside* the house," he protested.

"It wasn't fair, not to tell me," she insisted. "It made me feel like an idiot having to learn about it from the neighbors. You could have told me last night, when the picture of the little girl who died fell off the wall. That would have been the perfect opportunity, don't you think?"

He placed the bags on the counter and walked over to her, taking her into his arms. She pulled away from him.

"I'm sorry. I just didn't think it was a big deal," he said with remorse. "It's not like there was a mass murder in this house or something - a little girl had an accident and died, a very long time ago. It's sad, but it happens. Forgive me?"

She turned and looked at him with hurt filled eyes.

"Done. Forgiven," she said and kissed him quickly on the lips. "Are you absolutely sure there are no more secrets? I was kind of rushed into moving in here with you, you know - and I hate surprises."

"Really?" James said as he walked over to the counter and reached into a bag. "Because I do have one more little surprise. But if you hate surprises, it can wait."

He paused, keeping his hand in the bag, a playful spark twinkled in his eye.

"You've got a surprise in *that* bag? *For me*?" Claire asked, smiling slyly. "Yeah, right. What is it, a big cucumber?"

James pulled his hand slowly from the paper grocery bag. In it he held a small velvet box.

"I've been waiting for the right time to ask you this, but the more I think about it the only time that seems like the right time is right now," he said and got down on one knee in front of her.

"Claire Sheppard, I can't live another day without knowing that the rest of my life will be by your side. Will you marry me?" he asked, eyes eager and full of love.

"You big dummy," she said, and hit him playfully on the top of his head. "Yes, of course I'll marry you! But our gossipy neighbors will be disappointed to learn that we've quit shacking up."

***

JAMES WAS AWAKENED by a whisper in his ear as he slept beside his new fiancé later that night.

"*What?*" he asked Claire, irritated at being woken up, but she was sound asleep. He sat up and squinted at the alarm clock on the dresser across the room. It was two o'clock in the morning, the middle of the night.

Something moved at the edge of his vision, in the dark hallway just outside the bedroom door – not much more than a flicker of static in the shadows. He figured the dim light was playing tricks on his tired eyes, ignored it, and lay back down.

He closed his eyes but heard a whisper again, calling his name softly from somewhere outside the room.

James slipped quietly out of bed, careful not to wake Claire. He padded to the doorway and stuck his head into the hall, listening.

Then he heard it again, a singsong voice calling, clearer this time.

I need you, Jamie, I'm so lonely.

A soft breeze blew through the hallway, carrying the scent of jasmine and honeysuckle, intoxicating.

Words floated in the gentle wind, plaintive, wretchedly sorrowful.

Come to me, Jamie.

James followed the voice down the hall to the alcove. He began to slowly ascend the circular iron steps, afraid of what he might find, but unable to resist the urge to know.

He stepped into the darkness of the tower room. Every window was open wide, even though James knew he had locked them, had double-checked them. The five curtains writhed in the balmy breeze, illuminated by the light of the moon.

The wind gusted as James walked further into the room, lifting the curtains into the air to greet him. Sheer fabric and lace careened around him, caressing him. Every touch was a spark on his naked skin that sent shivers of pleasure through him. Rather than being frightened, he felt himself growing aroused.

The curtains seemed to grow longer as they swayed about him. James watched, enthralled, as the five curtains floated up into the air and met in the middle of the room. When the ends touched, the cloth began to twirl, twisting together as though alive, lengthening and taking shape until the solid mass of fabric grew long enough to touch the floor in front of him.

The mass of twisting curtains pulsed with desire. The column of cloth continued to take form as he watched, like soft clay being molded by invisible hands, some parts tightening, others separating, curving, straightening. At last a pale silken specter stood before him, wearing a little white dress, sheets of white curtains flowing out from its head like hair to the curtain rods above the windows.

James recognized the figure instantly. Ten-year-old Sophie gazed at him, her brilliant sapphire eyes gleaming with a fire of deep longing in the moonlight.

"I knew you would come back for me," she said, her little voice drowning in hope. "You promised you would never leave me, remember?"

James took a step back away from her, unsteady on his feet, unsure if he was awake or dreaming.

"Please don't let the lonely take my heart again," little Sophie pleaded.

"I don't understand," he stammered.

"You will, Jamie, I promise. I love you so much."

James stared in awe, mesmerized, at the little girl standing before him, so perfectly formed from curtains that glimmered as they flowed in the warm spring breeze.

"I'm not a little girl any more, Jamie. I just wanted you to see me as you remembered me. I'm all grown up now, and I need you so bad," she said, and let out a groan of desire that echoed through the rafters high above.

Little Sophie disappeared as the curtains swirled apart in the wind. After a moment the curtains came together once again, twisting and sculpting themselves into the most beautiful woman he had ever seen. She was naked, the silken skin of her swollen breasts iridescent as they glistened in the moonlight.

She held out her slender arms and a deep desire flooded through him, hot and uncomfortable in its intensity. Her full lips parted as she mouthed the words *come to me,* not asking, but demanding.

He was unable to resist. He practically ran to her and was immediately swallowed up in her silken embrace, the sensuous cloth of her being flowing around every part of his body, ichor pulsing warmly through her veins.

For hours they were lost in the rapture of each other's arms until, at last, James collapsed, satisfied and spent onto a bed of silk and satin on the tower room floor.

***

CLAIRE FOUND HIM THE NEXT MORNING, naked and snoring on the hardwood floor in the tower room, his clothes tossed into a messy pile in the corner.

"What the fuck, James?" she asked, as she prodded him awake with her foot. "What the hell are you doing?"

James sat up and rubbed his eyes, remembering what had happened the night before.

He quickly surveyed the room, but everything looked normal. The curtains all hung neatly from their wooden rods, the windows closed.

"I don't know," he said sheepishly. "I guess I came up to check the windows and fell asleep."

Claire inspected the room with a look of disdain. "I hate these curtains," she said. "I want them taken down. They give me the creeps."

After James showered and dressed, they said nothing more about the awkward incident; but Claire was quieter than usual throughout the rest of the day.

James' thoughts continued to drift back to what had happened in the tower room the night before. He knew it couldn't have been real, Sophie was long dead. But the passion that had been ignited inside him was very real and still throbbed; he desperately craved her touch, her satin caress. Even the thought of it aroused him.

Several times that day he crept back to the tower room, vaguely hoping to find something there. But each time he found nothing but an empty room and old curtains, hanging limply from the rods. Once he quietly opened a window to see if a fresh breeze might bring them to life, but the air outside was strangely still.

***

THAT NIGHT, James was once again awakened. The same voice, floating through the darkness, softly calling his name. Without hesitation he slipped from his bed and went eagerly to the tower room, unsure if he was truly awake or still dreaming.

The silken apparition was already fully formed and mobile in the room, sheets of hair flowing up to the rods behind her, her silken skin sparkling. The only clothing she wore was a sheer shroud, wrapped tightly around her sensual hips.

Tonight, something was different. The room was frigid, the scent of the air antiseptic.

Sophie swirled around to greet him, her blue eyes glowing with an icy fire.

"I won't share you," she declared. "It's her or me."

"What would you have me do?" James asked.

"Trade her life for mine," she said. "Bring her to me now and I will pull her breath inside of me, so I can be yours for always."

"I can't do that," he said "I love you, Sophie, I always have, you know that. But I can't hurt Claire, I won't. I love her, too. It's not right."

She turned away from him in anger, the loose fabric edges of her body rippling in the breeze, as she rose, streaming through the air towards the rafters. After several moments of billowing furiously about, her fit of jealous rage seemed to subside.

"I understand," she said, softly, resignation in her voice. "You always were a kind man, Jamie."

As she spoke, a warm wind blew through the windows once more and the scent of sweet jasmine on the breeze washed away the sterility of her anger in an instant.

She floated down to him like an angel on soft clouds, her smile a string of pearls in the moonlight.

"Then take me one last time," she said sweetly as she gently guided his lips to her silken breast, "and I will bother you no more."

Unable to resist, he took her into his arms, her porcelain body unfurling into sheets that wrapped around him, locking onto his every limb. Overcome with ecstasy, he collapsed with her onto the floor, consumed by passion.

Knowing this would be their last time together for the rest of eternity, James poured every ounce of his love and lust into their final coupling, entwined with her for hours until finally, spent and satisfied, sleep once again pulled him into the deep.

***

IN THE MORNING James awoke, relieved to find himself in his own bed and not on the cold floor of the tower room again. He rolled over to snuggle with Claire, but her side of the bed was empty and cold.

Panic filled him and he felt his heart clench tight like a fist. *Had she seen him with Sophie last night?*

A faint smell of acrid smoke stung his nostrils, and James jumped from the bed, alarmed. Something was burning.

"Claire?" he called in a panic, but received no response.

He ran to the end of the hallway and glanced up the spiral stairs. The door to the tower room was open wide.

He bounded up the stairs and into the room, but it was empty. Individual beams of sunlight were outlined in the light smoke that was beginning to cloud the air, but he saw no fire - not in this room, anyway.

He felt relief for a split second and then the realization struck him: the curtains were gone. Every rod in the room had been stripped from the walls, as though the curtains had been torn down in a rage.

"Claire!" he yelled again as a sickening feeling spread from his stomach and into his legs. His body suddenly felt like it weighed a thousand pounds. It wasn't supposed to end this way.

Then he heard a faint reply. It was Claire.

"I'm downstairs, in the living room."

James suddenly wished he hadn't found her, wished that she had gone, had left him instead. Now he would have to face her, would have to try and explain what she had undoubtedly seen him doing with Sophie the night before.

He had been such a fool, and for what? A figment of his own imagination? A lingering memory that refused to fade away into the dust of time as it should?

Claire was hunched over the massive fireplace, her back to James as she intently prodded something that burned there with a long iron poker. Thin tendrils of smoke streamed from the fireplace out into the living room.

James quietly walked across the room and stood beside her. "I think you need to open the flue," he said softly and turned the lever to allow the smoke to escape into the chimney.

Claire didn't say a word, just continued watching intently as the fire consumed the fabric, turning it from white to brown to a bright glowing red for an instant before it crumbled into a deep black ash.

"What are you doing?" James asked as casually as he could manage, even though he knew full well already.

"I'm getting rid of these nasty old rags. I spoke to Mr. and Mrs. Hill; they said we don't need to keep them hanging up anymore," she said, her voice surprisingly bright and cheerful. James was confused.

"They said you could get rid of the curtains? They didn't at least want them back?" he asked.

"No. They said to burn them. They're coming over this morning to visit, by the way" Claire said. Her voice was full of life and joy. "They want to make sure we're both going to be happy here, together, for a long time."

"So you're not angry?" he asked, still so nervous

that his stomach felt like a garbage disposal grinding tin cans. Maybe she hadn't seen him in the tower room with Sophie after all?

Claire set the iron poker down by the fireplace, then turned and embraced him, holding him closer than she ever had before. She laid her head on his shoulder and breathed in his scent deeply.

"Are you kidding?" she said as she held him tight. "I'm getting married to the love of my life and living in my dream house – what reason on earth would I have to be angry?"

James let out a sigh of relief and put his arms around her, nestling his face in her hair. It smelled of jasmine and honeysuckle. She felt so alive, so vibrant to his touch, almost trembling.

"So the old folks let you get rid of the curtains," he said bemusedly as he watched the fire consume the last bits of lace and fabric. In the bottom of the fireplace he spotted the two jewels that had been embroidered into the curtains. The heat and smoke of the fire had turned their bright sapphire-blue into a dull cinnamon-brown.

Claire noticed him looking away and placed her hand gently against his cheek.

"Hey, look at me," she said, drawing his lips to hers.

As James kissed her, he gazed deeply into her bright sapphire-blue eyes, so full of life, and he knew the truth.

"True love endures," she whispered.

***

A NOTE ABOUT *CURTAINS FOR LOVE*

Most stories start as small ideas, only growing over time through much nurturing and love as the writer tries to spark life into dead words to bring a new reality into existence.

Some stories, though, arrive without warning, fully formed from out of nowhere, begging to be set free upon the page. As an author the task of liberating these spontaneous incarnations is more akin to being a scribe rather than creator, simply the process of writing down something that already exists.

CURTAINS FOR LOVE is one of those stories. I was driving, music was playing. I distinctly remember it was the first time I had heard a song called THE LONELY by Christina Perri. As the music played, a bright flash of light burst into my consciousness and this entire story, every bit, arrived as a complete entity in my head and demanded to be set free.

I feverishly made several pages of notes, hoping I wouldn't lose what I had been given so unexpectedly and over the following days the entire tale was put to paper.

I'm not sure what to make of this story. I know it came from me, but still it doesn't quite feel like mine. I have no idea what it means, or if it means anything. Sometimes I love it and sometimes I don't, but it was a gift from somewhere and so I want to share it with you.

So how did an alternate ending come about then? After sharing the finished story with others, the general consensus was that the original ending was a bit, well, challenging. Eventually, I made the tough decision to change it to the final version published here, and I think the story is more satisfying as a result. But since this story came to me as a complete package from somewhere, I wanted to include the original conclusion along with it too, so you can decide for yourself which ending you like best.

If you love the ending you already read, then I suggest you not read the alternate ending that follows.

But if you enjoy treading deeper into darkness, then by all means, venture on.

Thank you for reading.

-Evans Light

CURTAINS FOR LOVE
ORIGINAL ALTERNATE ENDING

(picking up from final section)

...Unable to resist, he took Sophie into his arms, her porcelain body unfurling into sheets that wrapped around him, locking onto his every limb. Overcome with ecstasy, he collapsed with her onto the floor, consumed by passion.

Knowing this would be their last time together for the rest of eternity, James poured every ounce of his unrequited love and lust into their final coupling, entwined with her for hours until finally, spent and satisfied, sleep pulled him once again into the deep.

***

IN THE MORNING, Claire awoke to an empty bed yet again. Furious at being abandoned by James for the third night in a row, she rushed to the room at the top of the tower, her bathrobe flowing out behind her as she stomped angrily up the stairs.

Claire stormed into the room expecting to find James asleep on the floor with no clothes. Instead she found his clothes, but no James. They were neatly folded and stacked in a pile in the center of the otherwise empty room. On top of the stack sat her engagement ring.

Claire picked up her ring and slipped it back onto

her finger, confused. She felt a presence looming above her and looked up. What she saw caused her to instinctively put her hand over her mouth to stifle a silent scream.

Suspended high in the center of the room from the curtain rods that circled it, James hung, face down and naked with a single curtain bound around each of his wrists and ankles.

The fifth curtain was wrapped tightly around his neck just beneath his swollen blue face, dead bloodshot eyes bulging in their sockets.

Claire backed away in horror. As she did, she stepped on a sapphire bead that had come loose from the curtains. Her foot slipped from under her and she fell backwards as she lost her footing. She flailed frantically for something to hold on to, but came up empty-handed.

She staggered across the room as she tried to regain her footing. The cool glass of a window pane felt reassuring against her palms as she planted them in the center of the red stained glass heart.

The window steadied her for a moment, but the momentum of her fall was too great a burden for the single pane to bear for more than the slightest instant, and the glass shattered around her hands.

A sparkling explosion of tiny glass shards followed Claire as she plunged through the now gaping window on her journey to the lawn that lay waiting far below.

A fleeting look of surprise washed over Claire's face as she fell. Her mind was having difficulty trying to process what was happening and everything seemed to shift instantly into slow motion, as an enormous jolt of adrenaline pulsed through her veins.

Claire wondered if maybe she wasn't really falling. She was flying, she was in control. She thought maybe she could just set her feet down on the yard below and walk away. Her senses became hyper-acute as everything around her decelerated, and each fraction of a second began to feel like minutes, even hours.

She realized with amazement that she could see every little crack in the bricks, every single individual grain of sand in the mortar.

Every tiny streak formed in the splatter of bird droppings on the windowsill was vivid and crystal clear. Each was a rainbow of colors, incredibly complex compositions of interlocking swirls and splatters, miniature Jackson Pollock masterpieces.

Claire was stunned by the new world emerging around her, everything was suddenly so beautiful, she felt so alive.

As she fell, the distance between herself and the windowsill on the floor below growing smaller, Claire felt a sense of omniscience wash over her. She could see everything. It was all becoming clear to her now.

Knowledge surged through her at a dizzying rate. She could even tell what the birds had eaten the day before they painted that beautiful design on the ledge. She spotted a cluster of blackberry seeds hidden in the layers.

Yes! That's it! She thought. *And the bird that made that cream-colored sunburst pattern has been eating leftover winter seed from the feeder on the window of the house across the street.*

Just when Claire's newfound state of transcendence was about to catapult her into an entirely higher realm of consciousness, her forehead struck the rapidly approaching stone windowsill with a sharp *thwack*, sounding like an overripe melon hitting pavement.

The impact flipped her body completely head over heels a couple of times midair before she landed on her back atop the sharp iron cross in the front yard, the exact spot where little Sophie had met a similar fate twenty-five years before.

As Claire lay dying, impaled on the lawn, a little boy and girl walked up to her, holding hands. The colors of the world around them were washed out and faded like an old photograph, but their bodies radiated light. The little girl had a ring of daisies in her hair.

"Who is she?" the little girl asked.

"I don't know," the boy replied. "She looks kinda familiar."

"Then she can be our daughter," the little girl said, reaching out her hand to Claire. "Come on, daughter. Let's go make dinner in the playhouse in the woods."

***

THE PACKAGE

EVERYTHING DEPRESSES ME these days, makes me downright blue to the bone. Even just the simple act of reading the paper serves only to remind me of how far I've fallen. I'm a man living at the bottom.

Take today, for example: I hadn't even had my first sip of peppermint-flavored java and I was already reading about how the man with the world's largest penis got stopped by airport security under suspicion of smuggling a weapon in his pants.

It must be nice having the biggest dick in the world.

I sure as hell wouldn't know.

My belly let out a low churning rumble, must've been bad chili I had for dinner. Either that or the very thought of my own pathetic, minuscule manhood, quivering in the fetid darkness below my waistband, had sickened me.

World's Largest Penis. That's a title I wouldn't

mind having. God knows the old candy cane ain't what it used to be, way back when I first got started in this business.

I glanced over the top of the paper and past my bowl-full-of-jelly-belly to the missus at the foot of the bed, still hard at work scrubbing her wooden dentures - her *chompers*, she calls them. It's hard to believe, but back in the day she used to rock this big old sleigh bed until my head rang like church bells on Christmas Eve.

It's just sad looking at her now, those two saggy sacks of sand swaying back and forth like dead slabs of flesh in a slaughterhouse. If gravity wasn't kind to tits in general, then it must've been fucking rude as hell to hers, 'cause I've seen beef jerky with more sex appeal. I should've sent her off to the Mud Creek Shady Grove Convalescent Home years ago. At this point she was so repulsive that killing her would probably be considered an act of love.

Then I felt it.

It was only the slightest bit of a scrunch and a wiggle in the front of my britches, but I knew instantly what it was.

My penis had just shrunk a little.

The contraction was happening more often these days. I shouldn't have looked at her, I knew better.

Why had I done it anyway? The loss of length - a millimeter here, a millimeter there - might not be noticed by most men with a decent schlong. But my shrinkage appeared to be permanent, and I didn't have but more than a few centimeters left to go before it was completely gone.

I tried to resist the urge to look and see how much length I had lost this time, but after a few seconds I sat my newspaper down on the bed and lifted up the waistband on my red and green boxers to check out the damage.

It looked bad, real bad - like a fried pork rind, soggy from soaking in mayonnaise. Even I was afraid to touch it any more. The small pasty worm between my legs appeared as though it had nestled into my white bushy pubes and died alone, miserable and defeated. My little finger could've kicked its ass easily if the two had bumped into each other in a bar and got into a rumble tumble.

I let the elastic waistband of my underwear snap back into place and realized with horror that the steady sound of scrubbing at the end of the bed had stopped. A cold shiver scuttled from the back of my neck down along my spine and into my puckered asshole.

She'd caught me looking at my junk.

Crap.

The old bag winked at me as a hopeful look rose in her eyes, a dreamy smile spreading across her withered face. Her floppy jowls made her resemble a basset hound more than anything.

"You want to dig your Claus into me?" she asked coyly and lifted her skirt just enough to reveal what looked like a wet piece of driftwood lurking in the shadows underneath. Her attempt at a sexy voice was a dead-on impression of the evil witch of the west.

She lustily raked her swollen tongue across her crusty lips. I felt my penis shrink some more, but I didn't dare check the damage again - not with her watching.

I grunted at her fiercely and went back to my reading, to my dreams of someday getting stopped by security with a thirteen-inch trouser snake snuggling the inside of my left thigh. Ah, the sugar-plums I could pop with a mighty tool like that! After a couple of minutes, she sighed in disappointment and shuffled away.

A loud rap on the wooden bedroom door made me jump. The workshop that lay outside the bedroom had been dark and silent for the last few months, so I'd almost forgotten that Bernie was still here.

"Come in," I said, not even bothering to pull my stained t-shirt down over my bloated protuberance of a belly.

Bernie waddled in, the long grey knurls of his angry thicket of eyebrows curled up over several inches of his forehead. He was the last elf still on duty, since the recent spate of competing Snow White movies had cleaned out the last few remaining staff, who had headed for Hollywood with big dreams of stardom.

It's not like they would've had a job here much longer, anyway. Christmas is a high-volume, slim-margin business, not a charity - and the days of high cotton were long gone. I'd had to lay off just about the entire elf workforce over the last decade, hundreds of them. What had once been a time for joy and celebration in December was now nothing but a savage season.

The lucky ones had gotten jobs in Thailand's burgeoning sex industry; the not-so-lucky ones I'd found frozen in the snow outside the factory gates. It wasn't my fault that rising labor costs in China had wiped out the razor-thin profit-margin I'd made from outsourcing in the first place. The god of the razor was a cruel master indeed, and his victims had left a long trail of blood and gumdrops that nearly circled the North Pole.

I couldn't really justify keeping Bernie around, financially - but I figured Santa was entitled to having at least one elf to boss around; and after he ended up on the sex offender registry in Nova Scotia last summer for inappropriately propositioning a second-grader that he had mistaken for a sexy young elf, there wasn't really anywhere else for him to go, anyway.

"A registered letter arrived in the mail for you this morning, sir," he said, handing me an envelope.

"You sure this wasn't meant to go to Toys R Us?" I asked.

"No sir, it clearly says "TO SANTA" right here," he said, poking it with his stubby finger.

"Well, I'll be. So it does. July's kinda early for a Christmas list isn't it?"

"That's what I thought, sir," he replied.

I ripped it open with my antler-horn letter opener. It was the last remaining bit of Rudolph, may he rest in peace.

Inside was a contract of some sort, a single page of double-typed text with a duplicate behind it, sheets of carbon paper tucked in between.

"What the fuck is this, Bernie? An eviction notice? Because I will pack my sleigh with explosives and fly it into whatever building matters most on Christmas Eve if anyone so much as tries to tell me I don't own this here land," I shouted. Spittle was flying everywhere. "Fucking bullets and fire, I promise."

The veins on my forehead were throbbing. I pushed my glasses up my nose to get a better look.

It read:

"This contract is a binding and lasting agreement between Chamus Dundass of Wombat, Mississippi, and the great Santa himself.

This agreement specifies that in exchange for giving unfettered ownership of his immortal soul to the great Santa, Chamus shall receive from Santa both purse wropes to make him stand apart from other men, as well as the undying affections of whatever woman is capable of giving the best jowlbob in the world.

The exchange is to be completed at the crossroads near Dockery Plantation at midnight on October 31 of this year, or at any time prior to that date that the great Santa may wish to present himself to Chamus for the exchange."

At the bottom of the page was a bloody thumbprint next to Chamus Dundass's name, and a spot for my thumbprint beside it.

"What the fuck am I going to do with a soul?" I asked Bernie, who had been reading along over my shoulder. "Buy myself a nice white mule and a spotted pig?"

"Clearly it's a mistake, sir," the troll answered. "Should I mark it *'return to sender'* and drop it back into the mail?"

I noticed the headline of the article I had been reading earlier: "COCK BLOCKED," it read. I'm surprised they were allowed to print that.

It gave me an idea.

Mrs. Claus came over to see what the fuss was about, pulling back her floppy cheeks to slide her stained and mildewed wooden dentures onto her toothless gums. She'd had the same teeth for over two hundred years, and even though I'd offered to get her a modern, more natural-looking set a hundred times, she had refused to swap them out, said they had just gotten properly seasoned.

"What are you boys looking at?" she asked and smiled at us, her wooden teeth looking like the side of an ancient tobacco barn that had been used frequently as the backdrop for a firing squad.

As soon as her words reached my nostrils with their reek of nutmeg and rotten-meat-scented cedar, I knew the answer to her question.

Freedom.

"Bernie, go hitch the reindeer to the magic wagon and bring me one of those big velvet gift sacks from the warehouse. We're going out," I commanded.

He nodded in agreement, spun about on his heel and ran down the hall towards the stables, the bells on his curly-pointed shoes jangling as he ran.

"But it's not Christmas yet, dear," Mrs. Claus protested.

"It is for me, baby. It is for me." I said. "Now be a good girl and go get something sexy on."

Her droopy eyes grew as wide with surprise as her dilapidated face would allow. She let out a ball-shriveling cackle of delight and hobbled over to her wardrobe, and started rummaging through what she considered to be her naughtiest lingerie.

I buttoned up the big golden buttons of my red velvet coat with a newfound sense of purpose, cinching up the wide black belt and slipping on my shiny patent leather boots in twenty seconds flat.

I took one last look at myself in the mirror and adjusted the bell at the end of my long red hat. My rosy cheeks were absolutely glowing with excitement.

"Christmas for Santa," I said out loud to myself as I folded up the article that was about to change my life and tucked it inside my coat. "It's about fucking time."

"The sled is ready and the reindeer are ready to fly, sir," said Bernie, breathless and holding up the large velvet sack I had asked him to bring. "Nothing but sunset and sawdust between us and the sky."

I nodded approvingly, then cupped my palm over his hairy little ear and whispered the plan.

***

SHADOWS ROSE UP like dark men around us as the reindeer galloped forward, and then all the earth was thrown to the sky as we took flight into the darkening night.

It was just the two of us - I liked to call us the *nightrunners* - me in the back seat with my feet kicked up and Bernie up front at the controls. The big velvet sack was in the cargo area in back, tied closed with a giant bow.

We flew down along the western coast of the United States, turned east over Mexico and brought the sled to a lower altitude, just below radar surveillance, crossing the Texas border headed for Mississippi.

We spotted another treetop flyer as we flew over Nacogdoches, a beat-up single-engine Cessna that was no doubt carrying lots of presents for all the very naughty little girls and boys – the word is, they enjoy a white Christmas, too.

I tried to enjoy the summer breeze as we crossed over the Sabine River far below into Louisiana but it was surprisingly cold in July, and relaxing was difficult with the constant barrage of reindeer farts that assaulted our senses every few seconds, undoubtedly the result of feeding the herd cheap dog food instead of their regular, more expensive diet.

I saw the apartment building where Chamus Dundass, the man with the soul for sale, lived. I nudged Bernie and pointed below. He guided the reindeer to a silky smooth and stealthy silent landing on the roof, their graceful feet a waltz of shadows as they tiptoed to a stop beside the chimney.

I grabbed the special purse I had prepared from the seat beside me, and climbed up onto the chimney.

"Wait until I call you to drop the sack," I told Bernie.

He nodded.

Then quick as a flash I slipped down the chimney, with more gusto burning in my chest than I'd felt in centuries.

Chamus Dundass was a fat frumpy middle-aged man with his pants down around his ankles and a Miley Cyrus video playing on the computer screen behind him. There was a fine dark line between fun-loving and freaky, and it was clear Chamus had crossed it long ago. His apartment was old, cluttered and stunk of sauerkraut and freezer burn.

I climbed out of the fireplace, stood up and brushed the soot off my suit before introducing myself.

"Chamus?" I bellowed, and the man spun around startled and tripping over himself like he was doing the two-bear mambo, his face funny-looking and wide-eyed. He let out a frightened howl that reminded me of my dead dog Bobby.

"What the fuck! Who the hell are you? What the hell are you doing?" he shrieked.

"I'm here to make our trade, Chamus," I declared

in my jolliest voice, and held out the signed contract and the purse for him to see.

He gawked at me, speechless, as he pulled up his pants. Although he seemed to be in a bit of shock, a look of recognition crossed his face as he spotted the contract.

I pointed to my thumbprint just above my name on the paper, clearly stamped in a brown little smatter of plum pudding, Bernie's notary public seal impressed into the paper beside it.

"You're...you're..." he stammered incoherently.

"Why yes I am - the great Santa, in the flesh," I said and bowed smartly.

"No, I mean...they always told me at church that you were actually the devil and that Baby Jesus brings us presents, but I never dreamed it was true," he said.

"What are you talking about, fool?" I protested. "I'm not the devil, I'm Santa – and I'm here to collect your soul."

"So you're not Satan?" he asked, confused eyes blinking furiously, looking every bit like a jackass caught in a sandstorm.

"What part of this outfit makes you think I'm Satan?" I said. "Do you see horns? Is there a pitchfork in my hand, young man?"

"Oh shit," the man said, and then he began to laugh.

"What's so funny?"

"If you ain't Satan, then I don't owe you shit, old man," he mocked. "That contract was for him, not Santa Claus. You never once brought me what I wanted for Christmas, anyway, and I'm pretty sure they don't give out super powers and the world's best blowjobs at the North Pole."

I crossed my arms, frowned and slammed the contract down on the coffee table and roared at him. Most people don't know that in my youth, before I chose to become a benevolent spirit that bestowed gifts upon the poor folk of Bavaria, I once was a fierce Teutonic guardian of the woods. I used to eat legions of invading Roman Centurions like they were nothing more than a handful of skittles. It had been a while, but I could get rough if I had to.

"I don't know what you're going on about, but this contract in my hand says you agree to trade your soul to Santa, and that's what we're here to do," I declared in my most intimidating guttural baritone, the kind that only comes with hundreds of years of pent-up sexual frustration. "I've got the goods you agreed to trade for, and I'm leaving here with your soul if it means I have to reach down your throat and tear it out with my bare hands."

Chamus inspected the contract closely, desperately searching for a loophole. I poked my finger at my printed name. It said S-A-N-T-A, clear as day.

"God damn it," Chamus muttered. I think he finally realized I wasn't shitting around.

"Dyslexia is not a learning disability, it's a curse," he said glumly. "Do you know how many times shit like this has happened to me before? And now I finally get the chance to trade my soul to Satan for super powers and the woman who can give the best blowjob in the world, and stupid dyslexia fucks that up for me, too."

He screwed up his face in what was probably intended to be a pitiful look, but it came off as severely creepy instead - especially with the Miley

Cyrus video still playing in a loop on the monitor behind him.

I might have felt sorry for him once upon a time, but *fuck that*, I decided. He was clearly an asshole - and I felt a whole lot sorrier for myself, besides.

"It's time to pay up, Chamus," I said resolutely. "It says right here in plain English that you agree to trade your soul for *purse wropes* and the woman who can give the best *jowlbob* in the world. Here's the first part of the trade, delivered."

I slammed the purse down on the table, and plopped into an old Lazy-Boy chair to take a load off while he inspected it. It was an old knockoff Coach purse that I'd given the missus for Christmas last year. She hadn't even used it once and it was already starting to come apart at the seams.

Chamus scrunched his ugly mug up in confusion and then took a look inside. It was full of little pieces of rope.

"What the hell is this?" he asked.

"Your purse with ropes," Santa said, "as you clearly specified in the contract."

"Fuck you, Santa," Chamus said, brushing it brusquely off the coffee table and scattering the ropes across the dingy, matted carpet. "You still owe me a woman, Fat Man, or that contract don't mean shit," he growled hoarsely.

I smiled, turned towards the chimney and whistled. A couple of seconds later a big velvet sack with a giant bow on top dropped into the fireplace with a plop. Inside it, something wriggled and moaned.

"Your woman," I said proudly, hoisting myself back out of the recliner. I hauled the sack out of the fireplace and shoved it across the floor towards Chamus with my foot, smearing a grimy skid mark of soot across the carpet.

"Inside this sack is your woman – and not just any woman, either. This woman is equipped to give you what is definitely the very best jowlbob in the world. Her jowls have been prepared especially for your pleasure by gravity himself for the last four hundred years. Simply lubricate and enjoy."

Chamus hesitated at first, but then got down onto his knees to untie the giant bow. He opened the sack with much trepidation, folding it open to reveal in the dim fluorescent light of the apartment what appeared to be a shaved Bassett hound clutching lingerie.

He looked up at me with bewildered eyes.

"The trade is complete, and now your soul is mine!" I chuckled, unable to resist the urge to click the heels of my shiny patent leather boots together with glee. I could feel *mucho mojo* rising within me.

"But why Santa, why? What could you possibly need with my soul?" the poor man asked, his voice desperate and pleading. As he spoke his soul began streaming out of his mouth, eyes and nostrils like tendrils of green fog. I reached out and grabbed it in my hand, pulled the rest of it from him and stuck it in my pocket.

"Why do I need your soul? Are you serious?" I laughed. "I hear Satan gives out some good shit in exchange for a soul, and I already know what I want," I said. I whipped out the article about the world's largest penis to show him.

Chamus said nothing, simply sank to his knees, his face even more sallow and empty than it had been before. He was now truly a man with no soul.

"Have fun with your purse ropes and jowlbobs," I said as I made my way to the fireplace. "I've already explained to the former Mrs. Claus what a jowlbob is, and I have to say she's very excited to be here with you. She has the pent-up sex drive of ten-thousand horny teenagers, but she's completely unburdened by their pesky good looks - so you won't have to worry yourself about anyone trying to steal her away from you."

I winked at him, glad to finally be free of that salty hag and on my way to a better life.

"You kids have fun now," I said as I stooped under the mantle with care.

The last horrible thing I saw before I started back up the chimney was a buck-naked Mrs. Claus hobbling to her feet, leaving the sack wadded up on the floor around her swollen ankles. Her large nipples looked like two rotten tomatoes, splattered against a wall.

"Please, don't leave me here alone with that...that...*thing*," Chamus begged as he jumped up onto the couch, falling over the back of it as he scrambled to get away from her. The haunted look in his eyes was like a man standing at the edge of dark water, about to fall in.

I scuttled back up the chimney as fast as I could. I wanted to be out of there before Mrs. Claus lubed up her flappy jowls, wrapped them around his cock and began with the bobbing up and down. That old hag never could get enough, and I'm sure ol' Chamus will enjoy her efforts plenty eventually. I figure it won't be long before he's sitting on his stained sofa flipping through the channels while she goes to town.

It's not like he had much going on anyway.

I emerged onto the rooftop into the fresh night air, a happy man with a soul for sale in my pocket.

Bernie had the sled ready to fly.

It was time to go find us the Devil Red.

***

I love Joe R. Lansdale. He's an amazing author that I somehow overlooked for way too long. This story is a tribute to him of sorts, and fans will find it to be stuffed to the brim with references to the titles of his books and stories.

BLACK DOOR

THIS SUMMER has been a hot one – the kind that shimmers with a heat that looks like water puddles on the pavement. I can't remember the last time it rained. A month? Maybe three?

I wiped the sweat from my forehead with the back of my arm, and realized that I was now stuck with a sweaty arm. I dried it on the side of my shirt. Even without the rain, the air somehow managed to still be full of sticky moisture; my clothes became soaked with sweat the instant I walked outside. The whole world felt like a giant dog was breathing on it.

It's still early in the morning, but already it's so hot the trees in my back yard look wilted like celery that's been in the refrigerator too long, all shriveled and limp.

As I looked at the brown grass that used to be our lawn, I listened to my two brothers arguing as they packed for camp upstairs. Being the middle child, I usually mind my own business and let the two of them fight things out.

The three of us are in for one hot week in the woods at summer camp, though. I better make sure not to forget to take a fan.

I looked at my watch and realized dad had better get moving or we were going to be late. We were supposed to be at Camp Eustace for sign-in at ten o'clock sharp. Mom had gone to visit our Aunt Wendy for the weekend, and left us at home alone with Dad in charge. If we were late getting to camp, I knew he'd never hear the end of it when she got home.

It was almost eight in the morning already, and the drive to the campground took at least two hours – and that was if the GPS took us there the fast way. It almost never did.

"William – come get your stuff, we've got to go!" Dad yelled from inside. His voice sounded a little panicky; he must've realized how late it was getting.

Finally.

I stepped back into the house and the chill of the air conditioning made goose bumps rise on the back of my neck. I bet Dad was glad it was us boys headed off to camp this week and not him. A week of peace and quiet home alone with the air conditioner was probably all the adventure he could handle, anyway.

As soon as I got inside, Dad started really putting the pressure on for us to hurry.

"Come on guys, we're going to be late!" he yelled up the stairs. "Don't forget to bring everything you're going to need. Once you get to camp, what you've got is what you've got!"

My two brothers, Ethan and Aidan, came

barreling down the stairs like a herd of buffalo wearing cargo pants and baseball caps, duffel bags over their shoulders, sleeping bags under their other arms. The three of us were chock-full of summer excitement and the promise of thrills that a full week at adventure camp held for us.

Ethan, who was eleven - barely a year older than me - came down first; as he ran he somehow managed to simultaneously toss his hair with a strange twitch of his head that he thought looked cool. I don't know how he was able to do it without losing his balance and falling down the stairs.

"I call front seat!" he yelled as he shoved his way past me into the garage where the minivan was waiting.

This taunt caused an immediate spike in the stress levels of our youngest brother Aidan, who was following hot on his heels. They practically crawled over and under each other as they raced to the car, barely slowing each other down in the process.

"It's not fair!" I shouted. The fact that I was carrying at least my own weight in supplies didn't mean I should be unjustly relegated to the back seat for the entire two-hour trip to camp. The advantages in life my older brother gets for doing nothing more than being born earlier than me are totally unfair.

"I CALL FRONT!" Aidan's thunderous voice blasted inches away from the back of my head as he pushed his way through the garage door. We got stuck there for a moment; it was more bags and boys than the doorway could digest.

"Ethan already called it!" I hissed bitterly, enforcing the rules of shotgun with resignation even as they worked against me.

"Nuh-uh, I just did," Aidan insisted, with the truly innocent obliviousness only a seven-year old can muster.

"No Ethan did BEFORE you! BEFORE YOU!" I growled, as we popped out of the doorway, stumbling into the garage.

"Rotten eggs! Rotten eggs!" Ethan heckled in a muffled sing-song voice from his perch in the passenger seat, where he sat smiling and victorious.

I heard Dad let out a loud sigh in the kitchen as he scooped up his wallet, keys and sunglasses. It was going to be a long ride to camp. Mom had been smart to go visit our Aunt Wendy out of town. It meant she got to miss this magical weekend.

Dad locked up the house and tossed our bags into the back. In a few minutes we were on the road, headed to Camp Eustace.

This was the first time we had gone to summer camp at Camp Eustace. It was the third year in a row Ethan and I had gone to a week-long summer adventure camp; Aidan had gone with us for the first time last year. We all loved Camp Cherokee, but the campgrounds there had been overrun with an infestation of poisonous snakes and had been shut down for the entire summer.

Mom heard about Camp Eustace from some of her friends. From the pictures on the internet, it looked as though it might be even better than Camp Cherokee. For one thing, it actually had a pool; one with a water slide and a diving board, at that. We were also going to get to do some pretty fancy activities.

By contrast, Camp Cherokee was pretty much some woods with a few shacks, and a big mud puddle they called a lake. It had been fun, but I was ready to try something new.

Dad pulled onto the interstate and typed the address into the GPS. The GPS calculated the trip information: two hours and seven minutes it predicted – if all went well, we would get there right on time for sign-in.

The drive did go well. We talked about all the things we hoped to do this year at camp, about what girls might like us, about how we hoped Camp Eustace had Mello-Yello in the canteen like Camp Cherokee did.

There was barely any traffic on the road and after an hour Dad pulled off the interstate and took a left onto a back country road. We were headed straight for a mountain range that was looming on the horizon. Dad said Camp Eustace was in the woods somewhere below those mountaintops in front of us.

The direction from the GPS started changing rapidly as we drove - a "left in 200 feet" here, a "TURN RIGHT NOW" there – it seemed like the GPS was having a hard time deciding which way to go.

Each turn Dad made took us onto smaller and smaller roads, and I noticed the houses we passed were getting further and further apart.

I glanced at the clock on the dashboard. It was 9:57 a.m. We should be at the campground in less than ten minutes, but I still hadn't seen a single sign for it yet. *Shouldn't we have passed at least one of those blue street signs with a picture of a tent on it by now?* I wondered. I was starting to wonder if we were lost.

"At the next intersection, make a U-turn", the GPS bleated cheerfully in a pleasant computerized female voice.

Make a U-turn? That didn't sound good. I noticed Dad was frowning.

"What's wrong, Dad?" Ethan asked, looking up from his music player.

"Are we lost?" He said.

"No." Dad lied.

"WE'RE LOST??" Aidan bellowed from somewhere behind me after hearing Ethan's question. His brown eyes were wide with alarm.

"We're not lost, Aidan," I tried to reassure him.

"We're lost," Ethan whispered to him, hoping Dad wouldn't hear.

"I DON'T WANT TO BE LOST! I WANT TO GO TO CAMP! I DON'T WANT TO BE LOST!" Aidan's voice was so loud it was like having a grenade go off inside the car. It made my ears ring, and my whole body felt hot.

"We're not lost!" Dad repeated, as he turned the car around to go back the way we had come. I hoped the GPS knew what it was talking about.

"We *are* lost, aren't we?" Ethan asked calmly.

"I don't know, I think we missed a turn. We'll be fine – don't worry," Dad said, trying to keep his cool as he drove back the opposite direction.

"WE MISSED A TURN?" Aidan's shrill voice pierced my throbbing head again.

"I *told* you we were lost," Ethan whispered smugly. Dad ignored him and stepped on the gas, hoping to make up for lost time.

"At the next intersection, make a U-turn," the GPS cheerfully said again. I think it sounded more confident this time.

"We are lost," Ethan concluded aloud to no one in particular.

Then the car started to chime. I looked over Dad's shoulder at the lights on the dashboard; the words LOW FUEL were lit up in red next to the fuel gauge.

Great. We were never going to make it to camp this year. Mom should have stayed home.

"Take a left at the next intersection," the GPS suggested randomly.

Dad turned it off and pulled the car off to the side of the road, and turned the engine off. He gripped the wheel, breathing hard with frustration. He didn't look like he was feeling well.

"What are you doing?" me and my brothers all said in unison. We were feeling alarmed now – maybe Dad was trying to send a message when he read us the story of Hansel and Gretel – it was one of his favorites after all. Maybe we should have packed some pebbles and breadcrumbs in our pockets.

After a few minutes of uncomfortable silence, Dad spoke up.

"Well, guys – it's like this: we're almost out of gas, the GPS doesn't know where we are and neither do I. The closest gas station is at least thirty miles behind us. We probably don't have enough gas to make it to the gas station, even if I knew how to get back there, which I don't - thanks to this stupid GPS."

"What are we going to do?" Ethan asked. All traces of smugness had vanished from his voice.

Dad turned around to face us. He looked anxious and that made me feel worried.

"I guess we're going to sit here until someone drives by. Hopefully I can wave them down and they can give us the right directions to camp, it's got to be nearby."

He pointed out the window. "You see those

mountains right there? The camp is at the bottom. If
we can at least make it to camp I'm sure they'll have
enough gas to get me back to the gas station. Then I
can drop you guys off and get back home just in time
for your mom to say 'I told you so!'"

Just then, a loud rapping on the car window
behind me made us all jump. Through the windshield
just over Dad's shoulder I saw that a car had parked
on the side of the road right in front of us. A woman
was holding a screaming baby in the passenger seat,
but the driver seat beside her was empty.

At the window behind me stood a man,
motioning for us to roll down the window. He looked
like he was maybe in his twenties, and he was
wearing a dirty straw cowboy hat that looked like it
had been sat on one too many times. He had long
stringy hair, and a tattoo of a snake crawling around
his throat. Sweat was dripping down his neck, and it
made the snake look like it was crying.

The man wasn't smiling, and kept spinning his
finger in circles – he was saying ROLL DOWN THE
WINDOW in homemade sign language, apparently.

Not wanting to keep him waiting any longer, Dad
turned the key in the ignition halfway and rolled the
window down to talk to him.

"Hi!" Dad said as cheerfully as he could muster.

"Fancy car," the man said matter-of-factly and
then spit a long gooey string of spit down his chin
and onto his shoe. "How much did it cost?"

"What?" Dad said, clearly confused.

"So you guys need help or something?" he asked,
abruptly changing the subject. "I don't normal talk to
strangers be act suspicious like you, but my booboo
there made me stop an' ask." He tipped his head in

the general direction of the woman waiting in the car parked in front of us.

"Thanks so much," Dad said in the friendliest voice he could manage. "We're looking for Camp Eustace and can't seem to find it. I think it's nearby, though."

The man stared at Dad without blinking for a whole minute, not saying anything. My brothers crowded around me, no doubt to better ogle the man.

The man stared back at us with dead eyes. He started to spit out another brown loogey, but evidently he decided to save it for later, because he sucked the spit back into his mouth the second it hit his chin.

Finally, the man blinked – and spoke.

"Yep." He said.

Another awkward pause followed.

"Could you give me directions for how to get to the camp?" Dad asked hopefully.

"Yep."

Then more silence.

Then he started talking, his words all jumbled together and hard to make out. Dad grabbed a pencil and paper and started scribbling down the directions as he said them.

"Ain't hard, don't write it down, jus' listen – go that way two miles," he pointed over his shoulder in the direction we had been heading. "Take a right on Steely Branch road. Stay straight a half a mile, then left on Mule Creek. Go over the bridge and then left at the fork. Camp's a couple miles past that. Got it?"

"Right, left, left?" Dad repeated.

"Yep."

"Thank you so..." Dad started to offer his

profound appreciation, but stopped talking when the man spit a big gob of brown goo right onto the side of the minivan and then walked away, mumbling words we'd get a spanking for saying.

I heard the man screaming "SHUT UP!" at his booboo as he climbed into the car and drove away, leaving us in a cloud of dust.

The man's personality wasn't much to talk about, but his directions were perfect. Dad took a right on Steely Branch, then a left at Mule Creek. We went over the little bridge. A deep ditch ran along both sides of the dirt road, barely protected on either side by intermittent fence posts with rusty barbed wire strung along between them. I couldn't quite figure out the logic behind that type of protection; wouldn't being wrapped up in barbed wire be much worse than getting stuck in a ditch?

A little past the bridge we arrived at a fork in the road – right in the middle of which stood a faded sign that read: *"Camp Eustace arrivals, stay left. Two miles ahead."*

We all cheered.

"We made it! Yeah boy! We're at camp! WOO-HOO!" Ethan danced a little victory dance in his seat as he sang.

For a minute we all forgot about our little adventure, and Ethan and Aidan started discussing all the things they wanted to do this year at camp. As I listened to them talking, I noticed Dad was still keeping a nervous eye on the fuel gauge. Hopefully we wouldn't run out of gas in a long line of cars waiting to park and unload.

"I'm going to do archery," Aidan declared.

"You're not old enough," I reminded him.

"Yes I am," he insisted.

"No, you're not," Ethan turned around to offer his opinion as the resident expert on the subject.

"I told you," I said.

"I *AM TOO* old enough," Aidan said again, refusing to yield. "You were seven and you got to do archery."

"That's because I'm *mature*," I said, with the type of condescension only a slightly older brother can muster. "You'd hurt yourself – or kill somebody."

"I WOULD NOT!" Aidan roared.

One mile to go, one mile to go. *Where are all the other cars?*, I wondered, realizing I hadn't seen a single car anywhere down this road so far.

"Yes you would, Aidan," Ethan opined in his older-therefore-much-much-wiser voice of complete and total certainty. "You would."

I figured I'd go ahead and push Aidan off the precarious emotional ledge from which he was dangling. I smiled at him and spoke in my best fake-friendly voice.

"Don't worry. You'll probably get to do it next year… *if you're mature enough by then.*"

Aidan would've turned green and burst from his seat belt in a fit of hulkulean rage to rip me a new pie-hole if Dad hadn't distracted him at that exact moment.

"We're here," he stated simply. We strained forward against our seat belts for a glimpse of the summer camp wonders about to unfold before us.

Ahead, a single-lane dirt road led into the campground. It was covered with sparse gravel, full of potholes and lined with knee-high clumps of weeds. Fifteen feet above the road, an arched sign loomed over us.

It was the gateway to Camp Eustace.

The sign had a layer of rust working hard to eat away the last remaining patches of faded paint from the lettering and the background. In welded-on lettering it read: *CAMP EUSTACE: Founded 1879. CHILDHOOD IS BRIEF BUT MEMORIES ARE FOREVER.*

We all quieted down and stared wide-eyed in anticipation out the windows, each of us hoping to be the first to glimpse the Olympic-size pool with the three story water slide. I was surprised we had forgotten to tell Aidan that he wasn't old enough to do that, either.

Dad pulled into the campground, passing under the entrance archway. He stopped the car for a minute, trying to figure out which way to go. I was surprised we hadn't seen any other cars yet, no people, nothing at all. I looked around for teenagers in bright fluorescent yellow safety vests flagging us down, pointing us towards the parking areas.

The campground around us looked nothing like I had imagined. If anything, it looked a lot worse than Camp Cherokee. Several sagging wooden cabins slumped together off to our left, and a larger dilapidated building watched over them from our right.

Straight ahead was a military-looking brick building, a corroded copper sign hung above the door. I guessed it was the main office, since a crooked flagpole stood naked in front of it, thick weeds clustered at its base.

The most disturbing thing about it all was that there was no Olympic-sized pool or water slide anywhere in sight.

"Where is everybody?" Ethan asked, and Dad turned to look at us. His silence and the look on his face made reality sink in.

The place was deserted. We were all alone.

Dad turned the car towards the main building, eager to see what the deal was. Maybe we had gotten the date wrong.

Halfway to the main building, the car ran out of gas. It didn't even make a sound - no sputtering or puttering – the engine simply stopped and the car rolled to a halt.

We all sat quietly. Dad turned to look at us, and I realized we were all perched on the edge of our seats, eyes wide, mouths hanging open in shock.

"ARE WE LOST?" Aidan broke the silence like a gunshot in the middle of the night. We all jumped.

The more I thought about it, the more I realized there was no reason for any of us to be freaking out. We were here. Somebody would be here. We were early, that was all - or it was the wrong day. At the very least there would be a phone and we would call for someone to come get us, or bring us some gas. At least we were *here*, at Camp Eustace, and not broken down at the side of the road in the middle of nowhere.

I smiled at Dad in what I hoped was a reassuring way. Judging from the look on his face, I wasn't very successful. It was time for a pep talk.

"Come on, it's going to be all right. Maybe we came in the wrong entrance. It says Camp Eustace on the sign. We're here! We're at camp - come on… let's go check it out!"

With that I slid open the side door of the minivan

and jumped out. Everybody else followed my lead and a couple minutes later we were on our way to check out the campground.

The cabins were close, so I suggested we check them out before heading to the office. Ethan and Aidan quickly rediscovered their pent-up enthusiasm.

"Last one there is a rotten egg!" Ethan declared and he was off, with Aidan bumbling along in his wake, pushing and shoving me as he tried for a second place finish.

The cabin buildings were not much more than decrepit shacks, much older than I had expected, certainly not the "newly refurbished" facilities that the website had boasted about. I wouldn't have been surprised to learn they had been built during World War II.

It was hard to tell if the cabins were faded white from not being painted for a very long time, or if they were simply natural wood covered with dried mold. The tin roof looked like it was rusted through.

My brothers beat me to the first cabin by at least ten seconds, and they were on the small porch chattering excitedly by the time Dad and I joined them.

"This place is gross," Ethan observed matter-of-factly, as I stepped gently onto the porch with them, gingerly testing the rotten wood to make sure it would support me.

"I don't want to go to camp here," Aidan said.

I looked through the front window of the cabin. Only a few broken pieces of glass still remained, the shards hanging loosely from the frame like eyelashes around a dead man's eyeball.

Inside the cabin were a few rusty bunk bed

frames, but not a single mattress. Sunlight shone into the building through a large hole in the roof. It looked like there was a nest of some sort in the far back corner.

Dad put his hand on my shoulder as we silently surveyed the desolate scene before us.

"I'm sure this is just an old abandoned part of the camp," He said, trying to be reassuring. "I bet you the nice, new part of the camp and all the campers are over on the other side of the main office building right now. We probably came in through the wrong entrance."

We all looked at Dad with hopeful but dubious eyes. I really hoped he was right.

"Come on, guys! Cheer up! I'll race you to the office... last one there's a rotten egg!" Dad said, and took off running.

I jumped off the porch and started chasing after him through a bumpy sea of knee-high weeds towards the office. Ethan and Aidan were right behind me, and we were all determined to *not* become the dreaded rotten egg.

The air was cooler here than it had been at home, and the sudden burst of exercise invigorated me as I ran full-speed ahead towards the imposing brick structure.

I took in the desolate scenery as I ran – to my right was a sunken field that looked like it had once been a small lake but now was bone dry, its bottom covered with a bed of dried moss and weeds. The carcasses of small rotting rowboats lay scattered here and there on what must've once upon a time been its banks.

The administration building was the only

structure in the camp that appeared to have endured the test of time and passed. It was a sturdy and utilitarian-looking, with a tall façade on its front side that made it appear larger than it really was. The brickwork was drab and there were no visible windows. There was a small concrete staircase leading up to the entrance. Above the doorway was a green-tinted metal sign. It read, in smeary letters: *CAMP EUSTACE ADMINISTRATION AND CHECK-IN.*

I beat everyone to the steps of the office, and I could hardly hear my brothers gurgling and laughing in the distance behind me. I paused for a few seconds at the base of the stairs to catch my breath before going in. Maybe running hard after such a long drive hadn't been a great idea. I was out of breath.

The metal front door looked as though it hadn't seen a paint brush since Eisenhower was president. I sincerely hoped Dad was right, and that there would be a sharply dressed camp staff member inside laughing about how we had missed the main entrance to camp.

I climbed the stairs and reached for the doorknob. Before I could wrap my fingers around it, the knob turned and the door opened by itself – not much, only a few inches.

At first, I thought maybe I had actually pushed it open myself, but as I looked down at my still-outstretched arm and my empty grasping hand, I knew that I wasn't going to be able to fool myself into thinking that.

That door had opened by itself.

A cool wind blew in from the field behind me at that moment, pushing the door open a little further, revealing a small, dark room inside. A heavy-looking desk squatted in the middle of the room. Through the gloom, I could see that stacks of old-looking papers were scattered across it.

I hesitantly stuck my head inside.

"Hello?" I asked in a very soft voice, but not really expecting an answer.

As soon as I spoke the wind blew again, lifting some of the papers from the desk into the air. They looked like giant moths as they fluttered down to the dusty tile floor.

"Anybody here?" I asked again, a little louder this time.

I pushed the door open all the way so as much light as possible would shine into the windowless room. Then I took a deep breath and stepped inside.

It took a second or two for my eyesight to adjust to the darkness. On the wall behind the desk were several hand-painted boards with extremely neat lettering. One board read: *"DAILY CAMP SCHEDULE"*; and the other said: *"REGISTRATION INSTRUCTIONS & CAMP RULES"*.

There were no pictures anywhere on the walls. An ancient-looking light fixture hung from the ceiling above the desk. I found a light switch by the doorway and flipped it up and down several times, but the light didn't come on.

Dad ran up the stairs with my brothers just as I was reaching for one of the papers on the floor.

"Did you find them, William?" Aidan asked, hot sweat streaming down his crimson forehead. "Are we at the right place?"

"I don't think so," I said, and held the fragile piece of paper up to the sunlight, trying to read the faded words written there.

"Where is the water slide? Did they say where the water slide is? Where is the pool? I'm hot. I'm ready to go swimming. Where is the pool?" Ethan panted as he ran into the room. He stooped to rest with his hands on his knees.

"I don't know," I answered, still squinting at the paper. On it was a list of children's names, probably campers from years long ago. *Ben Hinkle. Andrew Smith. Sam Crowley. Madolyn Rose. Kirsten Larsen. Neil Allen, Andy McClendon. Ethan Rohl. Austin Logan.*

The paper in my hand felt so ancient, it made me wonder how many of those children were already dead from old age.

"If I don't go swimming I'm going to die of heatstroke," Ethan insisted.

"Is this the camp or not?" Aidan asked out of nowhere.

"It is and it isn't," Dad replied. I was sure his wishy-washy answer would only lead to Aidan asking several dozen more questions.

Ethan was closely inspecting the room, probably to see if any cold Mello-Yellos had accidentally been left behind.

"What's in there?" he asked, pointing to the left of the desk at a closed door. I hadn't noticed it before. It had a glossy coat of black paint that looked much fresher than anything else here, but for some reason, something about it made me feel nervous.

"I don't know Ethan, but nobody's here," Dad said, probably sensing my anxiety. "We should probably go look and see if we can find any gasoline in a storage shed. Come on, guys, let's get out of here."

He shooed us towards the exit with his hands. Before I could take my first step towards the door and the sunshine that lay beyond, I heard a noise behind me that made my blood run cold.

I froze.

"Dad, look!" Ethan shouted as he pointed excitedly to the wall behind me.

I didn't want to turn around. A rush of cool air rolled down the back of my neck, my arms, around my legs. I shivered.

"Look. Look. *Look!*" Aidan shouted, grabbing my arm and pulling me away from the exit, away from the sunlight.

Towards that door.

I turned around slowly to face it, knowing already it was open, knowing it had opened itself.

I turned around, hoping I was wrong.

I wasn't.

The black door stood open wide. On the other side of the doorway was a much larger room than I had expected. In fact, I must have underestimated the size of this entire building, because beyond that black door lay what looked like an apartment. Thin beams of sunlight strained to illuminate the room through windows hidden behind heavy curtains.

My feelings of dread disappeared the instant I looked beyond the doorway, replaced instead with the overwhelming desire to go through it, to explore what lay beyond. I took a couple of steps forward, trying to get a better look.

My brother and Dad seemed to be feeling the same way. The four of us began shuffling towards the doorway, until our heads were crammed inside its frame, eagerly trying to get a look at what lay beyond without actually having to step across the threshold.

"Can we go in?" Ethan asked in a hushed tone. I was wondering the same thing myself.

"I don't know," Dad mumbled.

"Please," Aidan begged, pushing so hard that I thought he might fall in.

Dad put his hand on Aidan's shoulder, holding him back.

"I think it's okay, Dad," I said with the most authoritative tone I could muster.

"Just wait," he said.

The rooms that lay before us were part of an elaborately decorated abode, barely illuminated in a musty gloom. Everything about the place was lavishly appointed, and ornate fixtures hung from the ceiling. Parisian-style furniture was crowded around an enormous ebony fireplace that lurked, cold and dormant, at the far end of the room. The mantel surrounding the fireplace displayed elegant craftsmanship, having been carved with an amazing level of detail.

The room had both the feeling of being lived in and of being empty at the same time. The scent of antiquity hung heavily in the air. Ancient newspapers and magazines towered in piles on end tables next to silken sofas here and there, as though the residents had set them down for a brief moment to run an errand that they had not yet returned from seventy-five years or so later.

"Hello?"

I was speaking that word into darkness for the second time today. My voice sounded as though it was being sucked into a vacuum, gone almost the instant the words left my lips.

No answer.

Then Dad tried. "Hi there... uh, my boys are here for camp... we don't want to intrude..."

He stopped speaking and listened. Nothing.

Ethan and Aidan looked up at him silently, their eyes wide as they listened.

"If you don't want us to come in, please say something," Dad continued. "If not, we're going to come in and cool down for a minute... if that's okay..."

A light, cool breeze from inside the room was the only response we received.

Dad took a deep breath and stepped into the room. We stood frozen in the doorway watching him, waiting.

"Well, come on!" Dad turned and motioned for us to follow him. "You want to look around, don't you?"

That was all it took. We elbowed our way through the doorway into to the apartment, Ethan and Aidan *oooh-ing* and *ahhh-ing* as they examined the amazing surroundings.

Once we were all inside, I realized that the room was even *bigger* than I had thought a minute before. The ceiling rose up at least two stories tall, but the room somehow managed to feel both elegant and cozy at the same time.

The room was densely packed with furniture, and the walls were lined with bookshelves and display cases, filled to the brim with a fine assortment of treasures and curiosities. I wondered how it was possible for the caretaker of an adventure camp to have living quarters this fine.

The walls were decorated with immense drapes and silken embroidered linens, their elegance diminished only slightly by the thick layer of dust that seemed to lie, long undisturbed, on the surface of everything in this place. The weak light coming through the windows left the contents of the cluttered corners still wallowing in gloom.

I felt like I had stumbled upon Ali Baba's treasure. Ethan and Aidan immediately started exploring, emitting small shrieks of joy at each new curious discovery.

"Look at this!" Ethan said, pointing excitedly to a rusty unicycle leaning in the corner, the padding that once covered its metal seat long gone. "Do you think I could try it?"

"Dad! Dad!" Aidan shouted excitedly from across the room. He was standing next to a barrister-style bookcase that rose from the floor to the ceiling.

I walked over to take a look. Inside the glass display case were gigantic models of World War II battleships, aircraft carriers, and submarines; all painted with painstaking attention, down to the most minute detail. There were dozens of them, all in pristine condition.

I plopped down on the sofa closest to the fireplace and began leafing through a stack of magazines. I couldn't believe my eyes.

"Dad, look at these," I said excitedly.

He came and sat down beside me, and I showed him what I had discovered: there were National Geographic magazines from as far back as 1918 and 1935; there were issues of Popular Mechanics from the 1950's with the words "Build Your Own Flying Car" emblazoned boldly across the cover. As I flipped through the pages, I couldn't help but notice that everything in the magazine looked bright and new, like it had been printed only yesterday.

We were entranced by shelves upon shelves of curious diversions; fragile stereoscopic glasses for viewing black and white three-dimensional images of national parks, Japanese pachinko machines loaded with shiny steel balls and garish paintings of abstract dragons.

Ethan called to me from another room; it startled me to hear his voice sound so far away. *Dad really should be keeping everyone together*, I thought as I went to see what he had found.

I found him in front of an enormous bookshelf laden with board games, grinning. It looked as though every game from every decade since board games had been invented was there, waiting to be played.

"Look, it's *Snakes and Ladders!*" he grinned, pointing to a game that looked ancient enough to have been played by Abraham Lincoln's children. There were literally hundreds of games stacked neatly on the shelves, some I had heard of, some I hadn't: *The Price is Right, Cipher, Ting Tong Tang, Ka-boom, Hi-Q,* and even the predictable *Monopoly.* They all appeared to be in perfect condition, if a bit dusty.

"Want to play one?" he asked. I couldn't think of a reason why not, so we set it up on the table by the fireplace. Aidan had found a chest full of stuffed animals, and he sat on the couch with a contented smile on his face as he hugged a ragged old teddy bear.

As Ethan set up the game, on the floor by the couch I found a little puzzle. It was made of wooden squares with letters on them that slid around in a tray. I figured the point of it was to see how many different words you could create with it. I shifted the letters around and held it up for Aidan to see. I had spelled the word "POOP" across the grid, and Aidan burst out laughing when he saw it. I got another idea for a word I could make, and started to work on my next masterpiece of hilarity.

Ethan grabbed the sliding word puzzle out of my hands, fiddled with it for a few seconds, and then held it up for Aidan to see. The letters now spelled out the word "BOOB". Howls of delight from Aidan assured Ethan that his sense of comedic genius was still in its prime. He grinned from ear to ear with satisfaction.

That was when I thought I saw something move, out of the corner of my eye, in one of the dark corners. I figured it was just another one of the collectibles. I looked hard at the spot where I thought I had seen it, but whatever it was had been lost in the gloom.

Then something moved again. For a split second it almost looked like an old woman, hiding in the corner. I thought my mind was playing tricks, but then she suddenly lifted her head and looked straight at me, and there was no mistaking it. Her black eyes were sunken, set deep into her wrinkled face, and she glared at me from beneath a floppy bonnet. I almost jumped up from the couch, but she lifted a bony finger to her lips and made the gesture, *shhhhh*.

I wanted to leave, right there and then. I glanced over at Dad, who was still flipping through old magazines, and then I looked back nervously to the old woman in the corner, but she was gone.

I noticed that the little bit of light we had in the

room was rapidly fading. I jumped up and almost knocked over the board game that Ethan was hard at work setting up.

"We *have* to go," I stated simply, motioning to the black door from which we had entered.

"But William, we just got here!" Dad protested, strangely content to stay. The other boys began to chime in.

"Yeah, Dad – we didn't even get to play the game yet," Ethan pleaded, making big puppy dog eyes and sticking out a pouty bottom lip.

"Dad, come on, it's getting really late," I insisted, as I scanned the room, trying to figure out where the old lady was lurking, watching us.

"But it's not even lunchtime," Dad said, but I wasn't in the mood to listen. I wanted to get out of here, now.

"Stay here if you want," I said, putting my hands on my hips to show I meant business. "I'm leaving right now."

I headed straight for the black door. A sinking feeling began to grow in my stomach as I walked. I felt like at any moment the old woman was going to jump from the darkness and block my path to the door, she was going to lock it and swallow the key, she was going to drag me back into the shadows with her. She wanted to keep us all here forever.

That thought caused me to start running.

"Can I take this teddy bear with me?" I heard Aidan ask Dad.

"Leave it!" I yelled as I grabbed the doorknob and pulled it towards me. To my relief, the door opened easily. It was so good to have the hot summer breeze feel warm on my skin. I closed my eyes in relief and breathed in the smell of the outdoors. It smelled like a grassy field that had been scorched all day by the sun. I relaxed a little.

"Please? Please can I keep it?" Aidan continued, as the rest of my family still lingering in the room behind me.

I opened my eyes, and my stomach twisted into knots at what I saw.

It was pitch dark outside.

The small room where we had first entered the building looked the same as it had before. The lonely metal desk cluttered with papers was still there, sitting beneath the neatly handwritten signs. The door to the world outside hung ajar, but nighttime had replaced the summer morning we had left only a few minutes earlier.

I turned back around to face my family who hadn't budged an inch. They still sat scattered across the sofas surrounding the fireplace. They hadn't even noticed how scared I was. They were still laughing at funny words on the puzzle, still cuddling tattered teddy bears, still setting up antique board games next to an enigmatically enormous fireplace – a fireplace where an unexplained fire now burned, casting a soft glow over the interior of the residence.

The part that bothered me the most was that none of them even seemed to notice that a fire had somehow started in the fireplace all by itself.

"There's a fire in the fireplace," I croaked. My mouth was so dry I could barely speak.

Dad and my brothers glanced at the fireplace for a moment before dismissing it, returning their attention to their playthings.

"Did you start it?" Aidan asked happily,

bouncing the teddy bear up and down on his knee.

"No," I whispered fiercely. "Did you know it's dark outside?" I asked.

Then I thought I noticed something moving again in the shadows, this time by the room filled with games. As soon as I looked in that direction it stopped.

"Hey Dad, can we stay here tonight?" Ethan asked all of the sudden. His eyes glistened with excitement in the firelight. "Please?"

"Yes, please Dad, *please*?" Aidan chimed in.

I turned and looked back out into the darkness of the night, straining to catch a glimpse of our stranded, out-of-gas car. It would be a long walk to nowhere, I thought, and an even longer walk to anywhere. I looked down at the floor in the front office and saw that my shadow from the firelight was dancing on the names of the children on the papers that littered the floor.

I closed the black door and walked back to the sofas.

"We can stay, but just tonight," Dad said happily.

Ethan and Aidan cheered and hugged him like he was now officially the best dad in the world.

Most oblivious dad in the world, I thought.

But then I found myself getting into the spirit of the evening. I quit worrying and joined in on the fun, despite the fact that I should have known better. We played old games for hours, laughed at the funny words we made up on the puzzle game, and we even found a bunch of stuffed animal friends for Aidan's teddy bear.

I forgot all about the old woman in the shadows as I rummaged through the forgotten treasures with my family like a delighted child.

Eventually, we tired from the fun, and the fire in the fireplace died down. Dad tucked us each into a soft, silken blanket on the sofas, each of us with a pillow fit for a king under our heads.

After kissing us good-night, Dad settled into a high-backed chair facing the fireplace, watching sparks as they swirled into the chimney. He smiled as he watched us, each with our favorite treasure in hand, and I thought he looked happier than I had ever seen him.

Then I saw her again.

The old lady was rocking gently in the shadows by the fireplace, watching us with what looked like a mix of joy and sorrow. The firelight glinted off a teardrop as it ran down her cheek.

I was terrified, I wanted to yell, to tell Dad she was there, but for some reason I couldn't. I was paralyzed. I couldn't do anything but hang onto the edge of the sofa; I clutched it so hard I thought the velvet upholstery might rip off in my hand. I lay there for what seemed like hours, watching the old lady watching me, watching my Dad and my brothers, from the shadows, helpless.

I began to grow tired. I couldn't stay scared forever. After a while longer I told myself it was okay if I closed my eyes, to rest them for a minute.

Only a minute.

When I opened them again, the old lady was gone, and Dad was asleep.

I kept scanning the room, looking for movement in the shadows, but all was still. My eyelids were so heavy I could hardly hold them open. The fire had died down to little more than a few dying embers, and darkness was fast settling over the room.

And then, finally, I slept.

***

SUNLIGHT HIT MY FACE, and I jumped awake. My body was covered in a film of cold sweat.

What had I done? I thought. *Why had I let myself fall asleep?*

I tried to jump off the sofa, but my legs were tangled in thick blankets, holding me down. As I struggled to free myself, a sickening panic filled me.

"What on earth are you doing?" a voice asked from above me.

It was Mom.

I stopped struggling with the blankets and rolled over to see my mom leaning over me with a bemused smirk on her face. I looked crazily around the room, disoriented.

I was in my own bedroom, in my own bed. I sat up straight, feeling giddy as a big wave of relief washed over me. It had all been a dream – the creepy camp, the crone in the corner – all of it my mind messing with me in my sleep. I felt a big smile spread across my face.

"Where's Dad? Where are Aidan and Ethan?" I asked, eager to know everyone was really okay.

Mom sat down calmly on the side of the bed, smiled and ran her fingers lovingly through my hair before she bothered to answer.

"Still sleeping, I guess," she said. "But everyone had better get up soon. You don't want to be late."

"What day is it?" I asked, still feeling confused.

"It's Saturday morning," she replied. "I wanted to

315

tell you goodbye before I left to go visit your Aunt Wendy. Don't forget to remind your Dad that you've got to be at camp by ten. I hope you have fun this week, and be careful."

Just then a sudden scream split the silence in the hallway outside my bedroom.

It was Aidan, and it sounded like he was in trouble.

"DAD!" he screeched at the top of his lungs.

All the relief I had from waking up from my nightmare was gone in an instant. I jumped out of bed and ran into the hallway to help.

Then Ethan started yelling for Dad, too. I was sure I was going to have a heart attack if I didn't figure out what was going on within the next three seconds.

Dad came running out of his room into the hallway and scooped us all up in his arms, hugging us. Ethan and Aidan were shouting over each other, not in fear, but in a cacophony of joyous excitement. I was so happy that everyone was alright that I felt a tear form in the corner of my eye.

"Dad! Look! Dad! Look! Dad! Look!" Ethan and Aidan shouted at the same time.

"What's all the commotion?" Mom demanded to know, as she followed me out of my bedroom.

I wiped the tear away to get a better look at what all the fuss was about.

Aidan stood there in his pajamas, a mischievous smile as bright as a birthday sunrise plastered across his face. He was hiding something behind his back.

He showed everyone what he had been hiding, slowly raising it up into the air with both hands, victory sparkling in his eyes.

I couldn't believe my eyes: it was the teddy bear from my dream, the identical one.

My mind reeled, trying to comprehend what I was seeing.

Had we all had the same dream? How on earth had Aidan managed to bring something back?

Mom shot a puzzled look at dad, but before he could say anything, Ethan was talking.

"That's nothing - look what was on my bed when I woke up," Ethan said, beaming with pleasure as he showed off a very expensive-looking antique *Snakes and Ladders* game.

Mom shook her head in disapproval. "I swear you spoil those kids," she said, not understanding the amazing thing happening right in front of her eyes.

"What did you bring back through the black door, William?" Aidan asked me. "You were there, too."

I didn't know what to say, so I just stood there wondering if I should pinch myself, to see if maybe I was still dreaming.

Then I felt something in the front pocket of my pajama pants. I slipped my hand into my pocket and my heart skipped a beat when I realized what it was.

"You got that puzzle game, didn't you?" Aidan asked.

He was right. I took it out of my pocket and my jaw actually dropped when I read what it said.

"Dad, look," I said, showing him.

"I see it, William. I see it. It's amazing," Dad said, a look of quiet understanding on his face. He appeared to be genuinely overwhelmed by the unreality of the moment.

"No, Dad, really - *look. Read it!*" I said, pointing to

the words spelled out on the puzzle:

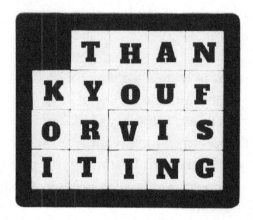

As his eyes grew wide, I realized something: maybe I didn't really want to go to camp this year, after all.

***

This was my first "all ages" fiction - gently spooky and dreamlike. Someday I'd like to develop this story into a horror novel for adults, where things take a much more sinister turn.

ACKNOWLEDGMENTS

Many thanks to my family, my friends and fantastic colleagues who helped to make this book a reality.

Special gratitude goes to my brilliant editors, each of whom shared their unique talents to help make each story the best it could be: my brother and lifelong pal, the amazing author Adam Light; my friend and mentor Doug Pryer; and to the gracious Catherine DePasquale, Andrea Harding, and good friend Wendy Bruss for their assistance. A big thank you to Cindy Pettit and Steven Beltzer for final proofreading.

Also sincere thanks to the kind Goodreads friends and readers who provided feedback and wrote reviews for early drafts of the stories in this book, and generously shared them with others.

Special appreciation goes to Laura Thomas and Mallory Anne-Marie Forbes for delightful enthusiasm and tireless publicity support.

But most of all, thank *you*, dear reader – for helping to make my dream of bringing nightmares to life finally come true. I hope we meet many times again.

Evans Light

May 2013

ABOUT THE AUTHOR

EVANS LIGHT has been in love with the written word from an early age, and works in a wide variety of genres, including horror, thrillers, sci-fi and humor - but stories of the "Weird Tales" variety remain his favorite.

Frequently drawn to uncommon experiences, Evans has thrown himself headfirst into a wide range of unusual situations, from testing low-level-entry parachutes with British Army Airborne units to travelling the vast reaches of inner space using sensory deprivation tanks.

Evans has lived here and there across the United States, from the mountains to the beaches to the desert, and currently chooses to reside in a southern state where the weather is warm and living is easy. He is the proud father of fine sons and the lucky husband of a beautiful wife.

His brother Adam Light is also a horror writer, and the two frequently collaborate as "THE LIGHT BROTHERS".

LINKS

www.evans-light.com

www.lightbrothershorror.com

www.facebook.com/CorpusPress

twitter.com/brotherslight

www.goodreads.com

Made in the USA
Coppell, TX
30 September 2021